Becoming is an Anti-Memory.

—GILLES DELEUZE AND FÉLIX GUATTARI

We're all born naked and the rest is drag.

—RuPAUL

I am rooted, but I flow.

—VIRGINIA WOOLF

you cannot bear to see it:
how i have made home here in your shame.

—ALOK VAID-MENON

Sea,
    Mothers,
        Swallow,
            Tongues

Prologue

For example, I never officially told you about "it." I just came over for coffee one day wearing makeup, with a box of Lindt & Sprüngli (the medium-sized, not the small ones like usual), and then came to Christmas dinner in a skirt. I knew, or assumed, that Mother had told you about it. "It." She had to tell you, because "it" was something I couldn't tell you. It was one of those things we couldn't say to one another. I had told Father, Father had told Mother, Mother must have told you.

Other things we never spoke about: the enormous birthmark on the back of Mother's left hand; the heaviness Father dragged into the house—like a vast, wet, moldering deer carcass—when he came home from work; your loud lip-smacking, your racism, your grief when Grandfather died; your bad taste when it came to presents; the lover Mother had when I was seven, the silver earring this woman gave her as a parting gift, which hung like a long teardrop from Mother's earlobe almost to her collarbone when she continued to put it on to provoke Father; the countless hours I spent—when I felt no one was watching—letting the earring glide from one hand to the other, holding it up to the sun so it would cast flame-like patterns on the walls, my intense urge to put it on, my unspeakable inner voice that forbade me from doing

3

so, my intense desire to have a body, Mother's boundless desire to travel the world. We never spoke about politics or literature or the class system or Foucault, or how Mother quit studying for her school equivalency certificate when I came into the world. We never spoke about how you grew a beard when you were pregnant with Mother, how this is called "hirsutism"; we never spoke about how you handled it, whether you shaved, waxed, or tweezed out the dark hairs, whether you took antiandrogens to halt the testosterone that your body "produces in excess," and we never spoke about how people stared at you, how ashamed you must have felt; we never spoke about shame at all, never about death, never about your death, never about your increasing forgetfulness. We spoke frequently about the family photo albums and every single picture in them, yet we never spoke about how ridiculous Grandfather looks in the photos with the young men from his Burschenschaft, how comically they fluff up their chests, standing wide-legged, grinning into the camera; we never spoke about the girl who, up to a certain age, wanders like a ghost through the photo albums, mostly hand in hand with you, sometimes with one of your five brothers; no, we never spoke about this youngest sister, whose name was Irma, and where she disappeared to. We never spoke about whether other families find it this tiring to act as though they're like other families, we never spoke about normality, never about heteronormativity, queerness, we never spoke about class, the so-called "third" world, and the hidden webs of fungi that are far more extensive and delicate than we imagine, we never spoke about all the paths that this world has in store for us, so we can run away from ourselves, the winding paths, the paths in the shadows of great poplars, the bleak, endless paths spooled around this world like thread around a ball of yarn, but we did speak about the paths that, added together, are called the "Camino de Santiago."

A few weeks ago, we were sitting on the sofa and you brought out one of the photo albums. I forced myself to feign the same interest I had the last ten times you explained the same photos with the same commentaries. We looked at a photo of your mother in which she's pregnant with you, a photo that surprised me the first few times I saw it: because there's this naked woman, in a bourgeois family photo album from 1935. Suddenly you interrupted your flow of words, looked at me, and asked: "But why are you never there?"

I'm sitting here at my writing desk in Zürich. I'm twenty-six, it's slowly getting dark, one of these evenings that are still winter evenings yet with a premonition of spring, a velvety scent: of overly sweet, blush-white blossoms; of people beginning to jog again, spreading their sweat through the excessively clean streets. I don't jog. I sit here and chew my fingernails despite the bitter antibiting polish, I chew until the white tips are bitten down and then further still, continually forcing them downward. Six months ago I took this ultraboring job in the public records office, where I spend all day long among shelves deep belowground, I catalog the medical records of long-dead patients, I speak to nobody, I'm content, I'm invisible, I let my hair grow, I go home and sit down at my desk. From here I can see the beech tree in the neighboring garden, from here the memories of our copper beech come to me, the large, red-leaved beech in the center of our garden. The copper beech, which in Swiss German we call the blood beech. I write. When my friends Dina and Mo, who are also sitting and writing somewhere, text me: "Coming out for a drink?" I don't reply. I try to write, and when I can't write, when I sink into the mudflats of the past, I shave, shower, and ride my bike to the outer reaches of the city, the "out*skirts*," as they're called in English, scour the gas stations and football pitches, prowl back and forth outside the gyms, the Grindr app my pale flashlight in the suburban night, leading me to the men I'm looking for, the men I need and need to need me, to use and get used by, the men I let push up my skirt and push inside me behind the bike shed, quick and emotionless. I have enough emotions and don't need more; what I need from them is a hard cut. I twin and twine with the rusty bars of the gym; I entwine with the railings of the deserted grandstand, they support me; and last, but not least, my cheek slams repeatedly against the Securitas break room door until I'm pounded out of my emotions and back into my flesh, then I go home, semen still inside me and the scent of a stranger on me, a warm feeling in my empty middle filling me up for the duration of my journey. I use the toilet, shave again, armpits, legs, crotch, always fearing the possibility of waking up in the night and smelling of somebody else, then I go to the toilet again to get the rest of the semen out of me, then shower, rub myself down with a pumice stone, moisturize. My skin is irritated from so much shaving. Then I sit back down at the desk, in view of the beech tree, and only then do I realize that it's you I've been writing to this whole time. When I'm not writing, I read, or think about the possibility of taking my body to the Camino de Santiago. I think about the possibility of walking until I'm no longer thinking about anything or until I reach Santiago de Compostela or the ocean, and I think about the possibility of not doing any of that.

We never spoke about the afternoon you didn't find your way home and how Mother got a call from the police. We never spoke about putting you in a home, and when you had a really bad turn a month ago and woke up in a rehab center and asked what had happened to your balcony overlooking Bern, Mother said, "But they removed it, remember, it wasn't safe anymore." And you said, "Oh yes, that's right," and laughed at yourself a little too loudly and then talked about the geraniums on the balcony. I hated Mother for her cowardice in not telling you the truth, I was annoyed at first, and then more moved than I wanted to be by her sudden concern for you. All at once she's the caring daughter, I thought, but not me, you don't get me as a caring daughter, Ma, and I said goodbye to her more coldly than usual. We don't talk about the high probability that you'll have another turn in the next six months ("a turn"—as though you were just making some slight detour), and we don't talk about the high probability that this "turn" will erase what remains of your memory.

It's nighttime now, and I imagine you also standing at the window of your room in the rehab center and staring the night in the face. I can feel you slowly disappearing. Dear Grandmother, I want to write to you before you completely disappear from your body or can no longer access your memories.

I'd like to be able to tell you I was afraid of you, that for example it was I who smashed the jar of raspberry jam that time, just after

you'd made it, the one you thought Mother had smashed, and that
Mother was actually protecting me, she took the blame and you
really bawled her out. I feel guilty about that to this day. I'd like
to know what happened to my great-aunt Irma, the girl who walks
hand in hand with you through the family albums and then disappears. I'd like to understand what it was like to be you: first
a lower-class, then a middle-class woman in twentieth-century
Switzerland. I'd like to understand why I have barely any memories of my childhood, and why the only ones I have are of you.
I'd like to find a language in which I can ask you: "Where are my
people?" I'd like to know how all this shit gets in our veins.

You were too loud, too demanding, too coarse. You never listened. You sent me money, accompanied by notes: "You know
you can visit me anytime." I'm sorry I'm such a bad grandchild.
I'm too delicate to be decent.

Dear Grandmother. When I think of you, I think of all the things
we never could and never can say to each other. I remember how
you always used so proudly the words that the Bernese German
dialect took from the French, and while I can understand that
pride, it also makes me incredibly uncomfortable. French was
brought to us by Napoleon; it was the language of the occupiers,
the language of the cultured yet barbaric warmongers. He brought
us the language and some laws, and in return he stole Bern's treasury, renowned all across Europe. Several hundred billion, if
you convert it into modern-day Swiss francs (even the name of
our currency comes from Napoleon, from the old French franc,
which literally means "a French"!). He used it to pay off his debts

and finance his Egypt campaign. I know these are my petty tears of white privilege, and that we've been world champions at high-finance robbery since the late nineteenth century. Napoleon's looting gave early nineteenth-century Bern and its surrounding region a very high emigration rate. By the 1890s a good one hundred thousand Swiss people had emigrated to the USA. And the tax implications of Napoleon stealing Bern's treasure stretched into the twentieth century: Bern had been a rich city and its residents were only taxed after he came robbing. So I find it strange that you proudly bear the fruits of the man who carries part of the blame for your poverty.

Traces of Napoleon that can be found in your vocabulary to this day:
dr Nöwö—the nephew—le neveu
ds Fiseli—the son—le fils
dr Potschamber—the bedpan—le pot de chambre
ds Gloschli—bell-shaped petticoat—von cloche
dr Gaschpo—flowerpot—le cache-pot
ds Lawettli—washcloth—von laver

You told me about Madame de Meurron, the legendary Bern character who was the first woman in Switzerland to drive a car: a patrician who spoke almost exclusively in Frenchified expressions in order to show how aristocratic she was. She didn't roll her *r*'s like the tanners from the shabby Matte district, but instead pronounced them nicely at the back of her throat, à la française. "Schaffed Iir no oder sid Iir scho ober?"—Do you still work or are you already somebody?—you mimicked her, sounding the *r* at the back, totally exaggerated, laughing and exposing your teeth. I didn't understand the question. How can a person move up in the world if they don't work? (I hadn't yet learned that genuine fat-cat capital can only be inherited, not acquired through hard work, in contrast to the rags-to-riches myth we shovel into one another practically from birth.) You're beginning to forget anything that didn't happen before your fiftieth birthday. You're disappearing. But the French stays with you. I think about how close to you I feel when I'm writing to you, and how far from you I feel when I see you. How you talk about going to Santiago de Compostela someday, and how happy that would make your mother and Maria, and how—after the long, long walk— you would jump joyfully into the Atlantic, clothes and all. I think about how you talk without pause, about anything—the special offers at the Migros supermarket, the days when there are double Cumulus card points. Your fear of silence. I remember how you continually protected me after Grandfather's death, so you wouldn't have to confront the loss. No, wait—that's not me remembering. That's Mother's memory.

In the language I've inherited from you, Bernese German, my mother tongue, "mother" is *meer*. It means both "mother" and "the sea," sneak-tweaked from the French; *la mer* and *la mère*. For "father," we say *peer*. For "grandmother," *grossmeer*. For "great-grandmother," *urgrossmeer*. The women of my childhood are an element, an ocean. I remember my mother's legs, I remember wrapping my arms around them, gazing up at her and saying: "You are my meer." I remember a feeling of home and of beingutterlyenveloped. The meers' love so big we couldn't escape it, can't escape it, even if we swam for a lifetime to emerge from its depths.

The language I've inherited is itself a sea; language herself an ocean, waving and mixing, ebbing and gushing, with no clear border, her shores are constantly shifted by storms, humans, more-than-humans, one language-sea flows into the next, they are endlessly weaving themselves into one another, jostling-cocktailing-throttling time and space; words are little *truckli*, as my mother tongue calls little trinket boxes; they travel through these times and spaces, slowly changing their meaning while always still speaking their past, and so languages are borderless spaces to me, lisp-whispering in undercurrents and riptides, melting and washing and vortexing, and another word has reached my consciousness, from my friend Mo who told me about his Irish heritage, told me a word that I realized was another word for meer, for this Swiss-Frerman word, this mother-sea-ness, because when he told me about the fairies in Irish folklore, the Sidhe, pronounced "Shee," I remembered that as a child I had a lisp, so the child cowriting these lines has too much tongue in its mouth and says *shee* for sea, and this many-tongued word clung to me as Mo spoke more about the Sidhe, those pagan creatures of land and forest, who I believe had traversed Europe in most celtic-germanic-heathen cultures, and I summon them here, dear Shee, dear fairies, please come, put your sparkly gay magic into these lines, because I believe you to be tangible beings, I believe you to be creative critters who do not inspire worship of a transcendent power, a power that has cut all ties from the Earth and matter and dirt and body, no, I believe that you *are* the Earth, matter, dirt, and body, and as the times have grown ever more dire while writing this, I need your fairy energy spilling and spelling itself into this many-tongued work of and about mothers, about the ocean, forest-ocean fairies, all fairies, and about the children lisping the sea into shee into meer.

There, there. I now return to the language that started me, to Bernese German, this language I've inherited from you, Grossmeer, my Meer language, in which there are only two ways to be a body. Growing up in the palate of the German language forced me constantly into this two-by-two, like a line of kindergartners.

In the language I've learned from you, my mother tongue, my smother tongue, I don't know how to write about myself. There's Mother's tongue and your eyes and me, my body, my bodies, my corporeality? There's this I, the writing I, and the child I once was, the child standing before that line of kindergartners, still needing to find a way through. And I'm permeated with the child, just like the moon in its entirety is held handlessly by the earth, but in writing I have to differentiate between us, because otherwise the childhood, because otherwise the childhood-body, because otherwise the flood of the past will wash me away.

And yet it's not simple in the Meer language either: because little detours, one might even say deviant deviations, crept in—the women were objects. Meer, admittedly, is given the feminine article *die*. But all other adult women, even the other nouns for mothers and grandmothers—like *mami* and *grossmami*—took the neuter article *das*, making them sound like objects, like pieces of furniture rather than people. And not just the mothers; all women when called by their names were neuter nouns: *das* Anneli, *das* Lisbeth, *das* Regini. And the children were objects too, sweet and tiny, like little mocha spoons: *das* Mineli, *das* Hänneli, *das* Hansli. I remember that this objectification infuriated me. I didn't want to be an object; I wanted to be a person, and grown up, and being grown up meant having a gender, a male one. As a woman, you were at risk of remaining an object or becoming an ocean. I didn't want either.

When I think of you, Grossmeer, I think of the Migros supermarket cafeteria, where you always invited me when you wanted to treat me to a "meal out," I think of the Urmeer, the primordial sea that emerged from the first bacteria, its temperature a rather precise thirty-seven degrees Celsius, I think of Meer and the life she sacrificed for me, and of the life you sacrificed for Meer, I think of how you've just been released from the rehab center, how at this very moment you're probably standing on your balcony and staring angrily at the half-withered geraniums, and I think of all the stories I've never written to you. In one of them, a bearded woman walks all the way from Ostermundigen to Santiago de Compostela. Halfway there, she meets a young person who has a beard too, and broad shoulders, a deep voice, a skirt and kohl eyeliner, and they talk about nothing, they walk silently alongside each other toward the sea, their footsteps dropping like flotsam between them, like lost ancestral lines drifting in the twilight.

1

The Search for Flotsam

Grossmeer, don't eat me.

———

I do not want the female gender that has been assigned to me at birth. Neither do I want the male gender that transsexual medicine can furnish and that the state will award me if I behave in the right way. I don't want any of it.

——PAUL B. PRECIADO

The gender binary is like a party guest who shows up before you get the chance to set the table.

——ALOK VAID-MENON

The wound is the land of healing.

——TABITA REZAIRE

I think you have to take me for me.

——HARRY STYLES

GROSSMEER'S HANDS

Grossmeer's hands were animals. They moved unceasingly. Mice in their restlessness, hairless mice, with skin as rough as cracked asphalt. Spiders in their form, humpbacked leg-monsters. Imprisoned in their coarse skin, they searched incessantly for a way out of Grossmeer, fumbling around like the recently blinded. They grab potatoes and peel them greedily. They grasp the little mocha spoon to heave sugar into the coffee cup—yes, the movement is a heaving, a foreign movement that doesn't match the object, as though Grossmeer had translated the harvesting of potatoes to the shoveling of sugar crystals. Half of the fine crystals always land on the red-and-white-checked tablecloth. The little mocha spoon: an object in a foreign language for these hands. The ridiculously beautiful detailing and flourishes on its handle. Excessive. Excess. When I saw a gloved Parisienne in a Disney film elegantly guiding a mocha spoon to her teacup with two fingers (the thumb and index finger; the little finger splayed out), I noticed the difference. The space between Grossmeer and the world I wanted to inhabit. Grossmeer grabbed the mocha spoon like a shovel, with her entire fist. Her arthritically thickened joints always reminded me of the enchanted thornbush in *Sleeping Beauty*. Those gnarled swellings. A hundred years of torpor.

I remember Grossmeer's hands reaching into me. In my memory, Grossmeer's hands are so lonely; one is constantly reaching for the other, and then the other clutches the one, they search without pause, search for something to hold, grab my child-legs and

child-arms and stroke them mercilessly. I don't remember my
child-legs and child-arms, all I remember is the feeling of intense
roughness and the knowledge that I have to endure it, that Grossmeer needs this.

GROSSMEER'S FEET

"I have men's feet," Grossmeer always said, proud, defensive,
apologetic, undecipherable. Grossmeer's feet were gigantic, the
big toe a little fist, and she had these lateral swellings she sigh-
ingly called halluces. I was always afraid another toe would hatch
from her skin. I learned at Grossmeer's feet that body parts are
beings that work against you, that they aren't the same thing as
you yourself, they might have another sex, be another species.
And that the feelings you have toward your body may begin in
the body, but they then spread out through the entire room.

GROSSMEER'S TEXTILES

Cloths—tablecloths, runners, fabrics and textiles of various kinds
lay on all the furniture, and they were constantly slipping out of
place. Crocheted, knitted, embroidered. The sofa was covered
with a gigantic, white, hand-crocheted throw. Grossmeer's pride
and joy. Every time I sat on the sofa when I was a child, or even
just touched the sofa, Grossmeer had to straighten the throw. It
had to sit perfectly. Grossmeer was constantly going from one
room to the next in order to straighten all the cloths on tables, side

tables, commodes, bureaus, and stands. They were never right. They covered the whole apartment, and they were never right. I think that for Grossmeer, these cloths were the constant, bothersome, burdensome proof that she was no longer poor. But her hands were still far too rough to pull these delicate doilies into place.

GROSSMEER'S TRUCKLI

I remember Grossmeer's little trinket boxes: her truckli. After Grosspeer died, Grossmeer traveled the world and collected these trinket boxes made of wood, stone, glass, ivory, plastic, bone, wire, steel, copper, silver, amber, leather, felt. The boxes were all over her apartment, on the cloths and coverings, and they were all empty and closed. Their emptiness unsettled me. When Meer and Grossmeer drank coffee together, the child wandered through the apartment, doing an inspection round, passing the truckli like you would pass someone who means you harm. You walk quickly, without wanting to create the impression you're walking quickly, and you look at them without them seeing you're looking. The truckli looked back. My fingers twitched. To this day, I can still feel emptiness of the truckli in that delicate bulge where cuticle becomes skin. Whenever I paint my nails, I always paint over that bit, even though that's not good form, not good manicurist form, *skip the cuticle*, but to me it often feels like this seam is a wave of the past, breaking in a bay. A messenger from Mesopotamia that I'd like to gloss over.

As a child, I was obsessed with the idea of secretly putting things in these truckli, regardless of what: pebbles, leaves, hair, a bitten-off fingernail—just so that something would be inside. But I knew this was absolutely forbidden, and I also knew Grossmeer would know precisely who had broken the unspoken rule.

I sensed things without understanding them. I sensed the truckli were Grossmeer's inner spaces that she had relocated elsewhere. The truckli were Grossmeer's accomplices; I knew she had cut off tiny fragments of her emptiness and was storing these in the boxes. Grossmeer acted friendly enough, but under no circumstances was her treasure to be touched. "One day you'll inherit all of this," she said, and it was always a threat.

THE CHILD

I write about "Grossmeer" as though you were a character in a novel, Grossmeer. As though you weren't constantly inside me, as though I could create distance from you. But this is the approach I need to take. I need to be in charge of you like a character, otherwise I won't write the things I'm writing about. I wanted to write in the past tense, but the fragments slip away from me into the present and back again, becoming blurred.

I can barely remember myself as a child. Or perhaps I mean: I can barely remember the body of the child. In the time I'm writing about, I don't yet have a body. I remember being an awareness rather than a body, a delicateness beneath the threatening bellies, roaming between the grown-ups' legs like they were tree trunks in a primeval forest, a tenderness against the coarse things, the asphalt, Grossmeer's skin. I didn't exist; there was my running, but there were no legs; there was the wind I felt when running, but no face or neck to feel this wind; there was the whooping joy unleashed by the running, but not the belly where this whooping rippled. A body was what others had. I remember Grossmeer's scary, wrinkled body, I remember Peer's thighs and penis, I remember Meer's breasts and hair. It's as though I had access to photographs, but not the actual camera that housed the photographs.

What a silly metaphor, this camera business. I can see myself tiptoeing around the actual things and resorting to analogies that have long been sucked dry. And what *is* the actual thing?

I remember my teeth, the milk teeth that felt like foreign bodies in the body and then began to wobble one day and that could be wrenched out. Another exception are toes, which—when you wake up during the night—aren't completely under the blanket, and how you need to hide them from the monsters that lurk under the bed. The nightly dilemma: Do you bring your toes to safety by pulling them back under the blanket, with the risk that if you don't do it slowly enough, the monsters might notice your entire body and devour it? Or do you leave the toes out, where the monsters will eat them for sure, but in the process save the rest of your limbs? An impossible dilemma.

Both—toes and teeth—are body parts I have lost and that, in a magical way, have grown back.

GROSSMEER'S MOUTH

Grossmeer's mouth was a landscape in perpetual motion, in time-lapse. She talked incessantly, and when she wasn't talking—because she was drinking or eating or watching television—her mouth made every noise imaginable: slurping, coughing, hemming, sharply sucking in air, snorting, noisily licking her lips, testing the spaces between her teeth with her tongue and clearing out any leftover food.

Grossmeer always wore lipstick, an old-lady color between traffic-light red and Barbie pink. It bled onto her teeth, and she would wipe it off with a white cotton handkerchief and precise, hard movements. The lipstick disappeared, and she reapplied it again and again, but it kept retreating—an ebbing tide. The fine creases split her lips: cracks in a brittle rock face. The child wondered how something like that could happen, it stood before the mirror, pressed both hands firmly against its own smooth lips and felt sure Grossmeer's lips had been torn through carelessness. This wouldn't happen to the child. It would make sure its lips didn't tear, not ever, it would hold them tightly. There were tiny holes above Grossmeer's lips where the dark beard hairs had grown while she was pregnant with Meer. The child knew that Grossmeer's mouth was what kept her alive, this restless machine.

GROSSMEER'S TEETH

Grossmeer never threw away a piece of bread. She bought fresh bread whenever the child came to visit. She gave the child the fresh bread. She ate the hard stuff herself. *There is no hard bread, no bread is hard.* The hard bread crunched between her teeth. Grossmeer was so proud of her teeth. "My parents lost all their teeth by the age of thirty," she said—she stressed, whenever the conversation turned to teeth, food, illness, hygiene, or the past. "My meer was so proud she could pay for us to see the dentist, you can't even imagine," she said with an eerie smile that bared her teeth. The child was afraid the bread could break Grossmeer's precious teeth. Each time Grossmeer ate hard bread, the child spoke to the bread first. Using its magic gaze and quiet voice, it said, "Dear hard bread. Please don't be too hard on Grossmeer's teeth. She's so proud of them. Look how soft I am, how delicate, please absorb a bit of my delicateness." The child tensed up its belly and made a magic spell there, gathered the delicateness in its gaze, and sent droplets of it into the hard bread.

Grossmeer's teeth were big and white, like mountains, and they were always glittering, because Grossmeer was always talking. If the bread was too hard, Grossmeer suddenly stood up, tongue pressed against her gums, and prepared a plate of milk and a plate of egg and salt and pepper. Grossmeer didn't say a word while she was making French toast. It was perhaps the only silence she had. The child knew it was to blame that the bread was too hard. It should have tried harder. It resolved to practice its magic gaze. At home, it found a stone, went into the chicken coop, sat down in front of the stone, and gave it all its delicateness. The child was very strict with itself.

GROSSMEER'S FRENCH TOAST

When Grossmeer made French toast, first softening each slice of bread in the plate of milk, then dunking it in the egg plate and frying it in butter, her tongue swept like a cat's tail over her gums, which were bleeding from the hard bread. The child always got the first slices of French toast. Grossmeer placed the cinnamon-sugar tin, decorated with gentian flowers, on the red-and-white-checked tablecloth; the tin was an heirloom from her own Grossmeer, one that she had already mended six times. The glue formed yellowish scars that cut the gentians into pieces. The mocha spoon was in the already-mixed cinnamon sugar. The child didn't like French toast, even though it was the only meal where the child was allowed to help itself to sugar. No matter how much sugar the child heaped on, the bitter aftertaste remained: the French toast was here in place of all the bread Grossmeer hadn't had. But what the child liked even less than the French toast itself was Grossmeer during the French toast. I remember how the child had to look away. I remember the child staring at the French toast. Its eggy, yellowish skin, the grains of sugar over it. And Grossmeer's noises. Choking it down, though the French toast was still far too hot. The gulping and slurping and panting and puffing. Balancing an overly hot morsel on her teeth, baring her teeth, drawing back her lips, clamping the morsel to the side of her teeth—because teeth aren't as sensitive to temperature—breathing out the hot air; this hissing, waiting until the morsel has cooled a little so she can swiftly gulp it down. The hunger that's older than Grossmeer herself.

The child never left Grossmeer alone in her hunger-loneliness. But it could only bear her when it was thinking about magical things. The nursery rhyme "Heile, heile Segen." Twinkling. Healing. Hex Hex. It also understood, in its belly, the color of the French toast: this smooth yellow, the same yellow as the glue that held the sugar tin together. This union of glue and French toast. It didn't like how Grossmeer dished up its glued-togetherness in such a way that the words for French-toast-feelings were always missing, and the child doused the French-toast-yellow with cinnamon sugar, a brown-white blanket. It wanted to tell Grossmeer it didn't like French toast, but sensed this wasn't an option, because Grossmeer didn't differentiate between herself and French toast, just as she didn't differentiate between her hand and the child's legs.

REMNANTS

Things that surrounded the child were never outside of it; the child had no skin, and the world flowed in and out. Sometimes things surface that I've learned are called *childhood memories*. They feel incredibly intimate, but are actually impersonal, collective:

Learning to count from one to twenty.

Saying thank you, always, constantly, and saying sorry.

Politely answering the questions "How old are you?" and "Are you a boy or a girl?"

Playing outside, lying on your back in the grass, hoping it won't get dark yet, not for a long time yet, that it won't ever get dark, not ever, that you'll always be able to run through this golden light, this fragrant air in which the entire day rests like a rose chafer beetle on a peony.

Playing games that grown-ups think you like, where they think they're doing you a favor by playing them with you.

Speaking the Meer language properly.

Being silent, which was called *being good*.

Being afraid of strangers, which was called *having stranger anxiety*.

Holding back tears, which was called *being strong*.

Being afraid of going to sleep; being afraid of not waking up again; being afraid of losing your eyesight in the darkness without realizing (because you can't see anything). This was called *being difficult*.

Finding your balance on the bicycle for the first time and the resulting giddy euphoria, as though the whole world were made of chocolate; the feeling of being able to ride to the end of the world, to America, around the moon and back.

Because I remember these things, I know there was once a child there, but this child doesn't feel like me. I don't know whether these things I've listed are my childhood memories or whether someone told me about them and I can no longer remember who, or whether I read them and can no longer remember where. I'm trying to write about this time that's missing inside me, that was stuck inside this child. Perhaps home isn't a place, but a time.

What I do remember, remember more vividly than anything, is Grossmeer. It's as though my memory didn't put much effort into holding on to me, but instead held on to Grossmeer. My Grossmeer's name is Rosmarie, and she was a monster.

BODY: TODAY

Even today, I don't properly feel my body; I'm always bumping into things, into table corners and legs, open doors and cupboards, I'm jostled and I jostle. I don't know where I start and where I stop. When I cook, I often cut or burn myself and realize too late. When I grate cheese or carrots, I grate myself too. Then there's skin missing, me missing. My body, this remnant, this transformed ancientness, this matter that has already held countless other forms: rock, earth, plants, air, bacteria, fungi.

I only feel my body when I give it away, when I offer it to others, when they push inside me, penetrating the self-erected boundaries of my body and leaving themselves behind. My primary need isn't to feel cocks inside me, I need to feel *myself*; the pulsating cloak around the cocks. This body is capable of taking in extraordinarily large things when it relaxes, without feeling the slightest pain. Pain comes when you resist the intruding object or when you want to push it out. I have never resisted when other bodies pushed into me.

I'm sitting here at my desk, writing you this, Grossmeer, on the MacBook Pro I bought eight years ago with your Christmas money, I'm sitting on one of the wooden chairs you gave me (you hardly ever receive guests anymore, as you said, and only need two chairs), I'm sitting on my backside, which was penetrated half an hour ago by a man I've met twice, a man who's no more than twenty and—according to postcoital small talk—is a butcher and wants to move to LA to make reggaeton music.

I'm writing you this, Grossmeer, because for a long time I've been trying to do what I want with my body: to talk about it as I want, to move it as I want, to enjoy it as I want. To say how god-damn heavenly it feels to be fucked, how devilishly good to walk the streets and feel the sperm leaving my body ever so slowly, slower than honey, slower than the pine-cone syrup you always drizzle on your last piece of French toast. That it feels so fuck-ing good when the semen, someone else's lust, trickles down be-tween my butt cheeks and makes tangible this shame-laden zone, these body parts that conventional language names in degrading, violent ways. How incredibly soft and alive a penetrated ass feels. As though I were made entirely of silk.

I'm writing you this with the beech tree in sight, and the blood beech comes back to me, a really early memory comes back to me, I'm lying in the grass, you lean over me, and behind you the sky is made of blood beech leaves. I'm writing you this to write against the contempt I've felt for this body for as long as I can remember, the contempt that may be partly responsible for my having so few memories of it. How can you capture something that always yields, blurs, dissolves? I'm writing this to write against the body negativity I've inherited; maybe not from you directly, but from the Christian Central European culture. It's not about attributing blame, it's about unraveling the threads that have woven us; disentangling the threads that knot together those of us who suffer under masculinity, that have shackled each of us in a cocoon of silence, shame, and hypocrisy. It's about being able to say: sex—regardless of whether it's penetrative or nonpenetrative—is something wonderful, and it's about asserting that penetrated bodies are bodies just as much as penetrating and unpenetrated bodies are. We are not objects, we're neither devils nor angels, we are dull-as-ditchwater creatures of the twilight just like everyone else.

I'm writing you this because I was afraid of you as a child, because I felt you never had a body, because I'm still angry that you used me, used my body; angry that you looked after me, held me, stroked me, so you could off-load your unprocessed story into me, just like your meer used your body and her meer used your meer. I'm writing this because I only exist through your body, because I'm your continuation and because I no longer want to continue certain things. I'm writing this because—like Meer and you—I can't talk about the things that really matter to me, I'm writing this because: as long as I'm writing, I may not be speaking, but I'm not being silent either.

GROSSMEER'S RASPBERRIES

Her rubies. Her treasure grew in the back garden. Grossmeer wore a shapeless white hat and carried various baskets, her chrättli. "The raspberry harvest!" she said, laughing too loudly. Grossmeer's hands scuttled nimbly over the bushes. The child didn't dare run away, because Grossmeer might have thought it was running from her. Grossmeer said, like she did every year, that she had grown up in this garden where the child is growing up. That her peer was unemployed. That every square inch of the garden was planted. That they squeezed food out of every patch of the large garden like juice from an apple.

Grossmeer picks methodically. The good raspberries are put in one chrättli; these will be sold. The overripe berries are made into raspberry liquor. The squashed berries are made into cakes, syrup, or jam. The fallen berries, if they still look good, go in the last chrättli, together with the squashed berries. When they're no longer "good," that is, when they're "just bits," Grossmeer eats them right there and then. Grossmeer only eats the moldy raspberries. Otherwise, once winter comes, you could find yourself thinking about those raspberries you didn't eat because they were a bit moldy, and then you curse yourself and feel a hole in your belly, and for the rest of your life you'll never be able to fill this hole, no matter how many raspberries you eat. Grossmeer harvests raspberries until she can no longer see herself. Her fingertips have become fingerberries: red from juice and swollen from prickles. Her eyes are red from all the raspberries she's eaten with her eyes, from fear she might miss a berry. Grossmeer, why do you have such a big mouth?

GROSSMEER'S HANDS, SECOND
INSTALLMENT

When I pictured your hands again now, Grossmeer, how they plucked the raspberries, how they "scuttled nimbly over the bushes," I also saw your hands knitting, your index and middle fingers and thumbs; this clattering, clacking, clanging textile machine that moved untiringly around itself, conjuring up firm fabric from loose threads; this thread-tying machine, like a body detached from your body, working like a spider's jaw; a spider that spins its threads into a tight cocoon around its victim before sucking it dry. Although—no, that's not right, spiders spin their threads with their hindquarters, so the image that came to me is inaccurate. Or is there some justification after all, were your knitting hands actually a second, independent body that was both mouth and hindquarters, that simultaneously devoured and produced while you were watching the daily news, while you were watching me, while you were forbidding me from doing this and ordering me to do that?

I was bewitched by your knitting. "Bestitched," wink wink, sound the subtlety alarm. I really wanted to learn to knit too. But Meer didn't want that for me, she couldn't knit, or at least that's what she told me. "It's girlie shit. While the boys did sports, we had to practice knitting patterns for hours on end. And while men made the world, the decisions and all the important stuff, women had to sit at home and darn the men's clothes. I forgot how to knit as soon as I left school, so I can't teach you." That's why you taught me how to knit, Grossmeer. I sit on your lap, your arms hold me, your hands enclose my little hands, your fingers pull the thread, across and over, tie the thread, it comes from the left and goes to the right, I feel the thread pass beneath my fingertips, and as I write this to you, as I write on the computer, my fingers feel the knitting, they're surrounded again by your rough, coarse, hard fingers, spider legs, your spider jaw, your back, front, your parts, I'm part of you; in knitting and in writing alike—I'm connected to you.

GROSSMEER'S TELEVISION

I remember that only Grossmeer had a TV. I remember the child's battles with Peer. *Sleeping Beauty*, *Snow White*, and *Bambi* versus football matches, ski races, and athletics. I remember the threat: *You'll go square-eyed if you watch too much TV*. This threat didn't apply to the grown-ups; their eyes always remembered their form. After each film, the child ran to the bathroom. It didn't trust the feel of its fingers, it had to check the eyes' roundness in the mirror. Once, while watching *Beauty and the Beast*, it starts to feel sick and its eyes begin to hurt. It was convinced this was the sensation of the eyes transforming. It sits down on the floor in front of the TV and looks in the mirror above the sofa. The mirror is round, the child watches the film through it. Watching indirectly like this feels safe. The indirect gaze is always safer. Concealed within the writing-about-Grossmeer is a wanting-to-write-about-Meer.

GROSSMEER'S APARTMENT

Grossmeer's apartment is the scene of my childhood that's clearest in my memory, clearer than the house I grew up in and where I actually spent more time. I was always afraid of Grossmeer's apartment. Entering it was like stepping into a lake. Dim light, falling in thin rays. Layers of the past that you could stir up but never get rid of. Thick curtains and dark furniture, masks from "exotic" lands, with real hair and cows' teeth. Every sound was muffled: the apartment was covered with thick rugs, even the walls. And there were clothes everywhere, coats in particular, with at least one coat stand in every room, and she had two wardrobes. It was as though she were expecting a lot of people whom she wanted to clothe. But nobody ever visited except us.

The child found every object in Grossmeer's apartment monstrous, ugly. These "exotic" masks on the walls, the Persian rugs, the heavy, dark-wood furniture, the truckli from all over the world, the few paintings, in pseudo-Impressionist style. Today I think Grossmeer was using these furnishings to communicate her social status. She had been a poor farmgirl with five or six siblings—depending on whether you counted Irma—whose peer was unemployed and had built with his own hands the house in Ostermundigen—still just a village outside Bern back then—in which Grossmeer, Meer, and I had all grown up. Grossmeer had been a beautiful young woman, and she climbed the social ranks through marriage. Only now do I really understand the extent to which her furnishings signal how often and far she was able to

travel, all the countries she'd seen, and the valuable items she was
able to acquire there. That the child thought the furnishings ugly
is something for which I now feel very sorry.

Nonetheless, for me her apartment was always filled with an
unbearable emptiness, as though she were living inside one of her
truckli.

GROSSMEER'S PLACES

There are certain places and spaces that I associate with Grossmeer. Most are spaces of the emerging middle class and many are
imbued with her life's great credo: saving money.

Old ladies' beauty salons, named with labored wordplay (e.g.,
the Hair Necessities, Jacqueline's Hairmony Salon, Hair Trade,
Bright and Curly, the Cutting Edge, Tress 'n' Impress, the Top
Knot), with the smell of cheap hair spray in the air, with bourgeois magazines for women (*Annabelle*, *Für Sie*, *Donna*, *Schweizer
Illustrierte*, *Glückspost*, *Emma*, *Mein schöner Garten*, *Zeit für mich*).
Orchids on the windowsill and dryer hoods. Although I don't
have a concrete memory of having accompanied Grossmeer, I
feel close to her when I see one of those hair salons. She had a
perm for many years.

Customs. Crossing the border to go shopping ("Everything's
so cheap there, you know, and it's just as good"), then getting the
VAT reimbursed on reentering Switzerland.

Kiosks, or more precisely: the lottery stand. The hope of winning the jackpot one day. Even though she was no longer in financial need. The same crowd there always: People who, when they

go to cafés, swipe those little packets of sugar from the tables to take home with them.

Apartments that were built or furnished in the seventies. Like many families who started to do well for themselves, Grossmeer and Grosspeer bought a second home in the mountains. Dark wood, heavy dark-brown leather armchairs with those little buttons, kidney-shaped tables, oversized lamps with a long, movable arm that you can pull over the sofa when reading, rugs or wall tiles in those yellow-orange-brown tones with circular patterns or abstract flower designs. The orange of Ovaltine packaging.

H&M stores. Grossmeer often took the child, and later the teenager, to this shop during visits. She wanted to buy it a present. I don't know whether other clothes shops were too expensive, or whether she just didn't know any other shops that made children's clothes.

Cemeteries. All the times the child went with Grossmeer to her husband's and Urgrossmeer's graves. She never visited the grave of her son Nico, who was buried in the same cemetery.

The space I connect most with Grossmeer is the Migros supermarket. Even though she now had enough money, her life revolved predominantly around food, and she went to Migros almost every day. She always looked to see when the special offers were on, and then, on the very first day, she would set off for the hunt. She went to Migros because it was cheaper than its competitor, Coop. She did her big shop on Thursdays, because that's double loyalty points day. When a friend told me these Thursdays were a store strategy to ease the load on the weekends—and the only people who can go shopping during the day on Thursday are, of course, pensioners—I laughed at first, then felt sad. I felt as though Grossmeer was being unwittingly manipulated. When I asked whether she knew why there were double points on Thursdays, she said: "Well, there have to be double points sometime."

Grossmeer often took the child to the restaurant at Migros. It was always happy to go. It gave the child a feeling of being at home. The food isn't great, but it's cheap. Even today I always stare mesmerized into the Migros restaurant as I pass. Most of the customers are pensioners, manual laborers, alcoholics. I can't bear to go in, though, it reminds me too much of Grossmeer. I've decided I'll go to eat there someday, after she has died.

ON PLAYING DRESS-UP

Grossmeer had a large wardrobe filled with children's clothes, girls' clothes. They were old, little white-and-pink skirts, frills, embroidered hems, hair ribbons, little white socks. There's a phase when the child is still very small—I can't remember now how it started—a phase when it always goes to this wardrobe and lays out clothes for itself, on Grossmeer's big bed, assembles an outfit and puts it on, while Grossmeer waits in the kitchen. Once the child is content, she goes to the kitchen, knocks on the door, Grossmeer says, "Who is it?" The child struts in, tossing her head to the side as though she has long hair, and Grossmeer throws up her hands in admiration: "How beautiful you are, no really, how gorgeously beautiful." And the child turns as though on a catwalk, showing herself, tossing seductive looks and blowing kisses, then gets changed, next outfit. This goes on for three or four outfits, then Grossmeer says it's time for a story. I believe the child was never happier than in these moments, and never loved Grossmeer more deeply than when—in a high, ecstatic voice—she was praising the child's beauty. When the child put her original clothes back on, Grossmeer said, "Don't tell Meer, okay, this is our little secret." She winked at the child. The child winked back.

I don't know how long this dressing-up phase at Grossmeer's lasted; it could have been six months or it might have happened just two or three times. I remember that once, when the child came into the kitchen in girls' clothes, Grossmeer said very roughly, "Get changed, those are girls' clothes, and you're not a girl." The child was hit by an immense shame that had already been lurking for a long time outside the windows, outside the door, and that then came bursting, gushing in. The child changed as quickly as it could, and it was as though everything had eyes, the walls, the lamps, the mirror; a wave of shame crashed against its limbs, a shame it had already felt from afar, and had only been able to hold at bay for so long, because all of this had happened in Grossmeer's apartment: a space without fixed whereabouts, a ship. This was when the child began to hate Grossmeer. Years later, the question: Whose clothes are they anyway? And why was Grossmeer keeping them? Or for whom?

PATHS IN THE SAND

A shift has taken place since I started writing to you, Grossmeer.
I'm slowly remembering other things too, not just you. Unearthed
things. But I'm still not anything fixed. I'm a sandbank, camou-
flaging myself as an island. The tides erode me, the ebb carries
me away, dissolves me, the flow washes new things ashore. In our
family, everyone always called everyone by the wrong names.
The women were inadvertently called by their sisters', meers',
friends' names. The men by their peers', cousins', grosspeers'
names. Meer always got so wound up when you called her
Ida-err-Rosmarie-err-Irma. But Meer herself would also call me
Nico-err-Hans-err-child. And I've begun to do this too, unin-
tentionally. I'm searching for paths into myself, into my body-
memory. I've started this manuscript a gazillion times already,
I've constructed plots ad nauseam. But it doesn't work, this plot-
ting business, these already-trodden paths in the sand. The path
has to emerge along the way.

I'm writing quickly, but am I writing quickly enough? I spoke to
you on the phone today, Grossmeer. Even though you're back
home now, you were very confused, and didn't know where you
were. "What did you do with that geranium?" you asked. "Meer
took it home to nurse it back to health," I lied. "Can't you take
it?" she said. "You know they don't survive at her house. Do you
remember when she let all my geraniums wither away, bub?" I said
yes. "Please, you take them." I made some vague assurance. You
don't know I don't have a balcony; you've never been to my home.

GROSSMEER'S GERANIUMS

Grossmeer's geraniums were everywhere. No: Grossmeer's geraniums *are* everywhere. They grew and grow on her balcony,
in borders, they run rampant through the landscapes of my
memory. Grossmeer loved her geraniums, Grossmeer spoke to
her geraniums like people speak to ailing babies. The geranium-
whisper was the only whisper Grossmeer had. *Chüschele* is Bern
German for "whisper," close to *bäschele* and *häschele*, "pamper,
tend, care for too diligently." Grossmeer had cultivated a different voice especially for the geraniums, a tenderness I don't otherwise associate with her. Once, when Grossmeer was traveling
and Meer had to look after the plants, one geranium plant died.
One single plant out of many. Grossmeer raged. Meer was silent.
I can't imagine Meer not being jealous of the geraniums. Even
the child was jealous of Grossmeer's concern for her geraniums.

Grossmeer's geraniums were relocated pieces of her body. She
only had the red ones, never the pinkish-red. When Grossmeer
prepared salad, she always mixed in thin slices of carrots or
beetroot that she grated, cutting herself almost every time. She
couldn't feel where her body stopped. Then she would cry out
loudly, the blood ran out of her, and I looked inside her. These
fine slices of her skin, of her insides, were just like the geranium
blossoms: blood-red bundles, bound together in frills.

Grossmeer checked on her geraniums multiple times each day.
Her flesh, her rampant flesh. Luminous; the geraniums were vis-

ible even from a great distance, like if you were traveling into Bern by train. Hung out for all to see, Grossmeer's flesh, growing, more abundant with every passing year. *Here, my body.* She poured all her loneliness into these flowers.

The city of Bern awards a prize for the most beautiful geraniums, and Grossmeer won twice. A bourgeois award for housewives who contribute to the beauty of the city's image. I can't remember what she won the first time, but the second time she won an apron with a bear on it. She didn't need it; she had numerous aprons, ancient ones, red-and-white-checked, blue, pink-red, and they never wore out. "You like cooking, don't you need an apron?" I was eight, I was *in a very different place* and said, "But, Grossmeer, I don't want an apron, that's for women." She looked at me in amazement. "You're right, how silly of me."

I carried out undercover investigations and wrote my thesis on the history of the geranium. I traced its origins, how it came from the South African hinterlands to Europe with the help of the Dutch East India Company, how it became a fashionable flower, an exotic jewel in the estates of the colonial rulers, how later it was cultivated on a huge scale so its essence could be extracted for perfume production, how it came via Switzerland to Germany, where it was ultimately claimed by nationalist discourse: red like the flag and resilient like the people. I felt very close to Grossmeer while I was researching, a wordless closeness that came by roundabout means.

THE INVISIBLE THINGS

One day the child was on the bus with Meer, and an overweight woman boarded. The child began to sing operatically: "Ohhh, I'm so big, I'm so faaat, no-ooo-one thinks I'm all thaaat . . ." Meer yanked the child's arm to make it be quiet. When she said, through clenched teeth, that this wasn't nice for the fat woman, the child, too clever by half, said, "But I said *I'm* fat, not her." Meer said, "Yes, but she knows you mean her." The child was stunned by this idea. "How can she know?" It visualized the words it had sung in a very material way; little clouds that, instead of dispersing into the air, buzz around and whisper to the woman, "*Fat* means you." And even after that they still didn't disappear.

I think this is how the child perceived things the adults didn't talk about. It had an intuition, a tuning fork, that vibrated with the things it didn't see. The things from the past, the feelings that were all the more present because nobody spoke of them.

Childhood feels like a dead hare beside a dirt road that's slowly being decomposed by ants, flies, bacteria, and fungi. This feeling of things disappearing, although it isn't a disappearing at all, but a transformation, a translation of body to another body, of hare to worm, to flies, to world, of present to ever-present-past, of stories into silence, of Grossmeer to me.

SPIDERS

There were spiders in the basement of our house. They scuttled
out of corners, drains, cracks in the floor. Meer never went into
the basement without a broom. Meer killed the spiders with the
broom, or vacuumed them up. "Sometimes I wake up at night,"
Meer said, "and imagine the spiders building nests inside the
vacuum cleaner. The children of the vacuumed-up spiders crawl
out of the vacuum cleaner when darkness falls." She scalded the
really big ones with hot water. Grossmeer said, "The spiders are
in the ground beneath the house. They're older than us. You can
kill as many as you want, they'll still survive." The spiders are
waiting until the humans have disappeared.

THE FEAR OF GROSSMEER

Grossmeer was always unpredictable, and could fly into a rage
out of nowhere; a devilish fury. Grossmeer was a dragon.

   When the child reaches puberty, it becomes a he, a teenager,
and the teenager has a conversation in the car with Meer. He is
seventeen; Meer in her early forties. They've been living in Winterthur, in northern Switzerland's Zürich canton, for about ten
years. Meer says she misses Bern since they moved away, that
she misses Bern like a body part. The teenager says, "So just go
to Bern more often." Meer says she can't. That once she went to
Bern, just like that, for herself. Without telling Grossmeer that
she was in the city. And of course she ran into Grossmeer, in the

center of Bern. And she says Grossmeer *annihilated* her. Meer re-counts a memory: She's fifteen, making out with a boy behind the school. When she gets home, she knows immediately that Gross-meer knows. Even before she sees Grossmeer, she senses it. As though the apartment had become a hostile ground. Then Gross-meer appears. "You're no longer my daughter." As Meer tells the story, her voice trembles, and her eyes have solidified. The teenager senses immense fear. He says, "Yes, but you weren't a grown-up then. Now you are. You can do whatever you want." Meer screams at the teenage boy, "No I can't, you have no idea what it's like, how Grossmeer is, she can be awful, no, I can't go to Bern while she's there, I can't go to Bern without having to visit her. She's a spider, lurking in the city, in her dark corner, spinning her web across the whole city. That's why we stay away from the city." This is when the teenage boy understands that childhood is never over, not even for adults.

It's nine years since I began to write about you, Grossmeer. I searched for a magical way of writing, for a magical language in which I could express your story in a witchy way, less text and more something that's alive. I searched and lost myself in linguis-tic acrobatics, writing in an endless spiral.

It's about five years since I admitted to myself that I was going around in circles with the writing and needed to speak to you. I went to visit you (a rare occurrence) and said I was interested in your past and possibly wanted to write a book about you. I asked questions about your childhood and youth. About the kind of in-teractions that were possible between men and women, the first time you ate an orange, the first time you went shopping in a supermarket, etc. I realized that you remembered almost nothing. You laughed, threw up your hands, and said, "I don't know." Or, "It's so long ago, do you know how long ago that is?" That shocked me. I'd made the common assumption that old people can still remember their childhood and youth really clearly. The topic we kept circling back to was the first Rosmarie, your eldest sister, who had died before you were born. But even here you repeated yourself endlessly. How beautiful the first Rosmarie had been. You spoke (unconsciously?) for your meer: How awful it is to lose a child. Emphasizing that you not only had the same name as the first Rosmarie, but also came into the world on the same day, some years later. When I asked why you were born on the same day— though your due date was weeks later—you shrugged.

The first time I visited you to talk about your childhood, I brought a truckli of Lindt & Sprüngli with me (a small one). But on my way over, it suddenly felt cheap, stingy, impersonal. I was walking through the market in Bern, and there were these giant bunches of over-cultivated, deep-violet hydrangeas. Hydrangeas have always called to me. They have an element of the baroque, an excessiveness I really identify with. When I saw these hydrangeas, they seemed the absolute opposite of your truckli: a sumptuous abundance. I bought one, but not so much for you; I bought the hydrangea more for me, as a weapon against the emptiness in your apartment. You didn't seem especially pleased with it; you took it, said thank you, and immediately began to tell me about your stuff: neighbors, problems with your computer, taxes, foreigners.

Last week I visited you at home for the first time since you were discharged from rehab. We drank coffee and you monologued. Suddenly you said, "Come with me, I have to show you something." You led me into your living room, to the dresser that's covered with a white cloth, on which there's a small (but still considerable) part of your truckli. And there, in the midst of the truckli army, stood the hydrangea. "Look!" you said. "The flower you gave me that time! It's still beautiful, and I look at it every day." I touched the hydrangea's dry, papery leaves. They rustled. There stood my weapon against the emptiness, years later, among the truckli. I bent down close to the hydrangea so you wouldn't see my tears. I resolved to visit you more often and to bring you flowers that dry well. Hydrangeas, baby's breath, sea lavender, lavender, asters.

GROSSMEER'S TALKING

It was impossible to have a proper conversation with you: You gave monologues, and we had to listen. You spoke about the smallest of things, worked yourself up about the neighbors leaving their clothes hanging in the laundry room for two days, cyclists who ride on the pavements, the weather, the *anarchists* who coat the city in graffiti, the *n*— who sell drugs, etc. (Always this racism, which is another piece of the past that still flows strongly into the present.) Your talking was like a waterfall, white noise, intended to drown out everything that genuinely affected you. Your talking hates writing, it's the exact opposite of writing: it tries, with its mass, to cover up everything that matters. Your relentless talking is a speechlessness. I believe this is precisely what sparked the writing in me a long time ago.

Meer inherited this talking. She held the talking scepter in our family unchallenged—when you weren't there. The two of you determined the climate of our family: speaking loudly, as loudly as possible, to drown out the others. Never telling stories about oneself or the past, never talking about feelings. You were both dominant, far more "masculine" than Peer, in a stereotypical sense of the word. He was sensitive, delicate, showed his feelings, listened and held back. And yet I only have one single memory of him:

Christmas, the child is five, perhaps. It receives numerous presents. Once all the presents are unwrapped, Peer pulls out one last present, a small one, and holds it out toward the child. Peer has written a little card too, which he reads aloud. "My dear son. Every boy needs a knife, and every Swiss boy needs a pocketknife. I love you very much. Your peer." The pocketknife is engraved with the child's birth name. I'm always trying to lose the knife. I lose all kinds of things, but not this damn knife; just when I think I've managed to lose it, it always turns up in a drawer or bag.

MY BODY: YOUR BODY

If there's a feeling from my childhood that I'm still very familiar with, it's the feeling that my body doesn't belong to me. That it's there for other people, other things, and not for me to be in. I was always like a piece of furniture, a little dresser for discarded items. I don't know how, but the adults deposited their things, themes, problems in me: their unwanted feelings, their fears, being a man, being a woman, wounds. It's also possible that these things were just lying around, ownerless, and that I gathered them up, that *I* put them inside me. It's possible that no one forced me to take on this legacy. Nonetheless, I knew it wasn't right for these feelings to be floating around in the room like that, without bodies. I've always had a very acute awareness of what's right and proper and what isn't, without people having to tell me, and I always felt this inhuman shame when someone did something that wasn't right.

I was also told that I was a piece of furniture. In the Meer-language, a badly behaved child is a piece of furniture, a Möbu: "Du bisch es Möbu!" they scolded us. Back then I didn't realize *Möbu* was a synonym for "rascal." I believed it, I believed in the language.

I presume that Meer, like me, was also a piece of furniture as a child. She told me she was constantly being told she was a girl. That she wasn't encouraged at school because she was a girl, that she was grabbed because she was a girl, that she was expected to be silent or speak quietly and wear skirts and produce children. I presume Meer converted herself fairly early on, that she carpentered herself into an archive for all women who experienced violence. She collected their stories and feelings and stored them inside her, so many that there was no room left for her own story.

It's possible that the reason I get so turned on by taking foreign matter inside me is because I've had so much practice in it. It's possible that even during my childhood I was in training to assimilate as much otherness as I could. Being used as a pure unloading station is such a turn-on for me. I love degradation; I get so wet when someone treats me like the cheapest whore. And even more so when I see how much someone *needs* to humiliate me, how much my physical powerlessness gives me full psychological control over their lust. Nothing makes me more willing than feeling how dependent they are on my sluttiness to get their cocks hard. They say, *Take it*, but really and truly it's me who's giving them something; I'm giving them a body through which they can access their masculinity. And nothing turns them on more than their own masculinity. My gift to them during our collision is the most important attribute of their gender: power over others.

MONSTERS, IN-BETWEEN BEINGS

I remember you had a gigantic plant in your apartment. It stretched up to the ceiling and was so heavy it had to be held in place with sticks and string. Its leaves were as big as my head, and they were hands. When I asked Meer what the plant was called, she said, "Monstera."

I always knew you and Meer were monsters, on the hunt for somewhere to put your seed, your seedlings. I've always known that I'm a bag, a repository; this is my purpose here. I didn't know it in these words, of course; I knew it with the Meer language before I understood it. The sentence "Du bisch es Möbu" told me. I knew you could do magic, and if I didn't love you enough, you would make me disappear. You would make me tiny and put me in one of your truckli, where I would turn into emptiness. I knew you merged with the monstera at night, that you—like me—feel closer to plants than people. Your name spoke to me, Rosmarie, and I heard the rosemary in our garden, and I thought I'd be safe if I became a blood beech, that you wouldn't be able to see me. I didn't yet know whose tree the blood beech was.

But I knew you didn't stop at the plants. That sometimes, when I was in another room, you transformed into a spider, a tiny spider I couldn't see, that followed me everywhere and spun its invisible webs, capturing all the creatures of the air. And you drank the light from us all.

I was at your apartment yesterday, Grossmeer, and you told me about the first Rosmarie again, same as always. How beautiful she was, how hard it was for your mother that you were born on the same day—I don't think it's an exaggeration to say that you constructed yourself around the first Rosmarie like a spiral staircase around a well shaft. An empty middle. Your language of your body consists of an alphabet with only these letters: *R, O, S, M, A, I*. No *E*, because it's silent when the name is spoken, and your language is purely a spoken one.

You had a little "turn," that's why I visited you yesterday (Meer *really* wanted me to). When I noticed that you couldn't remember my name at first, I wasn't shocked. Then all of a sudden you were lucid again, and we playacted normality. I detected within me a cold, analytical curiosity: What will you forget next? What will you remember until the end? And does that say anything about how important things are to you? I tested you. To my amazement, I discovered that you no longer remember Santiago de Compostela, or the significance this place held for you. I almost laughed. How absurd. I would have thought your faith would stay with you to the end, that it's so burned into you, so practiced, that it would still be there once "you" have already gone.

MEER'S LEGACY

I remember Meer reading lots of books, exclusively about women. It was as though she was lacking these in particular: stories by and about women. She read a great deal about the herstory of witches. Meer's favorite witch was Catherine Repond, who had been executed in Fribourg. The child was always irritated by Meer's stories about witches. They clearly weren't proper witches, because they obviously couldn't do magic if they couldn't free themselves. And even when the child didn't want to hear any more details, Meer insisted on saying what had been done to the witches. How their bodies were inspected, tortured. Because their bodies didn't belong to them, but the devil—according to the torturers. The devil always hid in hair, that's why the witches' entire bodies were shaved. It hid in this strange lump over the woman's slit, hence why this was cut away too. Only recently did I begin to follow the bloody trail of the witches, which has stuck with me from childhood. I read up on the herstory of Catherine Repond:

Catherine Repond was already old and a beggar and lived with her sister. One day she was captured by the landvogt. "People say you're a witch," said the landvogt. Repond denied it. "Show me your feet, I want to see whether they're witches' feet," commanded the vogt. Catherine Repond took off her boots. "What happened to your left foot?" he asked. "One autumn day I was collecting wood in the forest," said Repond. "A storm broke out. I sought shelter in a barn, but without permission. The farmer caught me and cut off all my left toes."

But the landvogt knew the real truth. Out hunting one day, he had encountered a fox and shot a bolt through its left paw. Despite the injury, the fox had leaped away. Much quicker than foxes usually leap away. That's how the landvogt knew: Catherine Repond was a witch. She was this fox. She could change her form. "Exactly," said the inhabitants of Gruyère, "sometimes she's a mouse and creeps through our cellars. If we refuse to give her food, our milk goes sour or our cheese won't harden or our children die." In 1731, at almost seventy years of age, Catherine Repond was "interrogated" thirteen times in Fribourg, tortured—for example, hung up from her shoulders with a "quintal" (fifty kilograms) on her feet—and subsequently strangled and burned.

I read in the court report what remained of Catherine Repond:

> From July 19, 1731. Inventory of furnishings found in the house of the sisters Marguerite and Catherine Repond of Villarvolard.

IN THE HEATED ROOM:

- two dozen fioles, i.e., little, empty bottles
- a large and a small bell
- three knives
- three salt loaves
- two small bowls and two cups
- a spinning wheel

- a large cushion
- two small pillows
- a poor-quality blanket of minor value
- a cover for a large cushion
- two small sheets in the bed, made of tow
- two poor-quality chests made of fir wood
- another two sheets made of tow
- sixteen old, poor-quality shirts
- a pair of brand-new stockings made of white cloth
- three pictures of Our Lady

IN THE ADJOINING CHAMBER:

- around eight half heads of corn, Gruyère unit
- around a head of barley and three-quarters of flour
- a small quantity of dried fruit, i.e., dried apples and pears
- seven cutting boards
- an old knife
- a low sideboard
- a container for butter
- a large basket filled with pieces of stale bread
- a hundred balls of yarn
- two poor-quality baskets to carry soil

IN THE KITCHEN:

- a copper pot weighing six or seven pounds
- a cooking pot
- a small box

- a stove and a saucepan made of copper
- a pot made of iron
- an iron stove, not worth much
- thirteen small clay bowls
- four hoes
- a fork
- two pickaxes
- a receptacle in which to carry everything into the chamber next to the heated chamber

IN THE SMALL CHAMBER NEXT TO THE KITCHEN THERE IS:

- a whole ham or bacon
- around a dozen pounds of melted butter
- a piece of molten gold
- assorted vessels made of wood

The aforementioned house also contains a number of other poor-quality items, such as vessels or rags, which aren't worth recording, as well as a table made of hard wood and a pothook.

Their house is surrounded by piles of chopped wood that reach almost to the roof.

All that remains of Catherine Repond are the things the "mourners" pilfered, the inventory of their greed—and the blank spaces: the absence of Catherine Repond's story as she would have told it. The I to which we no longer have access. We only have this "she."

GROSSMEER'S TREE

There were many trees in our garden. The trees are what I remember most, and the tree I remember most of all is the blood
beech. It was large and had low-hanging branches, making it easy
to climb into. I felt more connected to it than I did to people. It
had an element of the monstrous, the hermaphroditic: it was a
mixture of animal and tree. It was an in-between, and it drank
blood. The child talked with the blood beech. It sat beneath its
red foliage as though beneath a second skin. When the sun shone
through, the foliage was a skin from the inside. The child asked
for lessons. The blood beech knew so well how existing works,
how to find one's own form, how to fill out a body. How not to be
driven out of one's own skin. How to withstand a storm, the winter. Once the child said to Grossmeer that the blood beech was its
favorite tree. I'll never forget the look on her face. An alliance.
"That's my tree," said Grossmeer. "It's exactly the same age as
me. My peer planted it for me when I was born."

Dear blood beech, how does a person become a blood beech?
How does a person become as big and strong as you? How does
a person defend themself against all the names they're constantly
being given, how do you fight back against the Bärli, *little bear*,
the Häsli, *little bunny*, and the Käferli, *little bug*?

The lessons of the blood beech were: Stand there. Shed your
leaves. Endure. Create new foliage. Come into leaf. Transform.
People were far more threatening than the monsters under the
bed or in the cupboard. They always had this body, and the mon-

strous thing about this body was that it was never simply a form of being in the world, but rather always had a gender, no, *was* a gender—a man *or* a woman.

I suspect I was also drawn into writing because writing is one single wavy line, a wave coming from far away that began long before me and will flow onward long after me. Because fluidity is the element of language. A languid, latent, deep, sweeping, carrying, igniting, drowning, retaining, life-giving, inexhaustible, mirroring, monster-concealing, dissolving fluidity. Because I was always a body of water, my body always sensed how much it flowed, how it was perpetually in motion.

It seems to me that in the body language of men, an old legacy gets passed down that is learned in fear, practiced in competition, and spoken in war. Even today, it fills me with horror when I encounter this language. When young men come toward me with this aggression in their shoulders, this broadness in their gait, this certainty of being correct in their body, this goddamn-cocky rutting-roaring language of the limbs, of dominating, over-powering, suppressing, *Bam, here I am, this is my space*. When I encounter this body language, I become something very light. These bodies horrify and fascinate me. I can't say I'm not drawn to them. That I don't sometimes draw this language onto my body—when no one's looking—and enjoy it. But I feel closer to the body language of women. I often wonder how I would move if I'd grown up on an island without human beings, among animals. Probably I would move animalistically, cowlike, snake-ish, mousily or multibestially. But here, in this islandlessness, in this always-in-the-midst-ness, in the binary-fascism of body languages, my limbs speak a mishmash, a masticated elvish, a ka-put Denglisch, an urgent in-betweenness that reels back and forth in confusion.

I don't know how else to word it: I don't know a language for my body. I move neither in the Meer language nor in the Peer language. I exist in a foreign language. Perhaps that's one reason for this writing, for this carved-up, crumbling writing. For the fact that my hands produce only shards, their edges so splintered I can't build from them a beautiful, smooth, compelling, polished story. Perhaps writing is the search for a foreign language in the words we have available to us. The attempt to carve a tongue-sized hideout in what already exists, in what we've inherited, one that's large enough to dance in.

OUR STORY

Dear Grossmeer. I've tried to—our story. So far, it's a collage of scraps, an assemblage of flotsam and jetsam. I'm noticing that I'm Meer's child and your child, and less the child of Peer: I've inherited your avoidance of storytelling. Peer's family was always a counter model to your ancestral line: they exclusively told stories of the past. I'm not saying that's better. There's something compulsive to how, in Peer's family, the lived experience is formed into narratives. And of course, not everything gets told; it's only ever a selection.

It's naive to think the stories we tell one another again and again don't have an impact on us, that they don't make us, and it's just as naive to think they don't have their own agenda. I believe that these stories build themselves around us, that we see the world through their alphabet. And I believe that the stories we don't tell one another, that we don't tell even ourselves, are a different story entirely.

A memory: at my peer's brother's place, with Peer and Oma, their meer. I was about twenty-four years old. We were drinking in silence. We drank long enough to traverse the silence. Suddenly: a feeling of lambskin in the room. I knew it was imminent, and went to the bathroom, just to escape. It struck me that the Bernese Oberland dialect, in which my peer was raised and which he now only speaks with his meer and other Oberländer, has no genitive. These mountain folk don't say: Hans's father or the father of Hans. They say: Hans his father. I had never grasped that as a child. Relationships and family connections were always unclear to me when I was with Peer's family. The people blurred into one another.

Even today, a sentence like that is a little home for me, and when I write "it has no genitive," I feel ashamed. Am I really this city-student type who says pseudo-smart things about the farmers in the mountains, who lives in another world? I feel ashamed, and simultaneously angry at the shame, because it's never personal; it's been installed in us to keep the mountain farmers with the mountain farmers and the city-student types with the city-student types, the bodies in the clothes, and the "gender" in private.

Coming back into the room to Peer and my uncle was like slipping on a glove lined with the finest lambskin. Peer tops up his glass and begins: Bruno and Hans, his best friends, had come to his house one August morning to ask whether he was coming with them to climb the Red Finger. He usually always went climbing with them; climbing was their way of escaping the valley. Escaping the confinement of the valley, which closed so tightly around their young, newly bearded necks. To this day he doesn't know why he didn't go, this one time, whether he had homework or something. But no, he was nineteen, he'd already left school, he can no longer remember. "You were twenty," said Oma. "Nineteen," said Peer. They looked at each other. "It's my story," said Peer. "I was there too," said Oma.

In any case, Bruno and Hans didn't come home that evening, and so their parents came to see him with two mountain guides, and he went with them, because only he knew exactly where they'd gone, it had been their secret route, because it had the best view, from the Red Finger. "You can see the Aletsch glacier from there, the Blüemlisalp massif, and Lake Oeschinen." They reached a freshly fallen scree field, and that's when he knew. They searched until nightfall. One of the mountain guides who had accompanied them suddenly rounded everyone up and said they should light a fire and rest a little, given it was almost completely dark. Then continue on at dawn. Peer didn't sleep for even a moment. When dawn came, the mountain guide who'd rounded them up walked straight toward a certain spot, and Bruno his clothes lay there. Peer thought to himself: Why are Bruno his clothes lying there, so bloody and torn to shreds? Until he saw it wasn't just the clothes, it was Bruno. They found Hans farther up the slope. Hans his torso was peeping out of the scree like a candle from a hand, intact. The lower body was beneath, completely twisted, coiled like a lock of hair. Almost severed. But otherwise, Hans was almost intact. The intactness its eeriness.

Peer didn't just tell the story on that evening. He had already told it many times: after burials, at birthday parties, baptisms, retirement parties, inauguration ceremonies, graduations. It's the first time I'm writing down his story, and as I write, I realize there are a few parts he always tells in exactly the same way. The core parts: Bruno and Hans standing at his door, ropes over their shoulders: You coming to the Finger? Bruno and Hans's parents at the door: They haven't come home. The freshly fallen scree field beneath the Finger. Bruno his clothes, which are his body. Hans his illusory intactness.

These parts are always the same. In particular the description of the bodies. But the margins of the story are always a little different, as though they change each time. As though they fray and Peer knots them together in a new way, until next time. What he was doing that day. What he was wearing. Details like the weather, or plants, or snippets of conversation. Who was in the search team. It seems to me that a person can't do much with the core parts of their story. They're already fully told before you've told them. The core parts have you; you're at their mercy. They're telling you; not you them. But you can do a great deal at the margins of your story. The margins are where you can fight against it.

Unlike Peer, you didn't come from the Oberland region, Grossmeer, but the Central Plateau, the lowlands, as we call them; unlike Peer you always tell your stories—if you're talking about the past—in exactly the same way from beginning to end. How beautiful the first Rosmarie was. How loved she was.

How she died. How much your meer missed her. You narrate sentences that contain a distance, that are closed off, like your truckli, sentences you can put away. But your hands. They narrate relentlessly. The scraping of your raw skin, of hand upon hand, is deafening.

To me, your hands were always the most horrifying creatures in the whole world. Not because they threatened, grabbed, and stroked me. But because I always sensed I would inherit their story. That this narrative had already translated itself into my body and wouldn't find its way out again if I didn't do something, if I didn't do something with it, if I didn't transform it. For a long time, I rejected this legacy. I didn't want to belong to your family; I didn't want to be your successor. But a person can't go home if they deny their legacy. And in Western culture, ever since Odysseus, writing has been the attempt to find a home that perhaps no longer exists, that perhaps still needs to be told. The medium that Odysseus carries is both the ocean and language. The God of the Sea has cursed him, that's why Odysseus's journey home takes ten years. When the gods finally decide he can return home, he first has to relive everything, live through another cycle: he narrates what has happened, the war, the odysseys; he narrates in order to have a future, to return to the place that is no longer home.

So far I've had fewer memories of Meer than of you. But I want to remember. I'm going to sit down now and open myself up to the writing, to this skylight in the fog of things, and see what comes. Because what I don't tell will devour me.

What I've saved until now: the story of the red-currant bread, the Meertrübeli bread, as you call it. I've saved it because it isn't a memory, because you still tell it. The story of the first Rosmarie might be your cornerstone, the reference point to which everything you experience comes back. But actually, it's not a story, it's a fact, and after all these years you still don't have enough control over it to make a story out of it. The Meertrübeli bread story, however, really is a story, and maybe that's why I like it. It seems to me that this might be the direction to take: in order to escape the things a person can't escape.

YOUR STORY ABOUT THE MEERTRÜBELI BREAD

In the olden days, back when the sky was still properly blue and people were poor, they used to help one another. They knew exactly who lived where in the neighborhood, who visited whom when and how, who left their washing hanging overnight, and they helped one another. That's right. People were close at hand because everyone needed everyone, nobody could make do with nobody. A few streets away from us, there lived an old witch. She was ugly and mean, and nobody really liked her, but they helped her regardless. I especially didn't like her: she once tattled on me to my meer when I peed behind a bush. My meer beat me, because girls don't pee behind bushes, never, that's only for boys. But because people helped one another, my meer sent me to the witch from time to time, so I could help her, and once I went to her and she sent me to the baker with a ten-rappen coin. I went to the bakery and fetched a loaf. When I brought it to the witch, she didn't say thank you or anything, she went to her kitchen, pottered about, came back. She had cut off the mürggu for me, the crust, and spread it with Meertrübeli jam. In the olden days, when there were wars and people had so many mouths and always hunger and never any money, people used to give one another food. I took the Meertrübeli bread, didn't say thank you or anything, walked around the block and was so furious at my meer for sending me to the witch, because I knew she didn't like the witch either and that I only had to go there because I'm a little girl and couldn't ever do anything to defy my meer. I was so furious at the world that I was in it as just a little girl, that I wasn't allowed to pee behind the bushes, and the Meertrübeli jam reminded me so much of the witch and her flabby cheeks that I dumped the Meertrübeli bread on a dung heap. And I tell you, I tell you, that night I lay in bed with a Meertrübeli-bread-sized hole in my stomach, and I cursed myself thinking about the Meertrübeli jam, its sheen, the fresh crust, crunchy but not hard, the bread's soft innards, and I still think about it and still curse myself for throwing it away, but what else could I have done with my anger? I had to do something.

2

The Search for Childhood

About the things that only my body remembers

———

We have all been injured, profoundly. We require regeneration, not rebirth, and the possibilities for our reconstitution include the utopian dream of the hope for a monstrous world without gender.

———DONNA HARAWAY

We're all just mutations, and I think that each mutation should be celebrated.

———ARCA

A spell is a story we tell ourselves that shapes our emotional and psychic world . . . The counterspell is simple: tell a different story . . . And if we tell our own stories with enough intensity and focus, we'll start to believe them, and so will others. We'll break the spells that bind us.

———STARHAWK

Becoming woman/animal/insect is an affect that flows, like writing; it is a composition, a location that needs to be constructed together with, that is to say, in the encounter with others.

———ROSI BRAIDOTTI

THE HOUSE

There is the house. Around the house the garden. The garden is alive. The garden remembers everything. It remembers on the people's behalf. In house and garden lives the child. Or rather: In house and garden dwells the child. Or rather: In house and garden exists the child. In houseandgarden it's in the world. In houseandgarden it survives. In houseandgarden it nests. In houseandgarden it grows up. In houseandgarden it's present. In houseandgarden it hides away. In houseandgarden it sneaks through houseandgarden. In houseandgarden it becomes houseandgarden. Houseandgardenhouseandgarden. Here is the child in a thousand ways.

It sits in the house by the window. Surrounded by paper cuttings. Made with the Swiss Army knife. Holes scratched into the black paper. The child uses the knife frequently. So Peer will see. See that the child needs the knife. Now the child stands. It looks outside. Looks at the day. The day founders in the scant evening light. Across the suburban areas. *Sabinaaa. Maurooo. Lauraaa.* The houses cry commands into the sky. The day slips into the boxwood bushes. The boxwood bushes are smart, perfect spheres. They guard the entrance to the street. Where the main street turns into the neighborhood. They stand to the left and right. They are guardians of loveliness. Ensuring everything is in order. They cast far-reaching shadows. Onto the homeward paths. These shadows mean business. When the family men come from the city. With their workfaces in tow. And want to get back

in. To the lovely family neighborhood. Step back into the idyll.
They have to strip off their citybodies. Empty them out before
the suburban guardians. Like rain from rubber boots. Before
entering the sitting room.

The night devours all objects one by one:
    the sheer-spiked fences standing sentinel,
    the perfectly rectangular vegetable patches,
    the spick-and-span summerhouses,
    the hordes of hanging birdseed bombs,
    the fertilized rambling roses,
    the hollow bodies of garden gnomes,
    the view of not-single-family homes far away in the so-
        called distance.

The house is stuffed with orchids. The pink, white, plasticky ones.
And the ones dyed with blue food coloring. The house is up to its
neck in them. Grossmeer brings one on every visit. So the visit
has a purpose. Meer doesn't water the orchids. She puts them in
corners. In the cellar. Beneath the coffee table. And still they live.
And still they survive. Are they actually ghosts?

Streetlamps devour yellow chunks out of the night. Family
life spills out of the single-family homes. Shining yellow into
the front gardens. The night is small. But the town is smaller.
It drowns in the night. The family people drown in the IKEA-
kitchen-lamp glow. Their dreams drown in the pumpkin soup
bowls. The mothers drown in their motherhood-happiness. The

fathers drown in their pale-blue shirts. Their orchid-blue shirts. Are they actually dyed with food coloring? The fathers. The dinners. The single-family homes. So they look. Like fathers, like dinners, like single-family homes. Are they actually alive?

As dusk descends, the child flees the house. Penknife in front like a sword. The child's hand conceals the engraved name. It runs to the blood beech. Crawls beneath her leaves. The night slips over everything. An enveloping nightgown. Here the child is safe. Here it is invisible. Here it is there. A window opens in the house. A gash on the house's brow. The window screams the child's nicknames. *Bärli! Käferli! Häsli! Müsli!* The names are an airborne threat. Then they strike. They pull the child from its hiding place. They force it to say, "Here I am." And then, "I'm coming. I'm coming back to the house."

The word *Haus*, the Standard German for "house," means "throat" in the Meer language. This house is Meer and Grossmeer's Haus, where their voices live.

THE SWALLOW

The child walks home from school. It takes detours. To be out and about for longer. The detours know the child. The spot where the concrete is a mouth. The spot where there's a slat missing in the fence. The child sees the house in the distance. It's on fire. Grossmeer's voice. Snarling fire. The child takes a long detour. It walks between castles of concrete. The Serbian butcher with the knives. The Thai restaurant with the orchids. The cheese shop with the Swiss crosses. The nail studio with the smell. The masseuses with the smiles. The electronics store with the overalls man. The hairdresser with no hair.

The child doesn't live in a place. It lives outside of a place. No trains stop at the station. They hurtle past into the city, or out into the world. They whirl up dry leaves. The child stands in the gusts of wind. It imagines grabbing on to a train and being pulled along. Ending up in a completely different place. It turns around. The place name sign cries out: OSTERMUNDIGEN. The child goes into the parking garage. It goes to the rainbow wall. THE BEAMING MILES OF OUR PRIMARY SCHOOL STUDENTS. The s is missing from "SMILES." Meer said. Beneath the wonky rainbow stand fingerless children. The swallow hovers over the fingerless children. The child sits in front of the swallow. It tells the swallow about its day.

Today I was a donkey. I spoke only with *E* and *O*. Anna was the unicorn again. Tamara was the fairy. I have to become a better donkey before I'm allowed to be a fairy too. But I already have a lot of fairy power. More than Tamara, for sure.

The child imagines joining the swallow in the concrete. Being in the concrete is like being in water. And everyone will come. And finally realize. That the child is a water fairy, and they'll feel so stupid they didn't see it sooner, and they'll cry so many tears for the child that the whole world becomes an ocean. And then the concrete will dissolve. And the child will swim with the swallow.

But now I need to get home. It's getting dark, dear swallow. See you tomorrow.

The child pauses in front of the house. The dragon is still raging. Suddenly Peer appears next to the child. "So. Is it dragon time again?" The child nods. Peer takes the child by the hand.

PEER

Peer is tiny. Space is limited in the house. Peer has to make space. Peer fits entirely into Meer's fist.

Meer and the house are related. Meer will inherit the house from Grossmeer. It was built by Urgrosspeer, Meer's grosspeer. The house crept out of Urgrosspeer. Like Meer out of Grossmeer. Being in the house = being in Meer. The walls are skins. The corridors have hands. The doors are mouths. Every knothole is an eye.

Sometimes Peer sits wide-legged on the sofa. But this wide-leggedness doesn't come without a cost. He has to cut off a piece of himself. He cuts off three hours of voice. In exchange, the house allows him a moment of wide-leggedness.

Meer is a cemetery. She carries within her all the women of the world. The women pile up in Meer as she reads. Most of them weigh a million kilograms. Every single one. Meer carries inside her:

Elisabeth Kopp,
Jeanne d'Arc,
Virginia Woolf,
Anne Lister,

Lady Di,
all women beneath veils,
all women from the textile factories of Southeast Asia,
all women from the women's prison Hindelbank,
all women from Africa,
all witches from the history of Europe,
especially Anna Göldi
and Catherine Repond.

These women are immensely heavy. While she reads, Meer has to go on a diet. She sits in the greasy armchair and doesn't eat. She stuffs herself with women's unhappiness. "My body still thinks it has to store fat for the brood," says Meer. The brood: the child knows that means the young rabbits. The child is moved. That Meer's body is storing fat. For Urgrosspeer's long-dead rabbits. "But Meer," says the child. "It's no use. An uneaten potato for every unhappy female life. There's no way you can balance things out." The child doesn't say this directly to Meer. When the child wants to speak to Meer. It puts Meer's old pajamas on Barbie. Puts Barbie-Meer on the greasy armchair. When Meer is at work. And says, "So, sweetheart. Do I need to remind you who rules the roost?"

Meer tells the child: "I was my peer's favorite child. All parents have one. You should count yourself lucky you're an only child, because in your case there's no choosing. I helped my peer with all kinds of outdoor chores: gardening, woodchopping, house repairs. My brother hated the dirt, the earth. I loved the dirt, the earth. The potato harvest was like Christmas and my birthday rolled into one. My hands knew exactly what was a stone, what was a potato. My hands weren't a girl's hands.

"Once a month, a chicken had to be slaughtered. Before the slaughtering, Peer would traipse around. He would lose his voice. He'd clear his throat as though he wanted to say something, but never said a word. When the time came, Meer called from the house: *Are you doing it or do I have to do it myself, you featherbrain.* Then Peer would drag himself over to the chicken coop. I went with him, sensing I needed to. He always did the hacking really quickly, then let go of the chicken and covered his eyes. I had no sympathy for the chickens; they have such tiny eyes. I felt heartache for my peer, though, because I saw how much it hurt him. Once I asked why he didn't stop doing the slaughtering. He said his peer and Meer's peer in heaven would laugh at him if he did. Then I hugged him, and cleaned the blood that had spurted from the chicken as it darted around everywhere. It was still warm. And afterward, from then on, I slaughtered the chickens myself and cleaned my hands thoroughly so Grossmeer wouldn't notice I was the one doing the slaughtering and not Peer. Another time, Peer gave me a shovel as a present. I took it with me everywhere. Even to bed. We understood each other without speaking, Peer and I. We were very close. Physically too. That changed when I reached puberty and became womanly. One day I was sitting on his lap, like I always had. Grossmeer came in and looked at us. Peer pushed me off. I crashed down to the floor. 'You're too old for these games now.' Then he began to scatter these sentences, letting them fall as though they were of no consequence. Like farts. Or slug pellets. 'Women are dangerous. Women can turn you into the devil.' Peer insisted my brother study at the gymnasium. He even paid for him to have tutoring. From the money he'd scrimped and saved. In the evenings, Peer studied with him. He always asked how he was doing in class. When I reached that age, it wasn't even a question. 'What would you want with the gymnasium? You couldn't handle it. It'd be money down the drain, you'll marry and have kids.' I did an apprenticeship and started to work. And once I'd saved enough money, I paid to do my leaving certificate at night school. Meer was tough as an ice pick with Peer when she opposed him on something. He was the same with her. I always knew: I'll never be as ice-pick-tough as Meer."

Meer strokes the child's head. "My little bear."

BLOOD BEECH

With Grossmeer and Meer in the garden. Grossmeer talks and talks and talks. Grossmeer's words form waves. She has snow-white sea-spray around her mouth. Meer swims. She's up to her eyes in water. The child stares into the garden. Blood beech, chicken coop, walnut tree. They're almost drowning too. Grossmeer is in everyone's ears. She can't bear to be inside herself.

The child is afraid of Grossmeer. That she'll turn back into the dragon. The child has an idea. I'm going to draw you, it tells the blood beech.

The child picks a brown pencil for the trunk. A red pencil for the foliage. It draws the blood beech so many leaves. The leaves are ears. It gives the drawing to Grossmeer.

Grossmeer: "Oh, thank you, what a lovely drawing, how sweet of you, and he really didn't tell me about this motorbike, and now he parks it in the cellar all the time, and what can I do, am I supposed to say, no, monsieur, that won't do, and the other neighbor, the woman from upstairs, you won't believe what she's gone and done . . ."

The child goes over to the blood beech. I drew you, it says.

But you drew me wrong, says the beech. My leaves aren't ears. Do you always draw things that aren't there?

But Grossmeer needs more ears, says the child.

Can't you listen to her?

When I listen to her for too long. Grossmeer overflows. Then she lives in me. Her voices, says the child.

Well, they have to live somewhere.

But not in me, blood beech. I'm still so little. If I were as big as you. Blood beech. You can just grow. No one else decides your form. I wish I could be like you.

The child bites off a piece of its fingernail. A lot of nail comes away. There's a hole in the finger. Blood drips from the finger. Drips onto the roots of the blood beech. Seeps beneath the roots. The blood beech drinks it in.

Thank you, little one. Do you really want to be like me? asks the blood beech.

The child nods. One of the blood beech's roots twists upward. A thick, bulbous root. It thrusts into the child's open finger. The blood beech's juices surge beneath the child's skin.

MEER

Meer has three skins. The first is made of woman. She would have liked to be a man. To be allowed to be aggressive. To study. To be allowed not to have children. At the same time, she hates men. She makes the garden into a fortress. With yew trees growing along the fence. Dark and dense. A protective wall against the outside.

Meer's second skin is made of talking. Talking is an armor. An inherited skin.

Meer's third skin is made of dogged forgetfulness. Beneath it, she wears a truckli.

Meer works every day. She cuts hair. She drowns in the waves of her clients' hair. She sees lots of old women. Meer's work is one big permanent wave. The permanent wave has no shore. If the child had one wish, it would wish for everyone in the world to lose their hair. So Meer would never have to work again.

Meer works overtime. Meer is up to her hairline in work. She's a skin-sack filled with tiredness. When she closes her eyes. She sees all the cut-off hair. The back of her eyelids is one giant fur. That's why they're so damn heavy. And why they always fall shut on her. And Meer falls into her flowered pillow. The child makes a noise. So Meer doesn't fall into the pillow. Because it needs the pillow. And Meer's eyes fly open. And she's angry. And her eyes are empty. Empty like Grossmeer's truckli.

As soon as Meer has fallen asleep. The child steals the flowered pillow. Carefully, like stealing tiger cubs from a tigress. It bundles Meer's head back into place. Meer is so exhausted she doesn't notice. The child pulls on the forbidden magic shoes. Disappears behind the Meertrübli bush.

Why does Grossmeer always turn into a dragon? asks the child.

Don't ask us, little pill bug, say the pillow flowers. We can't even speak, we have . . .

Suddenly the flowers freeze. The leaves of the Meertrübli bush crackle. The child turns toward the house. A cool wisp of air. Something has awoken. A tremor goes through the earth. The windows are misted up and weeping. The house is already a shade of blue. The child knows what's happening. It can feel Meer through the house wall. Meer is transforming. It starts with her eyes. Her gaze becomes an icicle. Her pupils, a black hardness. The cold expands out. Her mouth becomes thin as a hair. Her body hard as a rock. She is now the Ice Witch. Hide. A layer of ice spreads over everything. Walls, floors, cupboards, glasses, windows, dust balls, sky. Houseandgarden is a freezer.

The child tries to run behind the chicken coop. But the ground freezes from the house outward. Spreading like a pool of white blood. A rapid, hard wave of cold. It reaches the child as it runs. The child can no longer move.

The Ice Witch opens an ice window. She screams. Her voice a nail on a blackboard. The child hears only the voice. It shoots through the child. It only understands a few words: stiletto heels, working, tired, brat.

shield

take cover

hide out

hide away

lie low

isolate oneself

entrench oneself

elude

duck away

crawl under

hunker down

creep away

submerge

shelter

bite one's tongue

keep under wraps

keep schtum

choke down

lock away in one's heart

conceal

mask

gloss over

suppress

withhold

contain

keep hidden

keep secret

not be seen

not show

camouflage

shroud

whitewash
cloak
draw a veil over
bury
occlude
obscure

O, you ambiguous word, *obscure*. You mean so many things. You even have a cure hidden inside you. Can you hide me inside you too?

THE BATTLE AGAINST THE ICE WITCH

To thaw Meer out from the Ice Witch. You have to be extremely brave. You have to go toward the Ice Witch. Like going home through an ice storm. You have to take one of the Ice Witch's hands. The hands are ice-cold spiders. Like an entire winter packed inside a glove. And then you simply have to be there. You can't let yourself freeze. If you let yourself freeze, you die. You have to carry a warmth inside you. Like a vast, vast desert. The thawing takes a long time. It always begins in the back garden. The ice spell wanes. The Ice Witch's strength dwindles. The ice begins to retreat. The ice creeps back into the Ice Witch. The plants thaw out, wet and limp. The ice lingers in the corners of the rooms. The Ice Witch retreats beneath Meer's skins. The thawing takes longest in her face. You can't look into her eyes. They remain ice-cold for a long time. Her gaze is a fist punch. Her hands remain moist for a long while.

The thawing is minor magic. Because it's so slow. But it's the most important of all the healing spells. Of those the child is able to do.

When Meer thaws out from the Ice Witch. She still can't speak for hours. She's a dry piece of bread. Trudges her way through the house. Bangs into corners. She crumbles away. In the Meer language, "crumble" is *brösmelä*. Meer is *brösmeling* away. The child collects all the little Meer *brösmeli*. Sometimes the child hides away under the bed. It lays out the *brösmeli*. Draws Meer's face with them.

Where does the Ice Witch come from? asks the child.

We're not allowed to say, say the *brösmeli*.

Why not?

We can't actually speak.

Why not?

We're only crumbs. We don't have a voice of our own.

If the child were to meet a fairy. And it had one wish. It would wish for a spark for Meer. A spark that never goes out. That she could hang inside her chest. It would always be warm. Then she wouldn't need the thawing spell.

One day, the child sees through the Ice Witch. Shortly after the thaw. Everything has thawed apart from her eyes. Then they thaw out with one blink. They rain down over Meer's skin. She doesn't say a word. She hugs the child. Her eyes flow onto its forehead. And when it looks up. The child sees behind the drained eyes. There could be a completely different witch there. A water witch. With a completely different way of doing magic. But. She's trapped in a block of ice. She's trapped inside this protective spell. *So. Now the laundry. It won't do itself.*

GROSSMEER'S PRESERVES

Grossmeer comes into the house. She turns the garden. Into preserves. Spring summer autumn. Quince jelly. Rose-hip jam. Apples with cinnamon. Cabbage into sauerkraut. Turnips. Beans. Sprouts. Grossmeer's favorite is making raspberries into syrup. She ties her apron as tightly as possible. Cuts off the blood flow. The large draining cloth in front of her, full of raspberries.

Grossmeer's arms vanish from the elbows down. The raspberries look like entrails. Grossmeer drinks the raspberries with her eyes. Gets drunk on the raspberries. Every blink a sip. Grossmeer is boisterous in this raspberry joy. She boils liters of water. Lets it cool. Filters off the chalk. Then she waters all the orchids in the house. The child watches from beneath the tables. Grossmeer waters spitefully.

The cellar is full of preserving jars. The Bülach brand. Sometimes the child walks between the shelves. This is forbidden. Something might fall. The child runs a hand over their cool, green bellies. The Bülach glasses have fat bellies. Their necks are tied as tightly as possible. The preserves aren't to be touched. The preserves are for the winter. For the *hard winter*. The *hard winter* is always the coming winter. And it's out to get us.

One time, the child is creeping through the Bülach forest. There's a noise from behind. It jumps in fright. As it turns, a jar of cherries falls. Grossmeer is standing there in the doorway. The child stands in the pool of cherries. They're still gurgling. The fruits like blind children's eyeballs. Grossmeer's eyes are glowing coals. She goes upstairs. The child waits. When the front door closes. It goes upstairs. The cherries cling to the child. Its footprints are made of children's eyeball juice. The orchids lean on their little plastic sticks. They crane their necks. Their heads pretend to be beautiful and white and innocent. But they see everything. Every misstep. There will be consequences, child. Very, very serious consequences.

BELONGING(S)

Dinnertime. Grossmeer is talking. Meer too. Peer is silent. The child is there. It feels the blood beech's roots growing inside. *Bloodbeech* is the biggest word in the world. Bigger even than *weepingwillow* or *meerträubelijuice*. No sentence in the Meer language has space for it. The child goes into the garden. Autumn is like baking parchment in front of the sun. Autumn makes the trees rust. They turn red and brown. They shed themselves. The child sits in the blood beech. Like in a cathedral.

FRÄNZI BETHLI JÖRG AND JÜRGLI

Peer told me a story, says the child. The story of Fränzi and Bethli. They were two sisters, one heart. They lived this side of the mountain. Then Fränzi was married off to Jörg. Jörg took Fränzi to the other side of the mountain. He gave her a son. The son's name was Jürgli. But Fränzi missed her sister, Bethli. So Jörg went to fetch Bethli from the other side of the mountain. But instead of bringing her to Fränzi. He took her to the depths of the forest. There he did her the most terrible violence. And cut off her tongue. So she couldn't betray him. And kept her guarded in a forest prison.

"A storm came to the mountain," he told his Fränzi. "The storm swept Bethli off the mountain." Fränzi was filled with grief. Overspilling with it. But Bethli, in the forest prison, was smart. She asked to at least be allowed to weave. Bethli wove an apron for Fränzi. She secretly wove her story into it. In a way that only Fränzi would understand. Bethli asked one of the guards to take the apron to Fränzi. Jörg didn't suspect a thing. But Fränzi understood the apron. She rescued her sister. Together they killed Jürgli. Because Jürgli was the extension of Jörg. Of Jörg's bloodline. More than Fränzi's son. That's how things were back then. Bethli and Fränzi cooked him. Fränzi gave him to Jörg to eat. Jörg ate him. Once he was finished. Fränzi showed him Jürgli's head. Jörg drew his sword. Pursued Fränzi and Bethli. God could no longer look upon this violence. He turned them all into birds. Bethli into a swallow. Fränzi into a nightingale. Jörg into a hoopoe.

The blood beech says: To become like me, you have to tell me *your* story. That isn't your story.

The birches exhale. Their breath is white. The birches exhale fog. It sloshes eerily against the child. The fog flows into its skin. The skin breaks open. The child sloshes against the single-family homes, the poplars, the streetlamps. It sloshes to the edge of this world. The child is filled to the throat with dark forest light. The leaves fall paperlike into the fog-child. They're fleeing the winter. I'll keep you safe, dear leaves.

The child goes to the walnut tree. Meer says that's where the potato field used to be. The child goes to the empty space. The weeping beech used to be here. Now there's just a hollow. Not even a hole. The weeping beech. That's what Grossmeer always says, and nothing more. In other respects, Grossmeer talks constantly about the garden. Grossmeer has to plow the garden every night. And she still can't. Eat. One. Single. Raspberry. Grossmeer ate the garden. And the child knows. From the garden. That the garden also ate Grossmeer. The night breaks out of the boxwood bushes. The child's animal names are being called.

MAN OR WOMAN, OR HOW THE CHILD WISHES TO FLY AWAY WITH THE MAGIC SHOES, AND HOW IT PRACTICES BEING HUMAN AND BEING A BODY AND DOESN'T KNOW WHAT IT WANTS TO BECOME, BUT MORE THAN ANYTHING IT LONGS NOT TO BE UGLY

The child stands in its parents' bedroom. Looking at Peer's leather shoes. They have a greasy sheen. Soles like planks of wood. Fattongued. Sour. Heavy. Mouths cracked where they've stretched. When Peer puts on these shoes. He also puts on their mouths. Takes off his own mouth. No longer has a language. Only the body language dictated by the shoes. This coarse angularity in his movements. Peer puts on the shoes only rarely. The shoes are for *weddings, funerals*, and *special occasions*. Or when Meer commands him to. Meer's magic shoes are made of refinement, of smoothness. When she puts on the shoes. The shoes walk through her body. Into her laugh. The laughter clacks with heels. Peer's shoes pull you into the earth. But the child understands Peer. It would like to have other mouths sometimes too. But the magic shoes. Are so beautiful. That they can fly. The child is afraid. That Meer will fly away with the shoes. Because that's what the child wants to do.

The child goes into the bathroom. Empties the mirrored cabinet. The mascara. The eye shadow. The lipstick. The nail scissors. The nail file with the two levels of coarseness. The child rotates the lipstick tube until the red comes. The shaving foam. The razor blades. The aftershave. The nail clippers. The child stands in the doorway in front of the mirror. It plays Peer. Puts on the jogging body. The bouncing. Arms slack at the sides. Puts on the football body. The broadness. The explosive run. The shoulders' transformation into double shoulders, into shelves. The crotch grab. Like this: Hrrrmph. Pronounced not with letters of the alphabet. But with limbs. The standing there. Hands on hips. The shouting, "Heey, that was a foul! Throw-in, throw-in! Corner! Fuck! Faggot!" The voice from the hips. It puts on Peer's after-work body. The trudging. The leaving-himself-lying-there like a snail trail. Setting down his bag. His gaze like a Sunday evening in January.

Now it plays Meer. Puts on the gardening body. The straight-backed bending. The quick tying-up-the-hair. The quiet monologue. It puts on the work and argument body. The armor: a layer of ice around the skin. The frowning brow. The swallowed lips. Voice like a knife. It puts on Meer's going-out body. The body made of dough. Soft and malleable. The slow brushing-the-hair-behind-the-ears. The gentle head tilt. Exposing the neck. Pushing out the chest. Shifting the weight to one leg. Not talking too loudly. The going-out body is the opposite of the football body.

The child wonders. When is it time to decide? Whether to become a man or a woman? It often poses in front of the mirror. But never for too long. It's afraid. That the mirror too will remember its body. The child knows: it can't become a man. Meer's love is immense. Meer's love is greater than the land. A lifetime wouldn't be enough to emerge from Meer's love. Meer's love is an ocean. And it has one single coast: masculinity. Meer says: "When boys become men. They walk like apes. They become so boorish. They get acne. Their faces become uneven. Their voices break. Women become objects to them."

But the child can't become a woman either. What would Peer do? But women have such beautiful hair. And they're allowed to wear makeup. And colorful fabrics. And they're allowed to sing. And they're allowed to wear trousers *and* skirts. And they're allowed to cry as much as they want. But men have such beautifully hairy legs. And beautifully deep voices. And they're allowed to belch.

Soon the child will have to decide. People are asking. *So. What are you then? A boy or a girl?* It looks at the other children. Most have already decided. They stand in the kindergarten two-by-two and stare expectantly. The child wonders: How does this decision work? Is it a magical process? Do you have to tell the Language Meer? The one inside your body. And she gives you a magic spell. You have to say it a certain number of times. Until the sentence meshes with your flesh. Gets embodied in your body. Floods into your blood. The child goes into the chicken coop. Invents witches' spells. But that's transformation magic. It's different to healing spells. The child has always practiced healing spells. For Meer. And Grossmeer. But transformation magic is a completely different science.

Brew, brew, I brew my magic potion
I'm not sick, but this confusion's an ocean
Brew, brew, hex hex
They say it's time to pick a sex!
This toy's a boy's
This pearl's a girl's
And what are you?
I girl, I curl, I twirl,
I hurl, I swirl, I whirl
I'm not nearly boy enough
And yet too much to wear Meer's stuff
Brew brew, make me now, this instant, into a woman!

No, I—Hocus Pocus, magic ban, now transform me to a man. Grr. Big. Tough. Buff. Hmph. Stomp. I'm no swamp. I'm powerful and grand! Like a trump card, I take a stand. Look at me, it's plain to see—I'm made of man!

Uh, no, dear Language Meer, please, oh please, turn me into a woman, I don't want to walk like an ape, I don't want to become boorish, for my face to get uneven or my voice to break. I don't want women to become objects to me, I beg you.

But oh, inside I hurt
Inside I feel like dirt
My muscles so inert
Of this I'm oh so sure
And what for others is true
To me is watery blue
But the skies above are always gray
A lifeline seems so far away
And Ostermundigen is harsh each day

And no, I'm no moaner
I'm secretly striving
to be a Casanova.
I'll head off on my quest
Become the very best
And someday live life at my own behest.

Language Meer, look at me,
I'm a chihuahua, see
Sitting by the TV
Like it's a gold rush spree
Watching sports so endlessly
The bodies there, a sight to see
But being a bully, it's not for me.

I wanna be the kid who escaped the Ice Witch's lair.
But I lack the know-how, the flair,
I float through the ocean, trapped and scared.
My hands, did I mention:
They overflow with chaos and tension
I need release, an intervention

I wanna be a peacock, plume aglow
Destroy them all without a blow
'Cause I'm a fun maestro,
I say "ciao" to the limitations
and "miaow" to the exultations
Oh, what a feat
ce n'est pas mieux, le vieux,
The old is now obsolete!

GROSSMEER'S SKINS

Grossmeer has five skins. The first is made of talking. Talking is a kind of armor. The armor protects her from her other skins. The other skins are made of the first Rosmarie. All but the last skin. Stomachskin. Hungerwall. Grossmeer often eats at our place. That's when Meer and Grossmeer fight. They talk against each other. She who speaks the loudest wins. Peer has disappeared into his skins. The child has to listen. After all, someone has to. Otherwise what would happen to people, if no one listened?

When Grossmeer and Meer talk. Their mouths grow over their lips. Their mouths grow over their chins and noses. Their mouths enshroud their skulls. Their first skins have turned inside out. The insides glisten like red silk lining. Two gullets. Abysses. Abysms. Abysmal. Dragging. Wrenching. The maelstroms tear the child in two. Which should it listen to? The child becomes invisible. Fades away. In a cramped place. In the air. As thin as paper. Like the crack between the fitted cabinet and the wall.

SWALLOW

Hello, swallow. Sometimes I think I'd like to be a boy after all, because it feels better, and I'd like to be allowed to be loud and wear those cool little hats and beat people up. I hit Anna today, and she cried and said unicorns don't hit, and I said fairies don't fart either, but you do, and I'd prefer to be the fairy anyway, because unicorns are dumb, all they can do is stand there and be pretty. Tamara said I can't be a fairy, because I hit, which means I'm bad, and that there aren't any bad fairies. But there *are* bad fairies, because bad fairies are essentially just young witches, and when they get older and powerful, then they become proper witches.

PEER'S SKINS

Peer is studying the history of Meer Earth. He's so deep in her rock layers. Sometimes he doesn't emerge for days on end. Then

Peer has seven skins. The first is made of dead deer. The second, of silence. The third, of granite. The fourth, of heaviness. The fifth skin is childhood. The sixth is made of God-fearingness. The seventh, of fragility. The fragility of a tiny edelweiss flower-fur.

Sometimes Meer Peer child are having dinner. Sometimes Meer asks Peer something. "How was your day?" By the time the question has reached Peer. Seeped through his seven skins. Meer has already washed the dishes. And put the child to bed. She smokes a cigarette in the garden. "My day was good," Peer tells the kitchen.

When the Ice Witch overtakes Meer. And Peer is fast enough. He grabs the child. And flees to the chicken coop. He puts the child on his knees. And tells the child a story. Peer has to tell a story. To hide his fear. His fear of the Ice Witch is immense. It's always bigger than him. The child always struggles. To focus on the chicken coop stories. It wishes a wish for Peer. It wishes for an internal pocketknife. A knife in the belly. So Peer can cut open his seven skins. From the inside.

If Peer has caught too much cold. And is staring into nothingness. The child says, "Tell me the story about the animal skin." Then Peer tells the story of the parchment. In days gone by, people made it from animal skins. It was used instead of paper. And it was very expensive. So the uppermost layer was always scratched off and a new story written on top. But you could never entirely erase everything. The skin remembered everything.

IT USUALLY SKIPS A GENERATION

Meer, Grossmeer, and child are sitting in the garden. The child is allowed to leaf through Urgrosspeer's herbarium. It's not allowed to look at the herbarium alone. Urgrosspeer collected all the plants himself. Meer is wearing a skirt. Her legs are covered with varicose veins. Little blue snakes beneath the skin. If you press them, they move. Grossmeer doesn't have a single snake beneath her skin. Where do Meer's snakes come from? Meer stares incessantly at Grossmeer's legs. Meer's gaze becomes a beanstalk. Meer never usually wears skirts. Skirts are a woman's domain. So that men grab us between the legs. Meer usually wears trousers.

"You take after my meer," says Grossmeer. "She had rough hands too. And she was quick-tempered." A glance at Meer's legs. "And she had lots of varicose veins. It's linked to temperament. You should be gentler. A woman should be gentle."—"I'm not Grossmeer. And you're not exactly gentle yourself," says Meer.—"But I don't have varicose veins," says Grossmeer.—"I'm gentle with the child," says Meer. "Gentler than you were with us." Grossmeer laughs. "You can't choose what you inherit," says Grossmeer. "It usually skips a generation."

THE VOICE

The relatives are there. Uncles, aunts, the entire herd. "So, how are you, child?" The child wants to say something. It can feel the blood beech seedling in its belly. It's growing. "You're a shy one, aren't you?" The child feels its voice. Something spiky in its chest. "Why are you afraid? There's nothing to be afraid of." The child runs to its room. It pulls out the watercolors, the Caran d'Ache brand. It wants to paint the things inside. The voice and the blood beech seedling. It draws itself. Picks a black pencil for the voice and a green one for the blood beech. The drawing doesn't come out right. The child gets angry. It can't make anything come out right. It can't draw things as they are. In other words: how they are for little magical children. Everything always looks so wrong once it's painted. Furious, the child eats the watercolors. They are soft and dry and bitter.

The child runs to the beech tree. The child's voice hangs out of its mouth. Far too loud. It pulls out the pocketknife and cuts off its voice. The voice entwines with the beech foliage. A skinned eel. It has no eyes. But it has seen everything. The beech leaves tremble. The rustling beech has a voice like a thousand whispers. The child spills over, crying watercolor tears. They mingle on its face. The face a muddled palette. All the colors trickling down its chin. It wants to stuff the voice back inside. But the colors have dried. Its mouth has dried shut. Where its mouth used to be, now there are colorful stripes. Far too colorful.

The beech leaves tremble.

Don't be afraid, little one, say the beech leaves. Leave your voice here. We'll keep it safe. Once you're big enough, you can come here. And get your voice back. Sometimes, when things get hard, you have to carve yourself up.

The child hacks a hole under the beech roots with the pocket-knife. Places its voice inside. When I grow up, thinks the child. I'll come back. And the voice will tell me everything. The voice has its own eyes. The child buries the voice. The beech leaves tremble. The trembling courses through the beech trunk. The trembling courses through the ground.

"Bärli, come on, Bärli, where are you, it's dinnertime. What have you been doing? You've got the whole garden on your hands. And your Sunday trousers are filthy. Shame on you. Only children with clean hands get dinner."

A CHICKEN COOP TALE

"Your meer doesn't have it easy, you know. She works while I study. That's tiring. And what's more, your meer has a gift." Peer takes a deep breath. On his lap are the garden shears. They're huge and rusty. He grips them tightly. "The dead visit her. She's close to them. She understands them. The dead who linger want to talk, after all. Otherwise they would have moved on. Not everyone can understand the dead. But your meer does. She has a keen ear. And she sees them. She has eyes where others don't. But your meer doesn't want her gift. A gift like that comes with responsibility. If a person understands, they also have to listen. We have it much better nowadays. Than our dead. They suffered. So we would have it better. You can't choose your gift. A gift is always a duty too."

The frost flowers on the chicken coop windows begin to fade. The wood creaks. The ice begins to retreat. The Ice Witch is releasing her ice spell. The child doesn't say a word. Tentatively, they leave the chicken coop.

Once they're inside the house, Meer hugs the child. Her arms are surprisingly warm already. But the child avoids her eyes, which are still full of ice. Suddenly Meer says: "I'm sorry I'm so cold sometimes." Meer carries the child close. "I'd like to tell you a story. Back when I was a child, I had a stuffed toy, my favorite thing in the whole world. When I had it with me, I could do anything. It was a teddy bear. A very old one: it used to belong to Irma, one of my aunts. I'd found the teddy bear in our attic. He was dusty, and missing an eye. Grossmeer said, 'You'll have to wash it yourself.' So I washed the teddy with ox gall soap, in the rain barrel by the chicken coop. I got the hair dryer and blow-dried the teddy bear. Then I picked him up and went into the garden. Like I'm carrying you now. The teddy bear peered out of his one eye as though he was newly born. And I walked through the garden and showed him the world." The child stares at Meer, its eyes wide. Meer carries the child through the twilight. She looks away. She looks into her story.

Meer puts the child to bed. "The end of Teddy." Meer sighs. "Teddy was already so old, his cloth skin threadbare and unravelling. I was so careful with him, but I took him everywhere: to school, on Sunday walks, to the bathroom, everywhere. It started with his mouth. Suddenly it tore open and his insides spilled out. He was filled with beans. The beans rolled out into the dirt.

Grossmeer said, 'Don't make a fuss.' I asked her to mend Teddy.
Grossmeer's good at mending things, as you know. Her whole
life long she's darned socks, sweaters, jackets, pants. It would
have been easy for her to mend Teddy. 'He's past mending. You
weren't careful enough. You were so rough.' I never saw Teddy
again." Meer looks at the child. Her gaze drives terror into the
child.

Then Meer sings the child its favorite lullaby:

> *There is a lad by name o' Fritz,*
> *Who runs so fast, and runs so quick,*
> *Who runs like lightning, lickety-split,*
> *He runs so fast, and runs so quick,*
> *That no one's ever seen 'im.*

The child decides to become invisible. To become a constant in-
visibility. To not be so unbearable. To not be so difficult. To not
take up so much space. So Meer can finally get her diploma. Become invisible, but not disappear. Disappearing entirely would
probably be hard on Meer. But becoming invisible would ease the
burden. Meer, I promise you. I'll become invisible.

> *And 'cause young Fritz, he never quits,*
> *And 'cause young Fritz, he never sits,*
> *Even this poet must admit:*
> *If he runs so fast and never quits,*
> *Does he even exist, this lad named Fritz?*

Meer's voice lulls the child to sleep. Her voice trickles into its little body. The child knots the voice to the spot where its own used to be. "Night night, Bärli."

"Meer?"
"Yes, Käferli?"
"Why is Peer almost never here?"
"His soul's stuck in his childhood. Like in a mole burrow."
"Meer?"
"What?!"
"Is your soul stuck in your childhood?"
"Listen, who is it that holds this family together? Who puts gas in the car? I don't have that luxury. Now go to sleep."

WARTS

Meer bathes the child. They sing together. The walls throw back the entangled voices. The child falls silent, so it can hear itself again. Then it feels the beech shoot. "What's that?" asks Meer. "What are these bumps?" The child draws its foot beneath the water. Meer pulls the foot up. "Warts," says Meer. The child doesn't contradict her.

The next day, Grossmeer comes by. She brings a bag from the pharmacy. The child has to take off its socks. "Plantar warts," says Grossmeer. Meer grips the foot tightly. Grossmeer pulls out a pen. She presses the pen against the foot. So cold it's hot. The child can't help kicking out. Into Meer's face. "Sorry!" Too late.

Meer cracks. The ice witch advances. Meer fights. She stands up and leaves the room. "I'll be good!" cries the child. "I won't kick anymore! I'll always put my pajamas on quickly! I'll stop waking you up during your afternoon nap!" Grossmeer stares at the child. "Now look what you've done." Her voice blazes with fire. Suddenly, the child understands the Ice Witch. How else can you fight a dragon? If not by turning yourself into ice. The pen hisses on the child's foot.

A week later, the warts are back. They grow quickly. They hurt when the child walks. Like little thumbtacks. They dig in deeper and deeper. "Those aren't normal plantar warts," says Grossmeer. "Look how brown they are! And so hard. Like wood." Grossmeer picks up a knife. Holds it in a candle. The knife turns black in the flame. Then red. Then yellow. Then the cutting begins.

Meer begins to brew a potion. She calls it a "decoction." Suddenly she has a piece of paper. Where did she get it from? She walks through the garden with it. Leans over the herbs. Pulls them out, roots and all. "The decoction has to be boiled for one moon cycle. It's a healing decoction. We'll soak your warts in it. Then we'll cut them out. Then they won't hurt anymore. Isn't that right, Bärli?"

THE MEER LANGUAGE

Meer makes syrup. "Are there Johannisbeere in it?" asks the child. A look from Meer.—"In the Meer language, they're called 'Meertrübeli,'" she says sternly. "Where did you hear that word?"—"The teacher used it," the child replies. "Don't go forgetting your Bernese German on me now," says Meer. "Bernese German is your mother tongue. Do you hear me?"

The child pictures the Meer language as a giant spider. She's bigger than all the mountains stacked on top of one another. The child calls it the language sea. When babies come into the world. They have no tongue. They can't talk yet. The tongue comes from the language sea. Every time a child is born. She cuts off her tongue. Her tongue grows back at once. It's attached to the language sea by a thread. It's tiny. The tongue crawls through the babies' ears. Into their mouths. While they sleep. They can't defend themselves. And when a person dies. And is laid beneath the earth. The tongue crawls out of their mouth. It crawls along the long, thin thread back to the language sea. That's why the mouths of the dead are bandaged shut. So the tongue only crawls back later. A person is nothing without their Meer language. The Meer language isn't a home. It's a threat.

THE STORY OF THE WOMAN WHO WANTED TO BECOME SOMEONE, OR THE STORY THE CHILD WOULD HAVE TOLD THE BLOOD BEECH IN ORDER TO BECOME A BLOOD BEECH, IF IT HAD HAD THE WORDS TO DO SO

There was once a woman. But she didn't want to become a woman. She wanted to become somebody. She wanted to pass her final-year exams. And then go off to university. In order to become somebody as a woman, you need armor. She forged herself a coat of armor from ice and steel. But it came to pass that she met a mole. The mole burrowed through her armor. Into her heart. Where he planted his seed. That's how the seedling came into the world. It was half mole, half woman. The woman disguised it as a child. The child didn't learn to speak until quite late. First it had to learn to write: it wrote *sorry* on the back of every word. Its language was a language of apology. It was afraid of the Meer language. Because the Meer language saw with its Meer eyes. And the Meer eyes didn't see the child. Instead, they saw the reason why the woman became a woman. And not somebody.

NINE WORDS

The child stands at home in front of the mirror. It practices Peer's sport: sitting. When they are at Grossmeer's. The child and Peer watch television. They watch sports. Hands on thighs. Elbows out. Taking up as much space as possible. Shoulders slack. Occasionally reaching for the trouser bulge.

Press. Scratch. Adjust. Hmph. Grr. Don't let anything captivate you. Peer gives himself a bodyful of sports on each visit. And saves this hard body to take home with him. The hardness only shatters once it collides with the Ice Witch.

The child grabs between its legs. Adjusts what it can. The child doesn't succeed. The whole thing is playacting. The child remains fluid. Sometimes it has to hit itself. When it meanders back and forth too much. Or bite itself in the arm. Or press a fork into its belly. Or a needle beneath its fingernails. Or push the back of its hand against a wall. And walk along the wall. So it comes from being-water back into its skin. Pushing itself back into what was assigned. Like cookie dough getting pushed into a cutter. At the end. Once there's nothing left to cut out. Just leftover dough. The butter already melting. The child knows it isn't proper. To be almost-melted leftover dough. To vanish from being-human.

The child hides between the raspberry bushes. It can feel the land. The land grows soundlessly. The invisible emperor goes beneath the earth. He makes the land. He has hollowed out the mountains. And he plans his campaigns there. He plants the light in the sun. And the fruits in the fields. And life in the bodies. And milk in the cows. And water in the taps. And beards in the men. And breasts in the women. He stretches his hands out toward the child. His many wispy, wiry, fleshy, inescapable hands. The child has to make a choice.

Dear raspberries. Can you help me? The kids at school make fun of me. Sometimes I'm a boy and sometimes a girl. But a person can't be both.

The child waits. Nothing happens.

And if you can't help. Can you pull me underground? Can you make me invisible?

The child senses the houses all around. All the single-family homes. They loom over the child. It feels their many-windowed gaze. The single-family-home gaze, this rectangular, geranium-lined gaze. The single-family homes are overflowing with families. All this loveliness. This terrible loveliness. Meer Peer child and done. And the child? What will become of it? Once it can no longer be a child? The raspberries are silent. The child touches the raspberries' long fingers. "Raspberries?" They don't answer. The child's hand is covered with delicate thorns.

The child runs into the house. Only Grossmeer is there. "What's wrong, Bärli?" The child can only cry. It runs into Grossmeer's arms. Her skin is wrinkled and delicate. Once the child has calmed down. She asks again: "What happened, Käfer?"—"The raspberries aren't answering me anymore. They normally talk to me."—"They normally talk to you?"—"Yes."—"Then you just need to be patient. They're a bit temperamental."—"Grossmeer?"—"Yes, Bärli?"—"Can you tell me a story? But it has to be true. From the past. From your childhood." Grossmeer is silent for a long while. "I can't tell you anything about my childhood. I barely remember it. I only remember the garden. But I've already told you all of that. I can tell you about my grosspeer. He had seventeen children. Imagine the work, with seventeen mouths to feed! There was no time left for storytelling. Once, at supper, there was a girl sitting there. My grosspeer asked: 'Who are you?' The girl replied: 'I'm your child, Peer.'"

The child is silent. "That's so. So sad."—"Käferli," says Grossmeer. "Why do you always speak in such short sentences? Why do you always break up your sentences like that? It's not healthy, you know."—"Promise me. You won't tell Meer? Cross your heart?"—"Yes."—The child summons all of its courage.

"I'm under a spell. The Ice Witch put a curse on me. I can't say more than. Nine words at once." Grossmeer pushes the child away. "You should be grateful. My meer never hugged me."— "Grossmeer, you have to help me! The Ice Witch wants to cut off my feet! And boil them in her magic potion! The beech tree wants to give me her power! But the Ice Witch doesn't want that! Because then I'll be stronger than her! And she won't be able to control me anymore! She wants me to disappear. Then she won't have to cook anymore! Wash for me! Clean! Shop! Iron! Work! Sing lullabies! Handle me with kid gloves! Struggle! Mend things! Bake birthday cakes! Take my temperature! Pick me up from school! Play the tooth fairy!"—"You ungrateful brat! That sick imagination of yours! Go to your room!"

THE ORCHIDS AND THE STORY
OF THE ORCHIDS AND THE MARSH
ORCHIDS THAT BELONG TO THE ORCHIDS
THAT URGROSSPEER COLLECTED,
AND THE CHILD'S WISH

One day they go into the mountains. Peer Meer child. Peer and Meer argue. Peer walks on ahead. The child takes Meer's hand. Her hand is hard, like a mountain. The child points at this and that. Look, how beautiful, it says. Meer has no gaze in her eyes. When they sit down to eat. Meer has a gaze again. The gaze is a knife. She points at a pinkish-red flower. "That's a marsh orchid," says Meer. "It was your urgrosspeer's favorite flower. Do you know why it's called a marsh orchid?" The child shakes its head. Meer digs out the plant. The plant smells of vanilla. It has two round tubers. A plump, light one. And a wrinkled, dark one. "Because it's got balls," says Meer. She laughs like a hyena. "Men are so in love with their gender. They think nature wants to be like them." Meer tosses the flower into the bushes. She shoots a look at Peer. Before they continue on, the child says, "I have to pee." It goes to the bushes. Grabs the two tubers in its ball sack.

At home, the child goes to the beech tree. Stands there for a long while. Until the beetles think it's beech bark. And the ants, a toilet. The beech, a foliage dumping ground. The child stays until it's completely invisible. Then it sneaks over to Urgrosspeer's herbarium. It finds the plant. Urgrosspeer collected so many.

Common Spotted Orchid

Military Orchid or Helmet Orchid

Man Orchid

Pale Orchid

Purple Orchid

Leopard Marsh Orchid

Elder-flowered Orchid

Beneath, he has written: "Marsh orchids usually grow in unfertilized wet meadows. Most marsh orchids are now rare in our latitudinal lines, especially the Elder-flowered Orchid. (I found this one in Bavaria.)

"There was a long-lasting superstition that women who eat the juicy tubers would bear a male child. The Greeks tell the story of Orchis, a beautiful yet impetuous young man who got too close to a woman. He was immediately struck by the wrath of the gods, who decreed he be torn apart by wild animals. A goddess took pity on him, however, and transformed him into a plant. His well-formed body remained above the earth; only his testicles, the corrupting roots of his masculinity, were banished beneath.

"Orchids are a young family. That's why the varieties are still very unstable. They like hybridizing among one another. This is why classification isn't easy."

The child doesn't understand much of this. It understands "wet meadow." The child hides the tubers. It puts them beneath its socks in a drawer. Sometimes it looks at them. Soon even the plump tuber becomes shriveled. One day, all of a sudden, they've disappeared. The child goes into the cellar. It goes to the preserving glasses. Throws a glass of cherries on the floor. Cherries are Meer's favorite fruit. The child goes into the garden. Lies on its back. Feels all of the earth. Transforms. Grr. Hmph. No. Hmph, and done. No grr. Un-grr. Ogre. Stomp. Swamp. Come, all you endangered species. All you unstable species. I'm a good earth, a swamp, a wetland. Come inside me. I'll protect you. I'll become a woman. And only in secret will I grow a garden. Deep down in my belly. A garden filled with marsh orchids, and no one will see it. And when I'm dead and buried, your flowers will bloom. You'll emerge and go out into the world, looking almost human, and if you are asked, "Who were your parents?" then you won't say a word. You'll smell like vanilla. And all the un-flowers will want to pick you.

A FAIRY TALE

I was once a little child whose Meer and Peer had passed away,
and who was so bitterly poor it hadn't a cubbyhole to live in nor a
cot to sleep in and nothing but the clothes on its back and a piece
of hard bread in its hand, but the child was good and devout and
went faithfully to the Lord God, who sees everything, who really,
really sees everything, and along the way it ran into a poor man,
who said, "Oh, give me a morsel to eat, I'm so hungry," and the
child handed him the little crust of bread and said, "May God bless
it for you," and it reached a dark forest, and dusk had fallen, then
another little child came and asked for a little shirt, and the devout
child thought, It's nighttime and dark, no one will see me, so I can
give away my shirt, and it took off the shirt and gave that away too,
and as it stood completely alone in the forest with nothing around
it but trees and not a stitch on its body, along came a pale specter,
a little ghost, who said full of bitterness that it had been slain by an
evil knight, and now no longer had a body, and yet its little brother,
who had no one else in the world, was waiting back at home, and
the little ghost asked very nicely for the little child's little body,
not for its own sake, but for its little brother's, and then the little
child gave its little body away too, because it had no one, not even
a little brother to look after. And while it was there beneath the
tall trees and no longer was anything and had nothing but its soul,
the rains began, until the entire heavens had rained down upon the
earth. And once the earth had become one great ocean, the child
dissolved and became part of the ocean. And if the child didn't die,
it's still a part of the ocean today, an invisible drop.

WHAT ITS BODY KNEW

Meer has been at work. Now she's lying down in the living room. She's "done in," as she calls it. She's sleeping so deeply. The entire sofa trembles with her breathing. The child is sitting in the same room. In the farthest corner. Making "paper cuttings." Scratching fairy sparks into black paper. It scratches so carefully. That it can't even hear itself doing it. It makes a heat spell in the sparks. It will give the sparks to Meer. So she can fight the Ice Witch. The child concentrates fully on the magic. Then it drops the pocketknife. Meer awakes with a start. Her gaze is a fist of glaciers. So hard. That the child's body screams. But the fist bores into the child. Into its mouth. Making the scream change direction. The scream drives deep into its body. The child runs into the garden. The scream screams through all its insides. Its entire body shakes. The child falls into its own middle. Stands beneath its rib cage. As tall as cathedral columns. In the ground is a hole. In the hole, a spiral staircase. At the bottom of the spiral staircase, a light. A tiny little light. The light is far, far below. The child climbs down. It goes toward the little light. That's when the child sees what the light is: its own life. It takes its life in its hands. Scoops it out of the depths like a tadpole. The little life nestles against the child's skin. That's when the child knows. Knows what its innerness has always known. Then the child pulls out its very biggest, most delicate tenderness, gives it to the little light to eat and says: "I'm afraid I can't take you back up there with me, little spark. You have to carry on hiding. She would extinguish you."

The child looks through the window. Meer has fallen asleep again. It goes to the cellar door. Takes off its shoes. Takes off its socks. Takes off its feet. Becomes an imperceptibility. Moves through the house. Not even the orchids see. It goes out. Goes to the copper maple tree. Plucks a leaf. Walks on, plucks an apricot leaf. Plucks a walnut leaf. Plucks an ash leaf. Plucks a blood beech leaf. Goes to the spot where the weeping beech was. Digs a hole with its hands. Places inside it:

    assorted drawings

    some watercolor pencils

    three cuttings from black paper,

        including the unfinished fairy sparks

    the word *obscure*

        with all its meanings

    approximately seven mouthfuls of spit

    the six plucked leaves

The child knows what its body has always known. Meer wants the child dead. It has disappointed her. It tried to become invisible. But it didn't succeed. Even invisible children are noisy. Even if they're not real human children. Even if they're little human-bears. Bipod-bunny baby-beetles of badly behaved Möbu. Now she'll want to kill the child. She'll send the Ice Witch. She'll say the Ice Witch did it. Becoming invisible is no longer enough. The child will begin to disappear. And it knows. If the disappearing spell doesn't work. It has to leave completely. Otherwise she'll get rid of it. The child buries its few possessions. Then it sings its favorite song.

There is a lad by name o' Fritz. Who runs so fast, and runs
so quick. Who runs like lightning, lickety-split. He runs
so fast, and runs so quick. That no one's ever seen 'im.
And 'cause young Fritz, he never quits. And 'cause young
Fritz, he never sits. Even this poet must admit. If he runs
so fast and never quits. Does he even exist, this lad named
Fritz?

But I was here.

URGROSSPEER

The detour has now become the usual homeward route. The
child stands in front of the house. The garden is a frozen waste-
land. It goes to the blood beech. She doesn't answer. She's an
ice beech. The child wants to reverse the ice spell. It begins to
word a fire in its mouth. But the child soon stops. It's no use. If it
thaws out the blood beech. The Ice Witch will notice. Notice how
good the child is at making spells. Not just the temporary thawing spell for Meer. It can't let her notice. The child has to hide
its true witching powers. Let them grow in secret. Until they're
strong enough to banish the Ice Witch, like the black spider was
banished into the beam, pooling all its magic into a single spell, a
glowing incantation that will thaw the Ice Witch once and for all
and free the imprisoned water witch from her ice prison, but—
and the child senses this very acutely—it will have to spend many
years scheming and practicing and formulating this emancipation

spell, because it knows it has only one chance to confront the Ice Witch and reveal its true being, to show its entire witchy nature, to use all its life force against her. Because if this healing spell doesn't come as a surprise, the Ice Witch will glacierize the child too. And the child will become an ice child.

The ice slowly retreats. It gets pulled into the house. After a while, Meer comes out.

"Where were you?" she asks sternly.

"I was here," says the child. "Meer, where does winter come from? Where does it go in summer?"

"Winter goes south, like the birds. And then it comes back up again."

"And us? Where do we come from?" Meer takes the child by the hand.

"Your urgrosspeer was one of seventeen, the eldest. A farmstead in Appenzell. He showed me a photograph, a negative: the farmhouse in Appenzell, a little toy block on the crest of a hill in front of the crests of other hills. The crests are white, the farmhouse whiter, the sky dark, the clouds black. Homestead. He was too poor to do an apprenticeship. Poor as a church mouse. His peer turned to alcohol. Your urgrosspeer went to the south of Germany in search of work. For ten rappen more per hour, he changed towns. He sent all the money home, he had to take on his peer's role. He was a very austere man. Your urgrossmeer didn't want to marry your urgrosspeer at first. Then she changed her mind. If you reject the hand of a real man, you're either stupid or blue-blooded. Then your urgrosspeer lost his job, man's hands here nor there. Urgrossmeer still had a job, two in fact: silk-spinning and in the chocolate factory. They scrimped and saved. Then they bought this plot of land."

"Your urgrosspeer built this house single-handedly, in 1927, during the economic crisis. They became farmers again. The garden and your urgrosspeer became one. Back then, people cared for their gardens like we care for our bodies today. There was always this one question: How to survive the winter? He measured the vegetable beds using little dibbers and cable; your urgrossmeer had to help. He double-checked her beds with the tape measure. If they weren't exactly right, he trampled them, and Urgrossmeer would start from scratch. Your urgrosspeer made a crop rotation plan: which plant grows where. He recorded everything. The potato record: which variety, how many kilos. The apple record, the chicken record. The last egg record is still there."

"Where?" asks the child. Meer goes over to the chicken coop.

"Here are the names of the chickens, and the days of the week. This is the total for the entire week, and this is for the entire year. For example: Agatha laid three eggs in the first week; Susi six. Susi laid the most by far. Susi was Urgrosspeer's favorite chicken. Vreni laid five, Romy two, Emmy four."

"Why does Romy stop here?" asks the child. It points at the middle of the table. "She got old," says Meer. "When chickens get old, they stop laying eggs. They become soup chickens. You cook them. Before the chickens, they used to keep rabbits, but Urgrosspeer wasn't able to kill them. They were too cute. That's why they switched to chickens."

"He could kill those?" asks the child. Meer nods. "Because

they have smaller eyes," says the child. "You can't see as far into their souls."

They left the chicken coop. "I only saw Urgrosspeer cry once, and that was when Susi died. A fox. Urgrosspeer was sitting here in front of the chicken coop, in the dirt, at night. He heard the fox, but it was too late. Urgrossmeer appeared with the lantern. Urgrosspeer was sitting with Susi on his lap. His hands soaked with blood, there's so much blood in a chicken like that. Urgrossmeer said: 'You two belong together. You and Susi. You chickenshit crybaby.'"

"And then what?" asks the child.

"Then he beat her so badly that she was sent away to recover."

"There were flat fingers hanging in the cellar: beans on threads. The potatoes were buried in the vegetable cellar. There was meat once a month, on payday. But not good meat, it was cervelat sausage, one per mouth. Pure luxury. But spring was the hardest, because by then everything had been eaten and there wasn't yet anything to harvest. Except wild garlic nettles linden leaves dandelions. The whole garden had to be used for vegetables. Urgrosspeer only permitted a few flowers around the perimeter. Urgrossmeer could beflower these borders, a second fence of tulips geraniums hyacinths and roses: whitish-yellow petals like tiny vanilla tarts. And oh: their scent. Like the perfume of the finest madames.

"This is where the *Suurgrauech* apple tree stood. Here the *Aargauer Herreöpfu*, here the *Winterzitrone*, here the *Frou Rotacher*, here the *Jonathan*. And here, the greenhouse they built. Grossmeer wasn't allowed to eat any of the tomatoes and raspberries, not once, because they could be sold at such eye-wateringly high prices. Every piece of fruit they ate was a loss.

"And still they had no money for the doctor. Urgrossmeer was frequently sick. She had this giant goiter, a sack of skin on her neck as large as a fist. When she pulled me onto her lap, I was always afraid it would burst. It reminded me of a baby's head. Bare, delicate skin. I knew it had something to do with Urgross-meer's sentences: she swallowed everything down, that's why she had such a fat neck. I knew that if it were to be cut open, there would be the most incredible mess. Of everything she'd swallowed down."

"Your grossmeer had eight siblings, two of whom died. The first Rosmarie and the stillbirth. Although your urgrosspeer was poor as a scissor-grinder, he planted a tree for every living child:

"For Robert, this birch. For Phillip, the copper maple. For Benoit, the apricot tree by the house wall. For Moritz, the walnut tree. For Hans-Peter, an ash. For Grossmeer, the blood beech. And for Irma, a weeping beech. But Irma's tree was felled. It used to stand where this hollow is now. I don't know why it was felled. Grossmeer doesn't talk about it."

"Where are Phillip and the other men?" asks the child.

"Robert: heart attack. Phillip: India. Benoit: heart attack. Moritz: disappeared. And Hans-Peter: heart attack."

"Urgrosspeer was interested in plants. Not just agricultural, useful plants, but beautiful ones too, ornamental trees, park trees, and especially beech trees. Common beeches dwarf beeches blood

beeches. He ordered the expensive trees even though he couldn't
afford them. He had saved a tidy sum of money he kept secret from
Urgrossmeer and used it to pay for the trees. And the geraniums.
After park trees, he thought geraniums were the most beautiful
plants in the world. When he couldn't sleep, he went around the
neighborhood planting homegrown geraniums. In front gardens,
at intersections, under benches, under bushes, along the roadside.
He believed Switzerland was the greatest country in the world;
and that the Swiss were the greatest people. He felt you shouldn't
mix with other countries," says Meer. "Your urgrosspeer was still
here, I could still feel him. He was still in the house, in the plants.
Things don't just disappear, you know. I heard him at night in
the woodwork. He was making sure that everything was in order.
After we first moved in, there would sometimes be a knock on
the front door. When we opened it, there was no one there. But I
knew it was him. He had this firmness to him. Like an old poker
in your hand. Cold and heavy and swiftly dangerous. I always
kept one by the door. One time, I shouted: *We're here now. You're
dead. Go away.* After that, he left us in peace."

FLOWINGTOGETHER

One day the child went for a walk with Meer. It can no longer remember when it was. But it must have been one day. They walked
through the forest. Meer and the child. It held Meer's hand. And
so did Meer. She held her own hand tightly. She was afraid of
the Ice Witch. The hand wasn't a body part. It was the bridge
between ice and child. But then the forest appeared. It opened

up. Around them. Then the forest was a sea of light. Made of green and humming and resin. And Meer and the child let go of each other. But they stayed close. And the hand became body again. And they leaped through the forest. Until they reached the river. The river was warm. It glittered and whispered. Meer and the child jumped. It was cool, but not cold, and they screamed, and Meer dove under for a long while. Then the water witch emerged, took the child, and pulled it under with her. She taught the child, taught them to fly, taught them how to glide over the riverbed. How to open their eyes where usually there are none. How to listen to the swoosh of the pebbles, to drink the light, talk with the rocks, to twist off the skin so the world can get in, so the water can stream into what's commonly known as the "inside" and soak the plants that grow inside the child, and the child now keenly felt what they had previously vaguely known: where their power comes from. It was a water magic, a streaming, a flowing.

LAST STORY

Peer is silent. Meer eats nothing. Peer eats. Meer looks at the child. Peer looks at the veal kidney pieces in mustard sauce. The veal kidney pieces in mustard sauce are smooth. They gleam dully like snails. The child eats the veal kidney pieces in mustard sauce. They secretly creep back up the wall of its stomach. Meer's pupils creep into the corners of the child's eyes. Meer, please don't eat me. On the table are spring roses. They separate Peer and Meer and child.

"I'd like to be grown-up now," says the child.

"But you're a boy," says Meer. Her pupils swim smoothly and gleam dully. "Your warts have grown again. After supper we'll scald them. The decoction's ready."

The boy goes into the garden. He feels the blood beech inside him. He feels it like fingers in his feet, like delicate, long claws, like spider roots. They break through the soles of his feet. The boy stands beneath the blood beech. The shoots reach through his skin into the ground. They begin to fix the boy to the spot. Rooting him. "One last story, blood beech," says the boy. "Irma's story. Irma was Urgrosspeer's favorite child, the smallest, the youngest, the sweetest, even more beautiful than the first Rosmarie. That's why Urgrosspeer loved her more than anything, and because he loved her more than anything, she wasn't allowed out. Because this world, it breaks you. Urgrosspeer sheltered Irma, and oh how he sheltered her. So she didn't go out, she didn't consort with men, but she got pregnant regardless, she got pregnant at fifteen, and then the van from Hindelbank woman's prison came and took her away. The very next day, Urgrossmeer had Irma's weeping beech chopped down. And Urgrosspeer cried and never spoke of Irma again." The boy pulls down his trousers and pants. He uses the pocketknife to make a sudden cut. He flows raspberry-red into the soil. The blood beech drinks the boy.

3

The Search for the Mother Blood Beech

Ey, Uropa, come with me on my "trip" through Europa.

———

For the human psyche . . . it is a mirror of culture. The relationships we have mostly known and the institutions of our culture are based on power-over. So our inner landscapes are those of the stories of estrangement, and they are peopled by creatures that dominate and must be dominated . . .

Yet power-from-within is the power of the low, the dark, the earth; the power that arises from our blood, and our lives, and our passionate desire for each other's living flesh.

——STARHAWK

And the best advice I got was keep writing, yeah.

——FRANK OCEAN

A turn toward the archive is not a turn toward the past but rather . . . an attempt to regain agency in an era when the ability to collectively imagine and enact other ways of being in the world has become deeply eroded.

——KATE EICHHORN

Bloody beech, bloody bitch, bloody stitch, bloody fucking hell, the wool's far too pale, yet again the wool's far too pale for the jumper I owe Grossmeer, and now the wound on my chin's burst open again 'cause I keep fiddling with it, and it's dripping onto this shit-pale shitty wool for the shitty-ass jumper I promised Grossmeer, promised her last winter at that, and now it's late summer, or autumn, actually, going by the calendar it's autumn, but summer's clearly not going anywhere, it's here to stay, and I'm staying too, wasting away here on my couch continent, and Grossmeer naturally obviously doubtlessly of course absolutely doesn't even actually need this shitty jumper in the slightest, what she needs is the occasional *Hey how're you I'm your grandchild remember we spent my childhood together*, but I can't, right now I just can't, because I'm wasting away here in this fucking heat (that's not a reason, I know, but the reason can't be crammed into a subclause), I'm withering away here in my apartment, in this frenzy, this cocktail of pain meds and gender pharma and green fairy, because I've been written off sick, haha, written and sick, I wish I'd written, I've spent this entire ridiculous boiler-pot summer burrowing around for the herstory or theirstory of the blood beech and trying to write about it, and I've written nothing, I've only gathered, and now Grossmeer's been put in the dinosaur home, now I should be visiting her and I'm knitting the pink jumper instead, or attempting to knit it, now (this weekend, I mean) I've been beaten femme-butch bloody, now the suburb-pigs have pounded a second, silent mouth into my chin, now I'm drowning in time and knocking myself out on the dregs of my bar, now I'm sitting on the fat folder of my blood beech research, now, finally,

I can make a start on the writing, with the blood beech, with this insane summer. But sorry, one thing at a time. Not in a straight line, of course, but curvingly and loopingly.

Perhaps like this:

Previously on *Sea, Mothers, Swallow, Tongues*

Part 1, "The Search for Flotsam": Check
Part 2, "The Search for Childhood": Check

Meanwhile (during the writing process, when I was at Grossmeer's, on a research trip disguised as a visit):

> Grossmeer sees my hand-knitted pink jumper and puts in an order for me to make her one.

Season: warmest winter ever

Part 3, "The Search for the Mother Blood Beech":

> This part didn't want to come, the writing libido refused to get itself up (though other libidos did), summer came, I left part 2 behind me, but couldn't leave the blood beech behind me, I dreamed of it constantly, and suddenly encountered *bloodbeeches bloodbeeches bloodbeeches* in every garden, park, and green space, and the question arose as to how this tree even ended up in my family's garden in the first place, whether this tree isn't pretty fancy if it grows in all these übercurated green spaces, and how it came about that this pretty fancy

tree arrived in our—let's be frank—pretty poor garden, and why the Beelzebub my farmer urgrosspeer planted this expensive tree in his garden, why he planted it in the middle of his vegetable garden, in the garden whose actual purpose was to feed him, the garden that was quite large, granted, but needed every dapple of sunlight to be as fertile as possible. This blood beech question arose, and it stayed. And because my meers were reluctant to tell me much about my manly urgrosspeer, and I, for certain already-alluded-to reasons, don't have the easiest of relationships with Meer and Grossmeer right now, I went to work on the blood beech, because this was something I could research without having to detour around pissed-off relatives. And so I went to work on this tree that was so important in my childhood, without having the faintest idea what kind of plant it actually is, where it came from, how it grows, and why—as I was suddenly noticing—it can be found in so many gardens and parks.

Season: another record-breakingly hot summer

Part 3, "The Search for the Mother Blood Beech," second attempt:

      In which I actually research, very conscientiously, the herstory of the blood beech.

Meanwhile Grossmeer:

      has a "turn" (perhaps the heat contributed?) and ends up in the nursing home permanently.

Meanwhile I:

> don't visit Grossmeer, research, research (Grossmeer
> who? lalalala), immerse myself in the bloodbeechmad-
> ness, gather everything I can find on this tree, trawl
> through all possible realms of knowledge in order to
> figure out why my early-adopting self-sufficient ur-
> grosspeer bought a tree that was essentially useless
> to him. Perhaps, by getting closer to this strange sylvan
> being, I'm attempting to get closer to the child I once
> was.

*Season: actually autumn, but upward of thirty degrees Celsius,
with the brief interlude of a flood*

I, in this summer-autumn:

> have, after a cruel season, gathered all the knowledge
> on this tree, but still haven't written a single sentence
> for this third section, and I can't find anything more
> on the blood beech, but some fists find me. A doctor
> sews me back together, so I know where I am again,
> from which body I'm speaking, and now I'm sitting here
> on my pharma trip, and I've started to *knit this pink
> willywooly jumper*, and I've bought the wrong wool (too
> pale) for the third time, and instead of knitting I find my
> way writingwards into part 3, the blood beech part, and
> that's where I am now. Finito Burrito. Or rather, at the
> beginning.

🌿

My blood beech summer began around three months ago, when
I ordered a kosher cinnamon bun. Well, it probably began before
that, when Dina called me: "Hey, so this Jewish bakery out by the
highway exit, it's totally hip now, I mean, not quite superhip, but
kind of hidden-gem-hip, we have to go right now!" And that's
how I ended up eating my first ever kosher cinnamon bun with
Dina, it was the start of summer, the kids' summer vacay-ecstasy
diffused across into our sluggish limbs as we sat in front of the
bakery, and somehow it was all very juicy: the cinnamon bun, the
weather, and us (I was wearing a new trouser skirt, kimono style,
and Dina was wearing my old broad-shouldered leather jacket).
The crème de la crème of Gen Y hipsterdom descended on the
bakery, which hadn't yet been entirely monopolized by capitalism's constant hunger for new colonies, and the ripped queers and
I ignored one another on common ground, given I'd renounced
their ruthless combine harvester kind of existence. I told Dina I
thought the kosher cinnamon buns were far juicier than the non-
kosher cinnamon buns I'd had in the past. And that I wasn't sure
whether the juiciness was only greater because: outing to a Jewish bakery and related quasi-exoticization. And whether we were
now gentri-hip-ifying the bakery away from the Jewish people.
And whether that was very bad. "Who knows," said Dina. "It's
probably as bad as your appropriation of pseudo-samurai fashion." I called her a bitch, she called me a cultural approprigeisha,
and we felt as hugely witty and annoyingly hyper-reflective as
trendy millennial writers and their #whitemaleproblems, then
immediately boring again in our self-hatred of our affluence-
ravaged whiteness, which is fixated on distinction, on distancing
ourselves through consumption from the poorer, richer, cooler,

gayer, woker, from the difference feminists, from the whiter and less educated, and portraying ourselves as more rational, more artsy, more gen-Z-y, as less-intent-on-disassociating. Back at mine, Dina talked about her newborn niece, whose life expectancy is twelve years at best; she talked about her mother, who'd been crying on Dina's shoulder, about her father, who has always used Dina to regulate his feelings; and Dina angrily crumpled my sofa cover and talked about her longing to write out this childhood rage and her fear of doing it. What would her parents . . . etc. "Probably I'll hide it all in poetry," said Dina, and then she cried so hard that my eyes filled with tears too.

Although, having said all that, how everything started with the kosher cinnamon bun, that's not technically true. It all began much earlier. Once upon a time there was an I, once upon a time I was an It, I was born and grew up as a human being, I came of age and moved to my country's biggest city, and back then there were only two genders, so my body didn't yet exist, and so I plunged neon-shoe-first into gay culture, where my body—or so I thought—had the best chance of coming into existence. I'd had enough of being human, I grew fur, fled my small-town friends, didn't want to know anyone anymore, I wanted to start over, I cast a protective spell around me through which my old life couldn't penetrate, I transformed myself from small-town baby into an otter, lived on pornos and fucked until I was so saddle-sore that even Bepanthen Plus salve couldn't help and the headmaster-like and Protestant-esque urologist cautioned moderation, I binged my way through the nights, watched CZECH & LATINO & CUM IN ASS & SLUT & ASIAN & PUBLIC & PRIEST

& BBC (BIG BLACK COCK) & TWINK & BDSM and and and, and then I evolved like a Pokémon, I tried on abs and pecs for size, I worshipped the moon, became a wherewolf, a whowolf, a who-can-I-fuck-today-woof, watch out, you horny hordes of sweet ass-lambs, or I'll bite you open. Here, chookchookchook, come to Daddy*Mommy. I hopped back and forth between Berlin and Zürich in ludickrous easyJet-orange exuberance, I blood-let and gave myself both cities' mainstream gaydom intravenously. I grew a beard, I waxed the beard, and I thought disco muscles and hard bodies and six-packs and interval fasting and cottage cheese and steely-slick-shaven necks were my life, I wanted to be an aestheticized-to-death Dolce & Gabbana, Tom of Finland queer. I didn't want to know the name of my fuckees, but I kept count and had them tattooed as notches across my bubble butt every few months, my cheeks hardened by countless hot-ass tutorials, and the ass antlers of my fuck sum grew, the sperm bank of the European ball herd sowed itself beneath my skin and grew rampant up my back like the hedge of thorns ran riot up Sleeping Beauty's tower; I wanted every new guy who set to work on my ass to know he was just another notch on the cellar wall of my ass-memory lust-prison body-archive. Number of notches = fuckability = self-esteem + desirability = looks × fucks = (style − fat mass) × (size of biceps + size of cock + bubbliness of butt) ÷ self-hatred. And I know I'm throwing all the pansies into one pot here, and generalization yawn, and I know this is a cynical, pumped-up narrative voice that's suddenly pontifiqueering over this part in such a labored pop-literary way, and I apologize for that too, genuinely, sorrysorry, but this time I want to write about, it's too close to me, too ridickulous, too ick for me to allow, from the arsenal of voices, even one not to make fun of it. Sorry, but it's simple. I'm ashamed. I'm ashamed of it all.

Perhaps a brief cultural-historical categorization for my early twenties might be useful here: In the twinkling icing of urban gayness, everything was about the steeliness of the gluteus maximus. These were dreams of an übermasculinity that didn't yet exist over in the center of hetero society in the late 2000s. The highly curated muscle-body had long been a fag-thing, and only crept into the mainstream in around 2010, from gay porn. I was part of this subculture, which wasn't a sub-version, which didn't tolerate women or anything feminine, and nor did the mainstream princelettes of the 2000s make any attempt to conceal this: *no fats no femmes no Asians*.[1] And I would probably have become a bear, if I'd continued to grow my body, to cultivate it, if I'd continued to colonize my limbs and let them be colonized, masculinities, come into me, I'm a fertile plantation, dámelo muchacho. But eventually enough hay had been made, as Meer would say. I got sick again, had a burnout, broke down in the weight-lifting room, and couldn't even cook for myself anymore.

So I wanted out of this ultraviolet Lana Del Rey–tristesse, this poppers-pop-rave-devoured-lostness, double-yaaaawn. And besides: I was never actually gay, because being gay only works if you believe there are two genders and that you fancy the same gender; and this horror story of just two genders, of two unmeltable glaciers that are the exact opposite of each other, is one I

---

1 "No fats no femmes no Asians" was the entry policy for many mainstream gay parties into the 2010s. Only the fuckable, please.

refuse to retell. Count me out, you peddlers of the status quo. I'm sitting on the perimeter of your oversubsidized playing field and somehow I'm surviving. I'm working to meet society's minimum expectations. And other than that, I accompany this madness, I accompany us scribing, I accompany us screaming, I accompany it all, sliding along the ocean floor of microplastics and microaggressions, my ink tentacles extended, and suck in all this dross without wanting to. I'm a witness for this time, for this body. I'm here, but I won't take part in your binary-coded firecracker game, paintball-madness, oppression fun park. I spurn the legacy of the protofascistic sexuality of gay masculinities.

What I'm unable and unwilling to reject are the memories, and when I write "protofascistic sexuality," I'm reminded of the Romans (or rather, of good old Latin class), who were, after all, the ones to lay the foundations of fascist aesthetics. And when I think of the Romans, I remember the chestnuts I collected with you, Grossmeer, and played with at your house: the fruit-bodies that transformed into food in my toy cooking pans, becoming raspberries, Meertrübeli, and potatoes, becoming warm, becoming berry syrup and pudding in the child's hands; the magical orbs that planted a sanctuary wherever the child played with them, the fruit-bodies that one day lost their magic and were suddenly just shabby old chestnuts. I can no longer remember why, or under what circumstances this disenchantment occurred. But I do remember the child being very angry with the chestnuts, and blaming them. When I think about the chestnuts today, it strikes me that it wasn't their fault, that presumably this was the moment when the child lost its magical thinking, and that the chestnuts' glossy matter remained just as magical as ever—chestnuts have been magical since time immemorial, the trees produce male and female flowers, can live for a thousand years, and are so magical that every autumn they enchant hordes of children, that they enchanted the Romans, trained and transformed them, assimilated the people into their propagation, and their magic melted the species barrier, the chestnut magic donned the legs of the colonialists, the chestnuts roamed all across Europe with these borrowed Roman bodies, allowing themselves to be planted everywhere and reach places they would never have reached without legs, and in turn they kept the poor mountain farmers alive through many winters, in Ticino for example. I think, Grossmeer, that as a child I believed you breathed life into my magic chestnuts. This was always a comforting belief.

This is what happened so far and led to *Sea, Mothers, Swallow, Tongues*. More or less.[2] And then I wondered about the conclusion of part 2, how to continue writing. The book was far from finished, I knew that, it wasn't finished with me, and so, stopping work early one day, instead of writing I ordered a cinnamon bun and some olive bread from the exotic kosher bakery, without realizing I was ordering a sexy cinnamon bun delivery guy too. He

2 For further details, you may want to read "Die Endlose Rose" (The Endless Rose) by Kim de l'Horizon, part 4 of the roman-fleuve *The Search for Sensitivity*, in which Kim offers very deep insights into their early adulthood.

wore this bike courier outfit, yummy sports pants, a kippah, and those narrow, knee-length underpants from Under Armour that have been en vogue for some years now. A filmic stored moment. Jump cuts. Eye meets eye. Slow-motion predator gaze. Eyelash flutter like a blue moonrise. Iridescent iris. Recognition. As I handed over the money, I saw a birthmark on his left hand. Whizz whizz and away, swallowed by the concrete jungle.

Cut. Close-up of my cell phone. Me on the Grindr app, which shows you willing men nearby. The nearer they are, the higher up the feed. One was called "Needygreedy27." Needygreedy27 had a boring profile picture: just his naked, hairy chest and mocha-spoon lady fingers framing a nipple, a gesture like in the double portrait *Gabrielle d'Estrées and One of Her Sisters.*[3] If there's no face in the profile pic, the men are either ugly, in the closet, or teachers looking for young boys (though not necessarily their own pupils). But that's when I recognized the birthmark on his hand. I wrote to Needygreedy27. We sexted a little; what he wanted to do to me, me to him, the usual. When I suggested he come over, he made an excuse. The following day, the same. The third day, yet again. Needygreedy27 was always online late at night, and I saw he lived less than eight hundred meters from me, but he was obviously one of those men who just want a few pics for a bedtime wank. I went outside, the night pulling me on its invisible leather leash, its blue was violet and fumbled my face, it was cool, empty,

3 I've always wondered, though: Where the fuck are the other sisters? Is it the seamstress? Or the naked torso in the painting? And what kind of "sister" would be tweaking Gabrielle's nipple anyway? I'm also a sister, Gabrielle, me too, I'm a sister, one of you, sibling, bling-thing, and I want to tweak your nipple, oh sis!

greedy. Cut, my searching gaze, cut, yellow streetlamps, cut, my footsteps on the asphalt, cut, quick check of the app, my desire taking me for a walk, me, a little stick figure in the pulverizing muzzle of the universe, I slice open the darkness with my gleaming eyes, cut, I come to a standstill, my voice says in the voiceover: "I'm not whole, not wholly real, my bones rust, I need the vinegar of raw tongues or I'll spoil within a day, I need the storms of garish hands brushing my skin new, ever new." Cut. I'm standing in front of a house. Close-up. Grindr shows Needygreedy27's profile. *Distance: 5 m.* The game is on, boy. Tiger Mama's come to chase you.

On the fourth day, when he had yet another excuse, I wrote that I knew where he lived and which delivery service he worked for. And that if he didn't want me to come by and reveal what was evidently uncomfortable information for him, he should come over to mine, and pronto, muchachito. He wrote back immediately, saying all I had to do was order some food, that he'd only come by during working hours. And that he wouldn't kiss me.

On one of my days off, I ordered olive bread and a cinnamon bun again, at 10:13, and at 10:38 Needygreedy27 rang the doorbell. I took the bread, he came in, glancing furtively around the stairwell, closed the door. "I've got fifteen minutes." Then he knelt down, naughty boy, right there in the hallway, pulled me out, then himself, then took me in his mouth. I stared at his birthmark, which reminded me of a beech leaf, we're standing beneath the blood beech, you tear off a leaf and trail it across my face; the leaf is young and has a really delicate pelt, a thousand times softer than your hand could ever be, and yet it feels like an extension of your hand, and Needygreedy27 came almost immediately. He came with a soundlessness born of practice. That's when I decided to follow the trail of the blood beech. Then I came too. He swallowed all of me. I was amazed. Then Needygreedy27 stood up, asked where the toilet was, washed his hands and mouth and wiped himself off the hallway floor. I was fascinated by his precise movements. Young man, I thought. You're cleaning away this desire you've ejaculated during working hours with such unrivaled thoroughness. "If you say a word to anyone, I'll pummel you," he said, imitating some soap opera bully. He was about to whizz away again. "It's not been fifteen minutes yet," I said. "Don't you want a glass of water?" He nodded suspiciously. I knew I had to proceed cautiously. We sat down. As rigid as two iguanas in winter. I knew I couldn't make eye contact with him. That would be too much. His hand rested on the table. Beautiful as fuck. I said the word *heat*. My hand moved closer to his hand. He said *global warming*. I cast my gaze on his skin, wanting to soften him with it, wanting to open him up and lie down inside him like he was a prewarmed sleeping bag. My gaze approached his eyes, orbiting them, and collided with a piece of ice in the center of his face. Then he stood up, shook my hand in a business-mannish way, and left. Cut. Me in front of the mirror. Three missed calls from Meer. My thumb hovering over the callback button. Putting the smartphone away. My fingers, reapplying eyeliner, repainting the black borders so my eyes don't melt out of them. Cut. Me eating alone at the table. The olive bread still warm. Cinnamon bun, moist. Blood beech, I'm setting off in search of you.

I research. I gather everything I can find on the blood beech. I know that the beech is called "Mother of the Forest" because she's the most important deciduous tree in Europe and makes a significant contribution to improving the soil, our beautiful, healthy European soil.[4] Soil pride is everything. But she's suffering from climate change and her uncontested number one slot in the European forest charts is under threat.

I now know that blood beeches are "common" beeches, but that the crazy motherfuckers have mutated away from their usual green, that the leaves refuse to break down the red pigment anthocyan, and I now know that hazel, plum, and acorn trees do similarly abnormal things, that the blood form occurs in many trees, but predominantly those that are strongly exposed to the sun—the blood-toned foliage is therefore a kind of protective spell. Hmm, I feel you, bloodleaf.

After my first research interval, I also know that beeches were often considered magical trees, that there were magic beeches and devils' beeches, around which the naughty witches danced until dawn, I now know that in Jeanne d'Arc's 1431 trial it was proven, evidentially, irrefutably, and in all probability even photographically—I mean, surely they caught it on camera—that she danced around a fairy beech, naked too, for sure, oh indecent girl, and that she was therefore quite rightfully condemned to death by

4 Urmi, 1989.

burning at the stake. Imagine if all girls were to do that. Wowzer. And besides, Jeanne wasn't girlie, binary feminine; she was more inter, but that's a different antinovel.

Andreas Hase writes in his book *Bäume. Tief verwurzelt* (Trees: Deep Rooted)[5] that beech wood, more than any other material, represents the transfer of knowledge; that Gutenberg invented the printing press with the help of a beech stick whittled into a letter of the alphabet. "The beech's smooth, silver-toned bark almost begs to be carved into, to have messages left behind in it. A small piece of oneself, entrusted to a majestic tree to be preserved and protected. Even thousands of years ago, our pagan Germanic ancestors preferred beech for these purposes: they carved into it emblems, magical signs and symbols. These were the symbols of the Germanic cultic script they called *runa*: secret. The priests of this ancient people used them for protective spells, magical cures and prophecies."[6]

And although I wanted to sink my teeth into the blood beech, a Netflixy pitch soon began to nag away at me: "Aaron, a young Jewish man, fuckdates his way through his drab day-to-day life. God's path is narrow. A pathlet. Actually it's a rope, stretched across the chasm of the flesh. His penis has belonged to his family ever since his bar mitzvah. Only on his delivery moped does he feel truly free. One day, out delivering a cinnamon bun, he stumbles into the clutches of a person who fascinates and distresses him, and falls ever deeper into their cat-and-mouse game.

5 Hase, *Bäume. Tief verwurzelt*, 2018.
6 The same Hase.

But what does this person want from Aaron? And why are they always going on about this blood-tree-nonsense?"

In order to banish this idea, I sat down—being the natural, thoroughbred writer that I am—and wrote: "Family is the connection that arises through the inheritance of personal trauma; culture is the connection that arises through the inheritance of collective trauma." I immediately crossed out this pathetic sentence. *Trauma*—this much I knew from listening to the psychiatrist back then—is what the ancient Greeks called their *wound*. A wound can be many things, an injury, but also torn tissue, something that has been ripped apart. Tissue that belongs together but gapes open. So to inherit a trauma means passing on a tornness, an unconnectedness, an absence of tissue.

Cut.

I'm sitting in the "Green Library" at the University of Zürich. A dusty book lies in front of me, I sink into it with my heavy tortoiseshell glasses, and it says, the blood beech originates—cut. The popularity of blood beeches in the nineteenth—cut. Cut. Cut! Shit! This film trick isn't working anymore. I wanted to "pull my finger out of my ass," as Meer would say, or "put my hind legs first," by which she means "step on the gas." But whenever I want to step on the writing gas, whenever I want to move forward by finally writing up my blood beech search, language immediately gets in the way—or rather, the body parts that have been placed and planted in the language, the masterless, mistressful, humanless, animalful limbs that wander around like ghosts—and then the language does something to me, even though I actually wanted to do something to *it*. When I write: "I'm pulling my finger out of my ass," it's not words, but rather hyperreal fingers that I feel poking around inside me (how did they get in my ass?), and when I hear "hind legs," I look down at myself and see hind legs, and they leap forward, before my front legs, and I'm running on these four legs (how did they get in my body?), and just a moment ago I was in the Green Library, but now I can feel the language-body, as though I'm a child, word-for-word, body-for-body, with massive hind legs, sinew, and fur, and I wonder whether my ancestors had a much deeper awareness of the animality of their bodies—did they have four legs still? And Meer and Grossmeer, who drink coffee in the garden and say: *So, now let's put our hind legs first and get weeding*, and then you both grow toward the ground, you weed as you crawl, and you grow claws, I can see it clearly, don't think I can't, and how can I tell my story when supposedly long-gone things keep butting into it, hopping in a seemingly disjointed way into the spokes of my narrative carriage, when my memory-images mix with language-images that are apparently much older. And who really believes that time is linear—what a cruelly absurd fairy tale, this successive occurrence of things, the nowness of the present! Everything is always so hideously simultaneous and entwined; a smooth, linear, unfragmentary story is nothing but a big fat lie! And I don't even believe in ghosts, by the way, but that doesn't stop them haunting me. And I only, merely, just wanted to tell you about my summer, during which I researched like a real person with a goal, like journalists or academics, like people with methodologies and pension schemes, I just wanted to proudly regale you with how

I've followed the trail of the blood beech, how I've dug my way through the internet, rooted through the botanical gardens of the German-speaking lands, sucked the sap from the German Dendrological Society and the German Arboretum Society, tracked down experts and squeezed every ounce of blood beech knowledge out of them, and how I even went to Meer to search through all the material on the garden (when she rented out our old house, she took all of Urgrosspeer's stuff to her place, all the old work tools, receipts, photos, lists).

Dutiful student that I am, bad girl gone good, bad girl gone super respectable, I wanted to rake together some knowledge, to wrap my brain around how a working-class, early-twentieth-century papa came to think: Yes, a fancy blood beech, that's what I'll plant for my little girl in the garden of the family home I built with my own two hands in the shabby suburban Central Plateau. What was the sociocultural fuss that linked Urgrosspeer with the blood beech? And not just with the blood beech, but all the other trees he planted for his children—the blood maple, the weeping beech, and the other ornamental trees.

At this point, the thing that usually helps helped: gazing out of the window. I saw a dude who I would describe as "tacky" standing in front of his Maserati, seemingly waiting for someone. His license plate revealed he was from the provinces. After a while, having clearly waited long enough, he drove off. It was obvious he just wanted to be seen in the city with his little machine. Then it hit me: the blood beech was like the nineteenth-century version of the leased Maserati, the fake Louis Vuitton bag, or the cheapest Rolex. Regal park trees must have been to Urgrosspeer what

holidays in the South Pacific, the truckli collection, and perfectly
arranged doilies are to Grossmeer. I had read, after all, that there
was a real hype surrounding park trees in the nineteenth century.
Especially blood beeches. The rich kids were to blame again, distinction distinction, we're fancier than you. We, the bourgeois
folk (just the men, of course) who rammed blood beeches into
their gardens. Initially only kings could afford them, then there
was a trickle-down effect, whereby the blood beech craze spread
through the gardens of the aristocracy into those of the more ran-
cid nobility and then, gradually, into the pleasure grounds of the
nouveau-riche victors of industrialization. The mainstreaming of
the blood beech. Classy stuff.

On my wild ride through the history of park trees, I stumbled across
a garden historian by the name of Clemens A. Wimmer. A really
shady character. Ostensibly, he writes about the development of
park culture in Germany, but he actually uses his academic text to
hate on the hoi polloi good and proper: "Originally, collecting
trees and shrubs was a kind of botanical game hunt, an exclusive
sport whose practice required vast quantities of money, time, expertise, and land ownership, and consequently, for a long time it
was the exclusive preserve of landed gentry or privatizing industrial magnates."[7] The arboretums (botanical gardens focused on
pretty trees) were, he writes, a typical phenomenon of the nineteenth century as the middle classes grew. Inside their homes,
people demonstrated their "taste" with painted landscapes; in the
garden, with constructed landscapes. According to Wimmer, in

7 Wimmer, 1997.

the nineteenth century all of Europe celebrated the cultivation of the garden. "By the end of the century, the trend for arboretums had reached the middle-class home garden."[8] The typical "middle-class" trees were the blood-leafed varieties, in particular the blood beech, which became one of the most-loved park trees.

But because the uneducated nouveaux riches fixated on showy individual plants, the picturesque design of the park as a whole, the "artistic concept,"[9] was increasingly neglected. Wimmer laments that "there was barely a park without blood beeches, they were even squeezed into small home gardens. A decades-long battle emerged between landscape designers who pleaded for moderation and those who defiantly pursued excess and the forbidden."[10] And so the blood beech fell from favor with the princes and duchesses. (It's understandable, right? Who wants the telltale traffic-light-red Louboutin sole if they can dress *really* exquisitely?)

Wimmer whimpers with well-to-do contempt that anyone can collect plants and brag about it, even "commoners and women"[11] (*sic* [yes, so sick]), but that only the male nobility understood garden design from an artistic perspective. He doesn't spare tasteless types among his contemporaries either: "The collecting of exotic trees and varieties was adopted by the lower classes, from Gründerzeit-era bourgeois villa gardens into their own front gar-

---

8 Also Wimmer.

9 Still Wimmer.

10 Yep, still the very same open-minded, antielite Wimmer: it couldn't get any grimmer.

11 I haven't made up this part either; you can find it in the same great essay.

dens and cemeteries, where to this day it holds its ground against artistic, home-nurturing, and ecological ambitions."[12]

Wimmer, the commoner-and-women-hating garden historian, isn't merely upset by the fact that, from 1900 onward, any Average Joe and Jane could afford a blood beech. He pursues the blood beech's historical trail all the way through the nursery gardens that cultivated her, starting in Germany, then across France and England to America. He irritably notes the botanist Richard Weston's claim in his encyclopedia that the blood beech originated in America. Wimmer isn't the only one to be bothered by this. A certain Alfred Rehder shed tiny tears of Germanness as early as 1933 in the *German Dendrological Society News*. Rehder observes indignantly that Weston, in his botanical reference book, defines the—noble Teutonic!—blood beech as the "American" beech variety. The blood beech, therefore, isn't just a projection surface for hatred of poor people, but also a provocation to nationalist narrative. Wimmer, Rehder, Weston: a boys-only club in which everyone lays claim to the blood beech for their own respective Faserland.

I've picked up some new, darker wool. I don't sleep, I knit, Grossmeer, I knit this pullover for you. You sit by me, or rather over me, around me. You guide my hands. The needles are too big

12 Well? Whose, do you reckon, is this inclusion-venerating quote? That's right: it's from Grimmer. I mean: Pond-Skimmer. Sorry, no, wasn't his name Pube-Trimmer? Feminism-Killer? Wannabe-Class-Wars-Winner. No, no, of course you remember his name. Empathy-and-Brain-Dimmer.

and too slippery, but your hands merge with mine, and the child's apron we're knitting for me, the fabric that's coming into existence, seems to come directly from your fingers. It's magical. You can create something from nothing. I tell you this. "It's magical."

Meer hates knitting needles. I've never seen her knit. And besides, you were the one I wanted to learn it from, Grossmeer.

I'm knitting this pullover so I can be with you without actually having to be with you. I knit and see all the textiles you knitted, crocheted, and embroidered, the textiles with which you—unconsciously?—wanted to show the world: "I'm no longer poor! I can afford completely superfluous things." I knit, and wonder whether I've betrayed you, whether I perhaps have far more in common with people like Wimmer than with you, whether I, in my apartment full of books, with my body language, my clothes, my choice of words, and all the things with which "I" express "myself," am not only expressing my queerness, but also my education, my urban existence, whether in doing so I'm not also—unconsciously?—wanting to show that I've left my suburban existence behind, that I've "moved up in the world" and am no longer a small-town fag. I wonder how much of my specific "queerness" is really a vital expression of my inherent personality and how much is merely the embodiment of the USA-influenced, metropolitan, citizen-of-the world queerness I identify with—also because it's cool and edgy. I mean: there are different ways of being queer, and I've chosen *this* way. Or, Grossmeer, to phrase the question differently: If Urgrosspeer were young today, if you were young today—where and who would you be in this society?

And: Is my entire way of life not actually the attempt to distance myself from the people you would be today? And doesn't this make me unspeakably similar to Wimmer? Now I've dropped a stitch.

While I was gathering the biological, botanical, sociological, classical, historical, and nationalist knowledge on the blood beech, I regularly ordered the cinnamon bun delivery guy to my home, over a four-week period. It never lasted longer than a quarter of an hour. Then a different guy suddenly brought the olive bread and cinnamon roll. I ordered three times before I caught on that Needygreedy27 was ghosting me. Biiitch. I waited in front of his building and smoked one and a half packs of Marlboro Reds. When he came home, he glanced at me then hurried inside. The next day I ordered again, and he brought my order, slammed the door shut, and throttled me. "Never do that again," he threatened, then he hit me, making my ears roar. "I'm not trying to rat you out," I choked out. "I just want to see you." He opened his trousers, pushed me back, and nailed me against the wall. Then he sobbed. I held him like you would hold a sick child. "Why don't you run away?" I asked. He looked at me uncomprehendingly. "Liking cocks isn't reason enough to betray and leave the place and people that are my home. Where would I go? To your oh-so-wonderful culture? To eat fast food alone every night?"

I went to work, researched the blood beech, slept, ate. It was like running around in a big fist that's a small fist, a tiny one actually.

I traveled on foot so the fist wasn't made even smaller by the bus walls closing in. The air was hot and muggy. A throng of blond teenage boys threw beer cans at me. And then they threw stones. And then the stones got bigger. And then the stones stayed in the air, hovering over the back of my neck, only hitting me once I turned around. And then the stones were throwing themselves, all the way into my dreams. Every night, I lay beneath an avalanche. It was so hot the houses melted out of their walls, and every street became a dead end.

When Dina nudged me in our group chat—the one with me, her, and Mo—to send the occasional sign of life, to tell them what was keeping me so busy, I sent her a chronological list of the blood beech's cultivated varieties that I'd grown fond of, which to me read like a family album, a walk through an ancestral portrait gallery:

"Dear Dina. Here's a selection of what's currently keeping me busy:

CUPREA, copper-colored, 1811, first cultivated variety

PURPUREA PENDULA, weeping beech, 1858, Potsdamer Landesbaumschule

ATROPURPUREA MACROPHYLLA, large-leaved

RIVERSII and SWAT MAGRET, both especially dark

PURPUREA TRICOLOR, 1873, Orléans

ROHANII, slit-leaved, cultivated in 1888 from the QUERCIFOLIA and ATROPURPUREA varieties in the royal garden in Sychrov, Bohemia

ANSORGII, slit-leaved, bred from ASPLENIFOLIA and

ATROPUNICEA by CARL ANSORGE in Hamburg, 1904

There are currently over 15 varieties of blood beech. "

The list of things currently keeping me busy that I didn't send to Dina:

STANTHEMAN, 20, butcher, small hands, big, dark-red nipples, my sofa, giggles

MEATY DICK DADDY, 46, railway employee, genuinely meaty dick, his shower, his kitchen table, his waterbed, screams HMMPHYESYESYES

SLYTHERIN SLUT, 29, French, unemployed, insanely sensitive earlobes, my sofa, cries

JACK40, presumably older, IT guy, pendulous balls, his living room floor, his sofa, his hallway, his bed, his balcony, makes startled Oh! noises

THAT ASIAN BOY, 31, Colombian, Spanish teacher, marble-hard six-pack, my sofa, my bed, my bedroom floor, can't cum

TOMISDOM, 25, banker, copper-colored glans, in a cornfield, verbally abuses me as he cums, Take that, slut, take it, take it, take it

AY PAPI, 19, Latino (identifies Latina?), high school student, absurdly ripped biceps, my hallway, cums after two minutes, apologizes

DADDY-D, 38, Austrian, sales manager, foot fetish, his bed, holds his breath

REAL MAN, 30, construction worker, incredibly sinewy shaft, in the porta-potty, says: Your ass is so white

RUDEBOY18, presumably younger, trainee postman, very
  hairy, in the park, grunts

My blood beech madness, my withdrawal from . . . well, everything, lasted the entire summer. I wandered aimlessly. The heat
mingled with the city, and I let myself be carried by its waves. It
washed me up in Oerlikon, driftwoodbody, and I walked along a
street where I used to live, colloquially known as "Balkanstrasse,"
where "Balkan" is interpreted very broadly: shisha bars and
kebab stands and Arab hair salons and lots of Middle Eastern–
looking people (meaning predominantly males, of course) which,
all combined, add up to "Balkan." At ten-minute intervals, young
men in sports cars race down the short one-way street. Their
dark beards are shaved with such precision that an arrow would
ricochet off them. I moved to this street at the beginning of my
studies, small-town-girlie me, the rents were pretty modest for
Zürich. I often sat at the window, looked down at the people below and felt so much smarter and better, because I didn't need
to flaunt my gender or wealth. What I didn't check back then
and I do check now, having guzzled Bourdieu and Eribon ga-
lore: naturally I was flaunting other things during this time—my
education, which I worked as laboriously to acquire as the Balkanstrasse guys do their Mercedes-Rolex-biceps-shine. We stood
at the window of our student digs, smoking (hand-rolled ciga-
rettes as another means of distinction: not supporting any of the
big cigarette companies) and literally looked down on the young
men, or rather, we looked at our preconceived images of them,
looked at these bodies that weren't individuals, that all seemed
the same to us, because we'd come from the suburbs and thought

"Balkanstrasse" was the city. Men who, just like me, decorated themselves with the insignia of the social class to which they longed to belong. Their penis extension was their car's horse-power. My ego injection, the many meters of Foucault, Bourdieu, and Butler I displayed on my bookshelves. We spat on economic capital, but lapped up cultural capital all the more greedily.

That was almost ten years ago now. After that, gentrification worked its wonders. The shisha bars vanished, the hair salons placed real flowers in their display windows. I sat down in a hipster bar and ordered a "Turkish coffee" (that, at least, had remained). It blew my socks off. I checked out the men. Meer texted me. "Grossmeer's not doing well, I think she's about to take a turn for the worse." I need your hands, boys, I need those arms dreamed from protein shakes and the 'gram, I need your tongues, cocks, asses, nipples, lobes, lobules, slobber, slime, shafts, juices, I need it all, I need your screwing, though this screwing will be your own undoing, but without it you'd wither with worthless-ness, I need your boyness, hyperboyish boys, take me, clear me out, and fill me up, my mouth is your doormat, yes, my mouth, so empty and yawning, come, fill me up, Grossmeer, you're stand-ing in front of me, we're standing on your balcony, you point to-ward the mountains, the snow-covered Alps that tower up behind the city, and you say, *So pretty, eh? So pretty*, and I'm barely as tall as the balcony handrail and I look at the mountains; they're teeth, white, angular, giant teeth, and then I understand that this world is a mouth, that this is the lower jaw and we live on the tongue of the land, the sky is the palate, and we're being digested. The world is devouring us. Meer arrives, picks me up, and thanks you,

Thanks for babysitting, and in Swiss German that's: *Dankä für ʒ'goume*, where *goume* literally means " the palate of the mouth," so, *Thanks for palating*, and I sit in the car and the word *palate* talks to me, reveals its connections to me, and now I know why I'm always so empty after you've palated me, Grossmeer: because I'm sitting in a palate within a palate, in the big world palate and the smaller Grossmeer palate, and it just makes total sense that you have to digest me, because you've been in the world so long already and have been almost completely digested by it, and you need me, you need my body, the nourishment, and that's why I'm so empty after being palated by you, and so filled with this emptiness that I can no longer feel myself, I sit with Meer in the car, and the car roof is so domed from the inside, and I can't not see all this, everything is a palate, and how can I put it, Meer talks and talks and overfills me, and *boooom*, a testosterone ride with tinted windows made my "Turkish coffee" vibrate. I was glad.

The fact that things are still as masculine as back when I lived here, when the dividing lines were clear, when I was just I and the fleshscapes in their wheels were still *them / the others / virility dummies*, this steadies me. The young bar owner told me proudly that he makes the Turkish coffee just like his grandpa used to, that he's the first on this street to also welcome "people like you" (genderfuckers? intellectuals? white people?), that he now earns enough that his grandparents, at long last, no longer have to work. I nodded as though I understood the life circumstances that would lead to this making him so proud. I glanced at his golden Omega. It had the diameter of my espresso saucer, but quite a simple clockface. Simple compared to a Lady Gaga video, that is. I asked suggestively why he wasn't wearing a Rolex. He laughed. His pecs, strictly measured excavated trench spoils from the battle of the sexes, twitched. "Rolexes are for dumb dudes with no style." Then he winked at me and served another customer. On Grindr, I would have messaged him. He would've posted a picture of himself that turned me on. He would've looked like the others, the men I used to call "Balkan machos." I wouldn't have guessed there were subtle differences among them too, between Rolex wearers and Omega wearers. I remembered the flora fawner Wimmer's elitist comments that the blood beeches had been "squeezed even into small home gardens" and that even "women and commoners" had started collecting ornamental trees, I thought about my urgrosspeer as a "dumb dude with no style," a wannabe social climber, I got sentimental, thought about how we look down on the "Balkan machos," we arrogant rich kids without money-richness, but our richness is our skin color and our Central European names and the narrative that we sprung up like mushrooms from the Helvetic soil. I thought about how we criticize the flashy masculinity of the "Balkan machos," their misogynistic culture. Since I moved away from here, political correctness has come into existence, and we may no longer say "Balkan machos," but we still think it, they're still "others," and we still secretly wish they'd grab our snow-white, bunny-like, trembling asses with their hairy hands and pound the portal of our intestines with their bullish balls until, blind with pain and lust, we grant their foreign seed admission into our native lowlands. I paid and let myself be swept through the ravines of suburban masculinity, I drank the pec muscles, round like milk breasts, hard like life, so masculine they're feminine, oh yes, daddies, give me your teats, testo mamas (what kind of I is this speaking, what voices are manifesting themselves? And what are they doing to me, why is it so damn tempting to let myself be ground like a nutmeg between these different selves, to be grated away between my homo-macho self, my Protestant self, my watery self, my figure-skating self, my history-student self, my appropriated self, my appropriated shamanic self, my more-than-human self, my gut flora, my inner child, my written self, my voguing self, my psychoanalyzed self, my Instagram self, my forced-heterosexualized self, my employee self, my sex-date self, my prostituted self, my shamanistic self, my sadistic self, my masochistic self, my success-lusting self, and my white, white, snow-white-privilege self), yes, testo mommies, I'm a naughty piece of alpine dirt, and more than anything, I'm drunk as I write this, sitting on my couch, I've been knitting this fucking pullover, attempting a Celtic cable stitch, I've brought five strands into the knit, but I keep losing the needle, whenever I cross it the super-fine wool slips through my fingers and I'm continually searching in panic for dropped stitches, but I just can't anymore so I've put the fucking pullover down and pulled out my notebook, it's slowly turned to autumn after all, the blood beech season is behind me, and that's why I can write about it now, drunkitydrunk as fuckety-funk, I'm not that innocent, oh, misters, no, I'm wild, untamed, a storm. I am a tempest, keeping my thunderbolts high up in the clouds, all these flashes of lightning, all these sudden strokes of white light, all these flashes of whiteness, all these bursts of internalized racism that I'm trying to hide from my white, leftist friends in the city, that's why I, why we, come to the edges of suburbia for fuck dates, where the screams screamed into us can be screamed out again, the screams that implant in us a *we* without us knowing, a tiny white *we*, a *we* cannot see, because it's everywhere, a supposed every-we, apart from the ones this *we* sees as *you*, and before we know it the *we* that only exists by constructing and negating this far-too-smooth, too-dull *you*, says: You're the unenterable zone, the color we're not allowed to touch—so tear down the white picket fences of our taboos and enter us screaming, we who are stuffed with the silence of our internalized violence. We don't want your headscarves on our daughters or your masculinity in our sons, but we secretly want it in our mouths for one night only, when we can moan against our political correctness, we want your strength in our economy and our pleasure centers, we want your flesh, your sweat, we want to lick you, we want to dream you, we want your bodies, but we don't want you.

Last night I was in Grossmeer's apartment. She had already died. I was afraid. When I opened the door to the apartment, I touched a kind of flesh. It smelt of acid. I turned around, Meer was there, she raised her finger to her mouth. Then she hugged me. The walls and ceiling were dripping. "It's too late," said Meer. She never let me go.

Meer and Grossmeer always drop Urgrosspeer into conversation so casually. When they're talking about other people, they sometimes say, "He's almost as much of a patriarch as your ur-grosspeer," or, "Your urgrosspeer was the only other person I've known to be that pedantic." But when I ask about him, they dodge the question and say, oh, I can't remember anymore, "he's been dead for so long." Then Grossmeer will often say, seemingly without any connection, "The young women, you know, if they were unmarried and expecting, were sent to Hindelbank, the women's prison. With the poisoners and lunatics and hysterics." And Meer adds that Urgrosspeer was happier about her brother's birth than hers. Because: son and heir. Sowing the family name deeper. Allowing the family tree to grow. But unfortunately, Nico was infertile. Says Meer.

August held me captive. I went to work early, didn't take lunch breaks, and at four I cycled to the Botanical Garden library on Lake Zürich. It was semester break and the deep cleaning was underway, there were more cleaning staff than students. For hours on end I pored over dusty botanical books, copied out passages, and organized the catalog of blood beech varieties according to new traits. I deleted all the sex apps from my phone, wanting to concentrate fully on the research. Ever since I kicked the neat gender molds out of their sandbox, I pick up fewer guys in the wild. The risk is too great that they won't be able to handle my blend of corporealities. A few days passed, then I couldn't hold out any longer and blew a cleaning man in the men's restroom. His hands smelt of cleaning fluid, his belly was hairy, and his penis kind of small, but the veins on it protruded massively, like a nest of serpents pulsing against far-too-thin skin.

His name was Farid, and we had sex whenever I went to the Botanical Garden. He was in his late forties, showed me photos of his wife and three children, and told me proudly how much money he was able to send home each month. Because he'd lived in England, he spoke good English. He liked it when I slapped his balls and told him what a stud he was, how big his penis was, that I was his dog, that he should inseminate me. After the second time he said, "I like you, but your ass isn't so tight. You're too fucked. It takes too long for me to come." I said it was okay if he takes a long time. After the first week, he asked what I did here every evening, and I told him I was researching my family tree. Well, I corrected myself, actually I'm writing about somebody I need to say goodbye to. "A love story?" asked Farid. "Kind of," I said. He liked it when I put my middle finger in his ass. He would protest each time: "But I'm not gay, you know, I just like the finger in the ass."—"Of course."—"I don't like the dick in the ass, you know." I nodded, like people nod obligingly at a child's insignificant fibs.

I kept a tally of our fucks. After the eighth time, we went and sat beneath a linden tree. I wanted to ask Farid where he was from. But I immediately wondered whether that could be racist, whether I would then reduce him to his nationality and from then on only think of him as the Syrian or the Lebanese guy or whatever he might be, and file him away in my archive of fucked bodies not as Farid, but as his nationality. Then it occurred to me that I didn't yet have anyone Lebanese in my archive, fuck and shit that this occurred to me, fuckshit, and it also occurred to me that I could never, ever tell any of my antiracism-committed friends this, doublefuckshit, and that we talk about hormone therapies and transgenerational trauma, but not about the racism that was forced down our throats with our pacifiers and that never stops having an impact, even when we set our minds against it, triple-fuckshit-shame on me, get out, you European upbringing.

"Do you always have a lot of sex?" he asked.

"Yes."

Silence.

"You're a bit arrogant for a half woman. I'm just trying to help. I could be your father," he said good-naturedly.

"You? You helping *me*? Take care of your own life, you closet fag."

"I can take care of myself, don't worry about me."

"I don't care enough about you to worry."

"Ah, yes, okay." Farid went.

Mo texted me: "Where are you hiding?" I didn't answer, instead I went to the books, read about the evolution of park culture in Europe, burrowed through the Renaissance and its Italian gardens, a bella vita for the grandi uomini. I bombarded myself with copper engravings of Italian royal gardens and began to actually find it fascinating, how this rigid garden image was imitated first by the French aristocracy and eventually by every European bigwig. The maxim was to make water and plants as geometrical and symmetrical as possible. After that, I plunged into the Era of Sentimentalism, the period from 1750 onward when the English garden was en vogue: closer to nature than the Italian garden, wilder, as though one were stepping into a "natural" landscape. But of course, here too nothing was left to chance, and "naturalness" is always propaganda. Because the actual model for the gardens wasn't so-called nature, but landscape painting, in other words the already-mediated and shaped and imagined and painted wilderness. And this was (finally!) also the time when blood beeches were swiftly gaining popularity and prevalence in the Western world. Blood beech, here we come.

Given that the good old blood beech had commenced the triumphant advance of her propagation in Germany, I focused my research on the development of parks there. I didn't find much, just one book addressing the historical development: *Umgang mit Bäumen* (Working with Trees) by a landscape architect called Heinrich Friedrich Wiepking. Right then. Hold on tight to your sustainably produced Eames chair imitations, my modern-day friends: enter Wiepking, another weeping king of another drowned kingdom. But as we know: anything that's drowned will eventually wash up somewhere. And anything that gets washed up, is always—read my lips: *always*—ugly.

Wiepking writes about the historical and ethnological significance of trees. He begins with the Thirty Years' War. In its aftermath, he says, everyone was completely loopy; they'd had enough of violence and hunger and severed body parts and missing family members (especially gunned-down fathers). And so people had an uncontrollable longing for beauty, according to Wiepking, and this beauty was arranged around their traumatized souls in the form of gardens. A picturesque garden as a symbol of peace. Wiepking writes that—watch out, here comes another Teutonic triple-barreled name—Prince Leopold Friedrich Franz of Anhalt-Dessau brought the English garden to Germany and gave it its "German manifestation." During his lifetime, the prince was nicknamed "Father Franz," or "Father of Humanity," and decorated with other daddy-issue-dripping nicknames. Papa Franz had numerous arboretums constructed, and created "one of the first big German nature gardens, a paradise of trees, the *Wörlitz* park, and other major arboretums in the triangle between Elbe and Mulde."[13]

Wiepking's *Umgang mit Bäumen* also contains numerous pages on our national überpoet Johann Wolfgang von-de-and-of Goethe, who visited Franz Park in Wörlitz several times. Wiepking cites the demigod garlanded Germanic citizen, who on May 14, 1778, wrote from Wörlitz to his beloved Frau von Stein about how immensely beautiful it was there, how unspeakably moved he, Goethe, was that the "gods have allowed the Prince (Franz) to create a dream around him."[14]

I need to request a little leap of faith here: this may all seem random right now, but Goethe and parks like Papa Franz's will be key to understanding how the blood beech ended up in my family's garden. I swear! And in order to unite father complexes and national poets in my argument, I can no longer avoid interjecting my two cents on the understanding of classical art, using Goethe, who has always made me uneasy. On the one hand, I mistrust his mastery of language, this total command of words, sounds, meters, genres, songs, tropes, themes; in short, things, wholeworldness—

13 Wiepking, 1963.
14 Wiepking.

and of course there's an element of envy in this, but for me clas-
sicism always holds certain totalitarian tendencies: the idea that
the author has complete sovereignty over *his* material, that *he* has
"everything under control," form and content thingamajigged together in absolute harmony. That art has to be perfectly formed
and "beautiful."[15]

15 And yes, I do know that even heavy-going literature has moved on a little since Goethe.
That there was such a thing as postmodernism, which set out to break down the traditional
structures, because the world had become too "fragmentary" and "complex" to be described
in a linear and pretty form. I know that armies of writers have worked their fingers to the
bone making "classical" art. That for a long time now the grandfathers and their texts have
been spat on, torn apart, and reassembled in a new way. I also know that the world has
continued to turn, and that it's become even more fragmentary and überübercomplex, and
I know that, nowadays, even a fragmentary text is too linear and too logical to portray this
fragmentary world. I know that for thirty years we've been searching for ways to get out of
postmodernism, whether above or beneath or behind it, and into this present.[15.1]
   I therefore also know that it's too simplistic to represent the fragmented world in fragmented texts. I know that because the postmodernists (male) have long since become classical writers—though that would be going a little too far—and the people who wanted to
escape postmodern irony and metareflexivity have also become classical writers (male).
Although these authors came from the margins, they've now become the new centers, for
example—and this is a random example, because it really would be going too far to explain
it here—David Foster Wallace, who wanted to escape the irony of the postmodern with his
New Sincerity. If we stick with the example of DFW, we can see that—without looking in
too much detail, because there simply isn't room in this footnote—yes, in DFW we see a
son who has become entangled in his daddy issues, who develops Papa Shakespeare's father
play *Hamlet*, whose *Infinite Jest* may try to disassociate itself from the male ancestors on a
content level, but is ingenuously and hyperreflexively trapped in *Hamlet* and its violence. In
DFW's *Infinite Jest*, we read a Hamletian text, from the title to the fathers who recur again
and again; the grandfathers who force the fathers into the tennis game, traumatize them into
profit-seeking; the fathers, who, like in *Hamlet*, return as ghosts and demand their sons fight
for their paternal reputation to the point of self-sacrifice; the sons, whose existence is solely a
son-existence. So. If we follow the trail of the Fatherness (almost) into contemporary literature, if we look at David Foster Wallace today—because anything else really, really would
be going too far in this small space—then we see someone who wanted to stop with Father-
hood, but who, precisely because of his Anti-Daddy Stance, has for many writers become a
new superüberpappy. If we stick with DFW, we see a twentieth-century child prodigy, who
further develops the ancient violence of men in his texts (and not only there). Thank you for
listening. It's necessary to examine male ancestors, but not *only* them. I hereby pronounce
that the Era of the Fathers has come to an end. And if not *its* end, then at least *an* end.
   15.1. The belief that the world used to be more straightforward has always been a false
narrative. It was only straight because it was viewed from one single societal and global
perspective (you know which). What's more, it's no coincidence that what is now regarded as the "normal" and "neutral" literary form, in other words the *novel*, evolved at
the same time as the European bourgeoisie—the bourgeoisie that saw "fraternité, liberté,

To me, the language of the classicists always seemed like Michelangelo's marble *David*: far too smooth, too large, too masculine, and much too white. And the proportions were completely misrepresented: Wasn't David, in the battle against Goliath, the small, youthful one? Why has he become a giant in this depiction? And back to the form: What happens if a content can't be "mastered" into "beautiful" language? What if the language flows out of its form or wants to flop into different forms? What if the long-silenced mouths in the language also have a say? What if languages have their own agencies, the sounds themselves, and by the same token, the themes that get written about—or rather: that get written *with*? How do texts look if a human master subject isn't at their center, deftly Goethe-ing the world into a mold? How do texts look if I am as much a part of the world as the texts, if I don't have an all-seeing vantage point outside of the text and world from which to examine them? I don't believe in people as sovereign agents. I believe that all materials have their own agency, that stories and themes and materials, as well as languages and media, always have a word of their own to contribute. That they cocreate themselves. I believe that everything we look at looks back at us, and that the gaze of the other does at least as much to us as we do to it. I believe that this is magic: the agency of all things. And I believe in this magic.

Damn, I hope I haven't scared you off yet again, naughty me— naughty who? Naughty this, naughty text that simply refuses

---

egalité" exclusively as the brotherhood, freedom, and equality of white men over twenty-five years of age. Men who paid more than three livres in tax (which in 1789 was worth roughly a kilogram of silver—so, in other words, those who had a decent income).

to be straight, instead constantly turning away, veering away, queering away beneath my badly painted fingernails. But don't worry, I can now make my way compellingly and superelegantly to Goethe and Wiepking. Things are about to get pretty intense, so stick with me! Wiepking, after writing a few pages about Goethe's visit to Daddy Franz Park, now preaches: "The era of the German garden has truly come into blossom; simultaneously heralding the heyday of arboretums as an art form, and of the German spirit. All those who move the world of the intellect in the 'classical' era are gardeners! They write one another enchanting gardening letters and offer assistance with gardening work in a brotherly manner."[16] Their aim, he writes, is to beautify the country: "To ennoble the common folk and lift up the lowly, in order that all civilized peoples can one day be united as one big family." Yep, haven't we already heard this rhetoric somewhere? Chestnut shoots. Brown. Didn't the brownshirts wear brown to show their connection to the soil? I was still in the library and didn't answer Mo's text. I had Wiepking's book in front of me and thought to myself: Yes, but wait a minute, surely this couldn't have been written before the Second World War? I looked, and no, it was published after the war. 1963. And then I stalked Wiepking online. Because he produced the knowledge that's accessible to me, knowledge about the evolution of German garden and park culture, and I swear, I searched as hard as I could, but I couldn't find any more recent nonfiction books on this topic. So, now a short, shudder-inducing résumé.

16 Wiepking, 1963.

Heinrich Friedrich Wiepking lived from 1891 to 1973. He was a landscape architect and, from 1934 onward, a professor of garden and landscape design. In 1941, Heinrich Himmler appointed Wiepking as *Special Representative of the Reich Commissioner for the Strengthening of German Ethnic Stock*. Wiepking loved dancing to Wagner and nationalist narratives. He legitimized the Aryans' superiority by claiming that Germanness was also in the soil, in this Germanic German soil, and that the newly annexed lands of the Third Reich must therefore be properly Germanized. In 1942 he wrote: "The Germans' landscapes are distinct in all ways from those of the Poles and Russians—just like the people themselves. The murders and barbarism of the Alpine race appear as razor-sharp furrows in the grimaces of their native landscapes."[17] The fact that he happened to be a particularly strapping Nazi certainly didn't hurt him any after the war. He became a high school teacher in the Federal Republic, and—just as he had been in the Third Reich—was responsible for training town planners. He received awards, and even had a prize for diploma theses named after him. He was able to further disseminate his fascist ideology, for example in the 1963 book *Umgang mit Bäumen*, the one I found in the library of Zürich's Botanical Garden, a library that is part of the University of Zürich. Perhaps two final depressing fun facts to round things off: In 1943 he supervised a thesis on the revegetation of Auschwitz. And in 1952, he assisted with landscaping the memorial at the former concentration camp Bergen-Belsen.

17 This delightful quote is provided by Wiepking's biographer, Ursula Kellner: Kellner, 2016.

Hmph. Grrr. Pfff. Okay. Thanks. That's Wiepking so far. And now what? Huge scandal, so a landscape architect shat his brown shit even after the Second World War? You might say it's common knowledge that the Nazis' minds weren't de-Aryanized. Yeah yeah. I don't mean to get all indignant. (Well, maybe just a little.) Initially I wanted to cut the whole park history thing so I wouldn't have to tolerate the Nazi's presence in my beautiful little book. It's not directly connected to the blood beech anyway, I told myself. But I realized that's not true. It's simply not true. Toward the end of August, I remembered Meer's descriptions of Urgrosspeer: "He thought Switzerland was the greatest country in the world"; all the neatly rolled Swiss flags in the attic; the rifle, not in a standard army bag, but in a velvet-lined box; the copper engravings of the Alps and lakes, the Bernese costumes, etc., etc. "People loved their country back then, that's all," said Meer, and I almost believe her, but I find it hard to swallow that well-educated people were also so fanatically Helvetic. My urgrosspeer wasn't a National Socialist, but he was a nationalist. I inherit that too, and I want to name this legacy, not to conceal this part of the blood beech history; not to cover up just how much the past fucks its way into the present. It wasn't a coincidence that Urgrosspeer planted the blood beech in the middle of our garden.

After weeks without messaging her, I turned up at Meer's, listened for half an hour to her tirades about work, about the chemicals that are ruining her hands and sense of smell (but in essence I only understood the overtones of *Grossmeer Grossmeer Grossmeer*), and said tiredly that she should join a union at long last or

start one herself and battle the beauty giants (but with what energy? And with what knowledge, how to form a workers' revolu-
tion? I know, I know), and eventually I didn't even try to hide the
fact that I'd only come in order to look through Urgrosspeer's
things, which she—since she started renting our not-shabby-
chic-charming house—had brought to her place. I mentally
thanked Urgrosspeer for having been such a pedant. Everything
was meticulously organized and labeled, with this absurdly beautiful handwriting that everyone was indoctrinated in back then.
He had noted down every single chicken feed receipt, and Meer,
who struggles to throw anything away, had kept the lot. In the
box "Garden: Trees and Animals" I actually found the receipt for
the blood beech. From a German nursery. Purchased: 1919.

So the blood beech would never have ended up at ours if German park culture hadn't been German park culture. If the blood
beech hadn't achieved the status of being one of the most beautiful park trees. If German gardeners hadn't merchandized and
distributed her across the Western world. If there hadn't been
dudes like Wiepking *man*dating what makes a garden beautiful; if
there hadn't been dudes like Goethe conceiving German loveliness. Wiepking and Goethe are progenitors of the blood beech,
whether I like it or not.

I'm still sitting, or rather sitting again, inwardly uninterrupted in
the same meds-induced delirium, drifting on my couch floe in a
writing flow, and I rashly up the ante with a Dafalgan. Or two.

After the Nazi story I had to distract myself from all the shit butting its way into my now-ness, and that's why I went to a forest rave, with Dina and Mo, and we drank early and then went up the mountain on our bikes, and we felt younger than our bodies, and the forest was big, but our half-cut youthfulness was bigger, and we could hear the rave long before we saw it, we followed our ears, and then we're suddenly there and in it and everything is lasered and we keep drinking, there's an astonishing number of people there and I feel astonishingly good for the number of people and then we've lost one another and I keep drinking alone and Farid is standing before me, in the jumble of hands, his hands in the air, his hands bewitch me, call to me, flashing red and blue from the lasers, and the booming that led us here marches rhythmically through our limbs, leads us to each other and we're only briefly in the sea of sweat and then I follow my hand and my hand follows Farid's hand, my gaze on his back, his back in the woolen pullover, his back in the semidarkness, in the semidarkness the stitches, lit only by candlelight, my hand shrinks on the stitches, becomes a child's hand, Grossmeer knits and knits and tells of how her Grossmeer taught her to knit, how on long, dark winter nights knitting was a lifeline out of the cold, the woolen stockings that grew out of Grossmeer's hands, the winds that knew the precise locations of the cracks in the house, the cold that at night became a snake that slithered everywhere, its ice-tongue finding every fleck of body that wasn't knitted; knitting as wisdom; how not to get cold, how to live in winter's heart without it winning, and Grossmeer tells of a walk on which Meer foolishly ruined her woolen socks and didn't want to darn them afterward, "she had no idea how good she had it, in this apartment with central heating, she didn't know what cold was, she didn't know what winter means: the fear that your fingers will freeze while you're washing," and Grossmeer's hands are animals, are older, are the hands of all Grossmeers, in the semidarkness of the ages, of the candles, the hands are everywhere, in the semidarkness of the trees that are the witnesses to our ritual, only a weak flash of laser lightning shows us where we are, and Farid stands before me, he stands sturdily before me as God created him, except what underworld God created him, because surely it can't have been a correct goddess, it must have been a human-made goddess, an Old Testament, Greek, cruel goddess, because she's tossing me this golden baby lamb, his dark little button eyes putting me to the test, oh yummy piece of meat for me the vegetarian, with his curls of shaved-off somberness, the goddess of propriety is testing me, she tears away my carefully constructed über-I and throws the mirror at me, Farid is closer than me, wearing only his Nikes now, he's already pulled off his face, dirty boy, he's pure flesh, pure muscle, and over his muscles he's completely covered in black sheep's wool, an unbearably fluffy dress, he says, *Take me, I'm yours*, I say, *I own you*, he says, *I belong to you, take me in*, I push into his mouth, he chokes, *You dirty bitch, I'll take over your body*, his eyes bulge, they've seen the dark, these night-bringers, *Your glans is so firm, oh master, like praying lips*, he rubs his lips on it, *Your foreskin is soft as an eyelid*, he says, *Open up and look at me*, and he pushes it back, pushes my foreskin all the way back, darting his tongue on the scar that binds the dome of lust to my sinlands, he's a flame, he pushes my penis so far back in his mouth that his throat bulges, he pulls on the foreskin till it burns, I burn ablaze, I burn white and blue and red, my foreskin tears, he opens the cathedral of pain and I enter in, he pulls off my foreskin, peels off my subtle skin and brings my second skin to the fore, I didn't know there was still a macho skin there, he peels me, I'm his lust onion, I bring him to tears, he pulls the skin up over my ears, and lurking there still is a body layer socialized as a man, *Flay me, turn me inside out*, he edges me, we're enveloped in the ocean's salamander skin, we wash in wild waves against the shore of our bodies, I'm on the cliff, reaching into nothingness, then I've given him enough power, *Now I'll make you beg*, I crash across his borders, storm the wonderfully hairy hills, storm his bowels, *I'm your fuck mare, give it to me*, his curls the bridle to chastise him into chastity, my manhood the whip to thrash him into depravity, our muscles the vessels to ship us to the bloodlands, *Tonight I plant my scions inside you, you're my plantation, I plow you, I sow myself in the furrows I'm tearing into you*, I lose myself in him again and again, I push his arm against his broad back, bite into his shoulder muscles until he screams and bleeds, *Oh sorry*, then he laughs and says, *No, don't be sorry, oh lord*, we tear down the fence of propriety, leave behind the pastures of our upbringings, and gallop toward the forbidden mountains, I shovel Farid out of his Faridness, I dig over his rolling hills, I lock down his language with my hand, I rebuild him, I board the spaceship *Farid*, storm him, run down the steps, deep below his ocean's surface, he howls, the two muscle snakes that usually run obediently parallel now entwine around his spine, they whizz and whirl, he's close to coming, *Please let me cum*, I slap his ass cheek, this naughty scoundrel's cheek, *What did you say?* He moans, *Please let me cum, sir*, I put on the brakes, *I'm not a sir I'm not a lord I'm your nemesis*, I wrench on the reins, pull my mare against me, wrap my fingers around his neck, tear out his Adam's apple and swallow it, open a portal so deep even Farid didn't know it was there, he screams and flinches away, my shaft shimmers darkly in the darkness, I've thrust open the rearmost chambers and the pig Farid can no longer hold himself within his ends, he leaks out, his pearls, incubated in secret, roll in their red sheen across my inner thighs, *Look how dirty you are, you dirty Arab, lick up your blood, you dog.* Silence. Panting. Staring. My sentence shocks me, was that really my sentence, it scares me. The sentence's breath breathes Farid. Then he says, *Yes, I am your dog, forgive me,* and licks himself from my calves, rubs his cheeks against my bloody thighs, I do nothing, I watch to see how far he'll go and he wraps his face over my blood-and-feces-smeared cock, he gags but doesn't pull away, we can't go back now, Farid is a field of sour clover and I'm mowing him, he peels off the last of my skins, I shed all my leaves, pull my roots out of the earth darkness, and ride him further further deeper into the undergrowth into what resides in me what terrifies me my last husk falls I'm afraid we're barges we're barques of the night of the fight no he's a barque I'm a three-mast I tower up high I've launched into a crossing beyond my knowledge drifting on the sea of my desire my storm surge rages I've seen the other side the ludickrous squishy tea-baggish jingling of my balls against his tears me away the pirate ship Farid has torn away all my lifeboats we drift on the crests of waves but don't see each other we ride the same waves but thrust each other into the depths I'm in distress my stomach reels those aren't butterflies they're caterpillars and they've pupated they've emerged as moths they've flown into the flame of his submissiveness *You've hexed me* and now the giant octopus of the deep stirs my blind flesh commands my fist pushes into his mouth every one of my fibers has left me behind I'm locked out I don't want that I want that no I don't who planted this field marshal violence in me who stitched this scepter into me who erected this granite pillar of domination desire in me who burned this hardness into me to tear down his catkin-willow-delicate hiding place who scripted these words into my fucking where's this vileness speaking from how does it have access to my inner voice I don't want this desire where's the tip of *I* that observes all this and doesn't stop it—*Are you crying?* my voice calls to him and he gags on my fist and I tear myself away and he says, *Please cum*, and I say, *Beg, you son of a whore—please please please I beg you*, and I say, *Moan louder*, and he moans in chorus and my skins contract in complete overripeness and rot off and I birth the sickest stars into Farid's belly of darkness and he cums too and I stand there without skin I glimmer away.

Farid lies there, sweating from his eyes. I stand in our ashes.

"But my name's Thilo," says Farid.

I bought new wool for you. Darker wool.

I had found the fathers of the blood beech, or at least two of them, but I hadn't found the mothers or a mother during my quest. I realized this while researching, when I stumbled across the Mother

Blood Beech, which is in Possenwald, near the Thuringian city of Sondershausen. I read that she's allegedly the oldest known blood beech, first mentioned in 1690, that she's encircled by eleven younger blood beeches, called *the eleven sisters*, and that the blood beech stock had commenced from these and all modern-day varieties can be traced back to them. Naturally, that made me a little distrustful. So all blood beeches have a matriarch? I searched on, wanting to know who had begun to capitalize the blood beech. After making inquiries with archives and botanical gardens and stately home libraries in Thuringia, I found an article, by a local historian named Hanna Nagel, that turned out to be the missing puzzle piece on the beginnings of the blood beech trade. In 2018, she wrote in the local rag *Sondershäuser Heimatecho* that in the early nineteenth century one Eduard von Michael, an Oberland forester, was the first to breed the blood beech. He took seeds or graft shoots from the blood beech and cultivated them. Von Michael began by marketing the precious tree to forestry commissions, nurseries, and private gardens. The trade became increasingly popular, and shipments were soon being sent from Sondershausen to France, England, and America.[18]

Using Nagel's bibliography, I padded on through the bloodbeech-madness and discovered there's a genuine fetish surrounding the Mother Blood Beech in Thuringia, as well as a battle over which blood beech is the oldest—because there are many of them in Europe. Set out below are the reports of three apple-blossom-

18 Nagel, 2018.

white old men, all of whom claim their blood beech is the oldest blood beech:

There's Paul Friedrich August Ascherson, who claimed in the mid-nineteenth century that the blood beech near Castellano in South Tyrol is the matriarch of all living blood beeches.

At the end of the nineteenth century, another bloodbeech-ologist, Günther Lutze, argued against Ascherson: The only true Mother Blood Beech is the one in Possenwald near Sondershausen in Thuringia, the heart of Germany. (Funnily enough, Lutze himself was a strapping Thuringian—purely by coincidence, of course.)

This Thuringian Mother Blood Beech was apparently so popular that all her children were stolen. Lutze, you see, wasn't solely interested in the true authenticity of the Thuringian Mother Blood Beech as matriarch, but also in her sexuality, or rather, her propagation. This tends to be important to these blue-blooded types. He grudgingly admitted that blood beeches cultivated from seed were less vibrantly red-leaved than varieties from grafted shoots. So the direct-blood offspring were unfortunately less full-blooded than the asexually reproduced.[19] But the fact that the children of the Mother Blood Beech were garden-variety beeches (I'd rather not say: boring, *green-leaved* beeches) apparently wasn't the Mother Blood Beech's fault, said Lutze in defense of the Sondershausen tree. Oh no, the fault lay with the other bog-standard green-leaved beeches that grew around her, imposing their inferior genetic material on this fine, ornate matriarch: "This minor percentage [of genuine blood beech offspring] is a result of the cross-pollination

---

19 Which doesn't entirely fit the blood-logic of the era: that the entire blueprint of a body is written in its blood.

that the Mother Blood Beech, entirely surrounded by specimens of the common beech, has to endure. If she could be isolated in such a way that the seed dust of other beech trees was kept at bay, this would guarantee that shoots taken from the matriarch would henceforth only generate blood beeches.[20]

In Lutze's ideal world, the blood beech would be surrounded only by her own kind. The Thuringian depicted his beech almost obsessively as the matriarch of all subsequently sold blood beeches—an übermother who would be even more potent if only there weren't so much impure riffraff clinging to her coat-tails, contaminating her genetic material.

But everything comes to an end, even mythical übertrees like the Mother Blood Beech. It seems that, in 1841, she began to suffer from topkill.[21] I read about how generations of German foresters toiled away at her, scraping off fungi and fertilizing her with cow manure. In the *Kyffhäuser Nachrichten*, I eventually found her obituary from the year 2017: "It was probably in 1926 that the Mother Blood Beech split, leaving just a small stump that is gradually becoming overgrown, and therefore difficult to find."[22]

I then searched for the real Farid. We did it ad exhausteam. Then we went for a coffee in the cafeteria. We small-talked pretty badly.

20 Lutze, 1892.

21 For those, like me, with only a mediocre knowledge of botany: this means her crown was slowly drying out. With my hair loss, I can empathize with how unpleasant this is. Humans and trees alike know that this is the beginning of the end.

22 *Kyffhäuser Nachrichten*, 2017.

I asked if he experiences a lot of racism. He laughed for ages, very loud and very high-pitched, and I knew all the biology students were looking at us, I knew they were all younger than me, not by much, but just enough to surely be more actively antiracist, and I didn't dare look around, I knew my question lay on the table between Farid and me, my stupid, well-intended question, and I knew I couldn't understand his laughter, couldn't interpret it, that I can only convey it as an empty space, a white space that's disguised by its whiteness. Then he suddenly stopped laughing and told me he was going home in two weeks. "Only home is home." He told me to drop by again beforehand. And with that, the conversation was over.

What isn't yet over—to make another Vaseline-smooth swerve—is the argument regarding the oldest Mother Blood Beech. Because there's another clue, one that leads to Switzerland. The third and final clue. I had, remember, been blindly collecting material at the beginning of my blood beech summer, and I was only gradually working my way through it as I continued to search. In my BB archive (blood beech and barebacking) there was a text by a certain Prof. J. Jäggi, which I'd found at the start of my history-rummaging but promptly laid aside. In 1894 Jäggi wrote an entire thirty-five pages on "The Blood Beech of Buch am Irchel." (At last! The first Swiss location, jawohl, we too can bloodbeech.) But he used such old-timey language that I was turned off and switched my attention to other blood beech texts.

That's why it was late August by the time I finally struggled through this text on the Swiss blood beech. Jäggi dedicates over ten pages to the plausibilization of why the oldest blood beech originated in Switzerland. I was amazed when I first read the location: Buch am Irchel, which is really close to Winterthur, where I lived with Meer and Peer after we moved out of Grossmeer's house. Jäggi names the three known locations of natural occurrence: the Stammberg near Buch am Irchel (Switzerland), the Thuringian Possenwald near Sondershausen (Germany), and a forest above Castellano in South Tyrol (which at the time—and until 1918—was Austrian). He adds, however, that these three locations had received very unequal consideration. Jäggi, every inch the irate citizen, rages that foreign botanists have "silenced and forgotten" the blood beech of Buch am Irchel!

Initially I was dubious about this Jäggi guy, thinking he was just another nationalist laying claim to the first blood beech for his patch of Europe. But he can actually prove that almost all German botanists deliberately falsified sources in order to claim that Germany was the place of origin. He verifies that the Swiss blood beech was already in existence in 1480, and that there was probably one there as early as 1089 (on account of the crest and place name). Jäggi stresses that the Swiss blood beech "significantly trumps the supposed matriarch of the Hainleiter Forest [Sondershausen in Thuringia] in age and that it had already been there for a long time when the latter was still in diapers."[23] He claims that the Sondershausen Mother Blood Beech couldn't, therefore, have been the matriarch of all blood beeches.

I was surprised to discover that Jäggi also found non-elite

---

23 Jäggi, 1894. No joke, he really wrote "in diapers."

forms of knowledge production pretty cool, and seasoned his little academic text with legends of Buch am Irchel's inhabitants. The most important legend goes like this:

A famine strikes the lives of five brothers. Now, women and other Others didn't exist back then, they were only conceived later—but because this is a legend, and legends, as we know, transform every time they're told, this time I'm making them three transfeminine siblings. When the three siblings are close to dying of starvation, they decide that one of them should sacrifice themself for the others. The eldest wants to do this, but the youngest beats them to it. They stab themself, and their blood swiftly seeps into the forest floor. Overcome with grief, the eldest wants to follow their sibling to their death, but then the beech tree starts to talk to the survivors. A choir of knars and the voice of the youngest. The beech talks the siblings into eating the youngest's body in order to survive. Eventually, they bring themselves to eat their own flesh. They survive the famine—many others don't. And so they decide to build a home for the many children who lost their parents to starvation, and become their guardians. When they eventually die, surrounded by their many nonbiological children, they ask to be buried by the blood beech.

I wonder whether Urgrosspeer knew about the Buch am Irchel blood beech. Whether he wanted the blood beech because she was so Helvetically pure and there just weren't any nurseries in Switzerland that sold her. Yes, perhaps he knew that, it's possible that the blood beech knowledge was passed down through the generations—and "forgotten" only in science. I wonder how he interpreted or would have interpreted the knowledge about the Buch am Irchel blood beech. Given that the oldest blood beech allegedly originated in Switzerland (this seems to be correct)—you can say that the blood beech is genuinely Helvetic. And as it can be found in all German-speaking lands, presumably in all Central European lands, you can also say that it's European. I don't know for sure, but I fear that Urgrosspeer was one of those men who would have needed the facts to back up his Helvetic nationalism or Europeanism. This is what I'm wondering, and I know I'm wondering this through the lens of my own era, and that this is pretty pointless, that being-in-the-world was completely different back then in a way that's hard for me to comprehend, that being-in-the-world was much more closely intertwined with nationality than I can imagine. And despite this, I live in this era when the specter of nationalisms is searching for—and finding—new sons.

Once the air slowly began to smell of autumn (though it was still hot as fuck), I texted Cinnamon-Bun-Aaron. He replied with just a quote: "If thou drawest nigh unto this place, it will befall thee as thou didst unto me."[24]

24 From *The Jew's Beech*, by Annette von Droste-Hülshoff, translated by Lionel and Doris Thomas (Alma Classics, 2008) [note from translator].

Farid got a major hard-on when I told him to hit me. Then it was quick, for both of us. Afterwards, he treated me to an ice cream in the cafeteria. I tucked a little money into his jacket pocket without him noticing. He asked me about my work-in-progress on the "family tree" and the person I needed to say goodbye to. I said I knew too little about what had really happened to get properly into the writing. Farid shared a saying from his homeland: "What you cannot say, you need to invent." "Oh, that's a saying where you come from? That's nice." "No," said Farid. "I just invented this now." We said goodbye to each other very formally.

I followed the trail of the blood beech. I had zero plan, I ran into the forest of knowledge, the undergrowth of propagation history, botany, nationalist discourses, class struggles, myths, park culture, I dove into the forest souls and eufloria and tree love *des boches*. I didn't push anything aside, but rather pulled into my little boat the ghosts obstructing my path, the ghosts of those who would never be saved by Noah's ark, who aren't part of his direct male lineage, who aren't reproduction-ready hetero animals, those who would be left behind.

The circles of my writing don't close, they're spirals, journeying on, out of the garden of my childhood into even earlier times and directly into my present, they move from the blood beech into my desire, they loop once more from this computer back into the paper, this erstwhile wood, and I wonder how much the writing is my agency and how much its efficacy lies in the wood itself. And it seems to me that when I look at the blood beech material, all the authors (all boys) were searching for a mother figure. They all wanted to lay claim to the Mother Blood Beech for themselves, for their nation. As though there were a great absence of mothers.

When I was at your place a while back, Grossmeer (before the blood beech summer), to talk to you about your past, you set your family trees down in front of me. You had your peer's family tree and your husband's family tree—my grosspeer's. "Your blood-line," you said. One family tree extended back to the fourteenth century, the other to the thirteenth. Only after I'd studied both family trees in detail did it occur to me that it wasn't, in fact, *the* line of my blood. It was only half of it. The patrilineal thread. To follow the thread of the women, you would have to trace it across multiple male trees. But I didn't tell you that, of course. Just like I haven't told you that I'm writing this, that I'm finally knitting a pullover for you, that I'm now weaving in all the pink wool I've used so far, even the one I used to start part 3, with the speck of blood from the wound on my jaw, this speck of blood is part of it now, yes, I still haven't visited you, but instead I've found the right pink by pulling together all the different threads, and so I knit here and tell you nothing, but I'm writing this, writing about how when "autumn" came I searched for the fake Farid, Thilo, I'm writing about how I wandered cluelessly through suburb-land, through the places outside the places, thinking he might be there, laugh-ably disorientated, the Grindr app my compass, and about how I approached people who looked like him and asked whether they'd seen a man who was about their height, with night-black hair and the same neatly shaven nape of the neck, that fade-cut, this thing-amabob with the edgy undercut, just like them, and the same per-fectly trimmed beard, a man who had broad hands with beautiful dark hair on the backs of these broad hands, as thick as a field of rye at night before the harvest, even thicker than the hair on the backs of their hands, and who was so deliciously hairy all over his body and had well-trained biceps like them and eyes like fresh teardrops, and whether they could please, please tell me where, Thilo, that for me it was more his dark things, but that's not why, I mean that he was also, he was German, well, a German accent, here a few weeks ago, in the forest that is, and something happened and I wanted to, I had to, something really important, and I asked so many men and kept going and asked again and again for so long until eventually a few men hit me, they broke my jaw and I woke up in the ICU, I was written off sick and came home pumped with pain meds, in a bad way, but finally high enough to write up my blood beech crap, and Dina and Mo came to visit and cooked for me and scolded me because I'd lost so much weight, and eventually asked whether I'd told my family, and then I was finally able to cry and said, No, please, anything but family, and Dina and Mo took me to the forest and we made a big fire and danced around it and I took all the things that are inside me, that have an impact on me, and threw them in and tried an invocation, a counterspell, and I called out: Oh big thingamajig, oh universe, everything that's there and no-longer-is and isn't-yet, oh planet that creates us, and oh you interplanetary space, oh my sense-transcending doodads, I invoke you so I can be strong:

Make me strong! Give me force!
(Any force, not necessarily The *Force)*
Here unto my claw. I worship thee
Exorcise all voices that speak with my voice

that lust with my flesh
Close the looks that lick with my eyelids
Please give me another tongue
to enthrall enchant entrance my thicket
to beguile bewitch bechime
With all the little forces
Lay out a sacred circle
A barricade of spoken singing, broken clinging
As far as song carries over concrete chasm.

But what if—woe is me, my oh! My voice can see
My tongue can say: shantay we stay
These tongues; these hoes to hoe our woes
These tongues can fly; can flee my disenchanted me
Can call the shee, can lol the me! me! enemy
Can fell my ego, me-go, please go, my unfairy unamigo
The transformed swallows swallow me whole,
Perform a weather spell to mellow the most annoying Mr. Bello
But what if—like the frog prince in the wart-thicket-dress—
I've left my spell-weaving there in the well?
Among pebbles the size of babies' skulls,
surrounded now,
by nothing but where-wolfish mold.

But then I grasp: you are already here, inside me
You super-duper force creating subtly wispish things.
I gather horizon around us
I stitch the texture of naughtiness to the sacred-circle ball-dress
    zebra-stripes

I'm the transient who never arrives
O thingie-thangie, whose name I do not name
'cause it has all names
Surrender to my shield and scheme
Wrench out the rungs of my career
Sprinkle half-dried ketchup on my business plans
Spear the knights in shining armor with your red-lacquered
    thorns
Skin me to my ears
This skin from which our evolution
made us epilate all the hair
And transform me into a skinless she-wolf in heat
And lead the night back home to me
And then into temptation
'Cause I want to stand at the big beech with my legs splayed
Come on, Incu-Bee-Demon,
Gimme your Mummy-Semen
I'll receive the spores of the night
And hatch centaurs, crytures, hoards of boho-boohoo boars
Low no-lords, moonsters of mildew,
agents of decay
And the stones that will be sown
narcosis-less
into our bloated bellies
Shall not plunge us into waters nor the depths
For we are made of the depths
And we are made of flowing
And we'll deliver you mold
no vinegar can fight

4

The Search for Rosmarie

The same branches, different threads

This is how we must read the attack against witchcraft and against that magical view of the world which, despite the efforts of the Church, had continued to prevail on a popular level through the Middle Ages. At the basis of magic was an animistic conception of nature that did not admit to any separation between matter and spirit, and thus imagined the cosmos as a *living organism*, populated by occult forces, where every element was in "sympathetic" relation with the rest. [. . .]

Eradicating these practices was a necessary condition for the capitalist rationalization of work, since magic appeared as an illicit form of power and an instrument *to obtain what one wanted without work*, that is, a refusal of work in action. "Magic kills industry," lamented Francis Bacon.

—SILVIA FEDERICI

Holy father, we need to talk . . .
I'm not the boy that you thought you wanted

—SAM SMITH

we got to know everything else, just not ourselves. and if we want to learn again the wisdom of the witches, then we really can study ourselves. all knowledge is within us. it really is. we have knowledge in our bodies that's three million years old. yes, three million!

—DORIS STAUFFER

1

Meer said, "Maybe it'd be nice if Grossmeer could grow old in Ostermundigen, so close to the house she grew up in, here, in the Elder Tree home," and I said, "She's already old and there's no growing left to do, she barely even remembers your name now, Ostermundigen means nothing to her, so it's completely fucking irrelevant where she gets looked after," and Meer said, "Oh and you would know," and we looked at you, how you were staring into the new emptiness in front of your bed, and Meer didn't say another word. I don't know whether you noticed us watching you. You straightened up until you were sitting almost regally. "Where are my geraniums?" you asked. Meer said, quietly, "She always was such a dictator."

No, that's not right. Meer said the sentence differently. In Swiss German, besides the pluperfect there's only one past form, the perfect tense. Meer said, "Si isch scho immer ä Befähli gsi— she *has always been* a dictator." The absence of the preterit is so acute in Swiss German; this form that's more written, more formal, more official—and which describes a past that's been concluded. In Swiss German, every past is in the perfect tense; it juts into the present and isn't yet finished with us. When we talk about the past, we're not in control of it.

And this present here is in the subjunctive, Meer is speaking only in the form of possibility: "Grossmeer *could* grow old, she *would* be happy here, we *would* have to do this and that." Meer

wants to talk about this present as just one possibility among
many. But not me, I'd like to come into a simple present. After
my blood beech summer that swallowed the autumn, I'd like to
arrive in this November. After so much evading, I'd just like to be
with you, Grossmeer.

A black cherry plum, its leaves blood-red, grows to the right
of the care home entrance. Next to this blood plum is a sign in
gray lettering against a white background ELDER TREE HOME—
FOUNDATION FOR LONG-TERM CARE, and in purple on white, WEL-
COME. You can buy brownies and blondies for sixty rappen. You
can craft, cook, have themed roundtable discussions, do memory
training, gymnastics, R & R, sing, and read aloud. There's an in-
house hairdresser, a cosmetic podiatrist, a clothing alteration and
repair service. You pay extra for all that. Only the pastoral care
and hearing-aid support are free.

You get categorized as a nine, which means you cost us 187 francs
per day. That doesn't include the basic telephone charges, radio
and television fees, insurance, chaperoning to the doctor, brownies, blondies, the hairdresser, or final cleaning on departure/
death. (If you depart or die within seven days of moving in, the
final cleaning is discounted by 50 percent, but we've already
passed that date anyway.) And I say to Meer, "But it doesn't really matter about the brownies anymore, sixty rappen a pop, it's
her little treat, really, she always had so much chocolate, she just
hid it from you, I'll pay for them, don't be such a skinflint, it's not
like it matters anymore whether she eats healthily."

Once we walk past the blood plum, this guardian of the home's entrance, we're entering your foxhole, and we have to be careful. There's no direction in these rooms. Time is full of holes. You all move in spirals here: from the in-house hairdresser to the imitation in-house village square to the hairdresser—village square—umbrella stands—hairdresser. In the corridors there are pictures of trees in sunshine, snow, or fall. People with a laugh. And orchids lurk on all the window sills.

Only people from outside can move around from floor to floor. There are doors in the corridors, but instead of leading to places, they lead to eras. They've put a different decade behind each door. Behind the blood plum there are only entrances, no exits. Meer says words to you that you don't understand; *nursing home*, *caregiver*, and *supplementary services*. I don't say words, I say looks. You tell me your life, the same thing over and over, it spills out of you, I scoop it up and place it inside me, like I used to. Grossmeer. You are not alone with your story, I listen to you, I carry it with me, I'm a good earth.

2

I'm sitting next to you, Grossmeer, and when I close my eyes, I hear the roar of your heavy breathing, you surround me completely, wholewretchedly, to the end. And I barely feel myself, even when I close my hands so tightly that there's no more world in them, no more Grossmeer; I don't feel myself even when I close my hands so tightly that my fingernails cut into me.

I'm sitting with you at the fake bus stop outside the home, which role-plays especially for all of you. We're sitting beneath the big linden tree next to Herr Füglister, who never speaks, because he's so eager to get home. Herr Füglister sets off for home every morning, sits here the whole day, and when dusk falls, they come out to say the bus won't be leaving until tomorrow. Herr Füglister's room is next to yours. Once they forgot Herr Füglister in the bus-stop-dusk. When the care assistant led him back to his room late that night, Herr Füglister apologized, saying he'd probably missed the bus. It doesn't matter, they said. Sleep here tonight and head home tomorrow. Their voices were gentle, their hands firm. They say you're all happy in these things that know you. That the rooms and objects take on the remembering for you. They say words I don't understand, they say *dignity* and *habits* and *blablabla*. Here they don't say *I*, or *you*. They only say *we*. How are *we* doing today, not how are *you*. I'm always happy to leave this place. Everyone loses their *I* so quickly here.

This morning, when someone you met at seniors' tennis came to visit, you stumbled and fell on your chin, and because of the pain you're now quiet. I don't know how to deal with the fact that you're not saying anything, it's not normal, not something we agreed on, my mouth feels superfluous in my face. Normally I know who I have to be, normally I'm the child again, normally my name is Ear, today my name is Mouth.

A nurse walks past and says, "Good morning, Frau Häfeli." He has a broad gait that says *man*, over and over with every broad step, but he looks at me for a little too long. Or perhaps: *and* he looks at me for a little too long. I drink his gaze, and we say, " ," and once he's passed by you ask, "Who was that?" That was Nico, your son, I say. I tell you this because two weeks ago you mistook me for him, and because I couldn't bear to be mistaken for your dead son, your favorite son. Meer is still jealous of him even now, two years after his death. You say, "Oh yes, that was Nico, he's loading my holiday photos from my phone onto the computer, that's why he's here." Then you rest your chin in your hand, and I nod.

The past moves through the folds of your skin like it moves through the home, getting entangled everywhere. Wing-backed chairs and little kidney tables, shit-brown and Ovaltine-orange, greasy-leathery and Formica-shiny. In the home there are replicas: a butcher shop from the sixties, a post office branch from the fifties, a village square from the thirties, with a historically accurate fountain, advertisements, and cars. The forties don't exist, they're not coming back, what were they again, was anything even there, did they even exist?

I look at the linden tree and say, "Look, that's a linden," and you say, "Yes, that's a linden," and I say, "Look, that's the bus stop," and you say, "Oh yes, that's still there too, the bus stop," and I say, "Look, there's Nico," and you say, "Yes, that's Nico, he's loading my photos." My hands are far too big for me, they're two giant gloves on my knees, I put them in my lap and then on the bench and then in your hands. You immediately start stroking them, like you stroked my legs when I was a child, and the gloves melt from my hands, my hands are bare in yours, and I immediately start to cry. So I can pull them away from you, I say, "Look," and take out my phone, "I wanted to show you this," and I go into the chat between Meer and me, because I can be sure there aren't any racy pictures in there, and I show you some photos Meer sent me.

"There's our house, where you grew up too. The chicken coop after the storm. The chicken coop before the storm. My new ear piercing, inflamed."

"You're so thin, child, you should eat more."

"Your geranium on my windowsill. Nico at the model airplane championship in 1999. Me after going to the hairdresser."

"But your hair's long, if that's after. We had to fight to be allowed to cut our hair, you know. I don't know why you boys want long hair again, it's so impractical. Ah, that's the blood beech."

"That's right, the blood beech, your tree, they planted it when you were born."

"No, that wasn't my tree, it was Rosmarie's tree. Listen, your meer told me she's worried about you, about your body, the way you treat it. She probably meant you should eat more. Would you please eat more? You know, it's funny really, we never had enough to eat, and you don't eat enough even though you have plenty."

"I eat enough. That's not what Meer meant."

"Don't tell her I told you that she told me, okay? Oh, who's that?"

"That's Alex, in Meer's kitchen."

"Oh yes, that's right. Alex is your . . . ?"

"Alex is Meer's partner."

"Of course, I know that."

"Of course you know that."

Grossmeer, oh grandmother, grandmither, grandmyther, you've become a myth, you repeat yourself, you move in set phrases, you're a piece of the past haunting us, you're a big girl now, peeing in the umbrella stands if no one makes you go to the bathroom. On the Saturdays when I visit, I sometimes just stand in the doorframe and watch you. You probably think I'm one of the nurses. You don't recognize me at first. Nor I you. You've become so gentle. You speak to the cushion as though it were a kitten. There's so much more I wanted to write to you, Grossmeer, and through writing, so much more I wanted to understand.

When I started writing to you, I thought I wanted to write "our story." But it turns out people like us don't have a "story"; not one that can be hammered into a pleasant family narrative, in any case. And besides, what interests me more than "our story" is our feelings, our inner lives, the layeredness of our boringly ordinary experience.

I wanted to tell you about my constant fear of my body: about being under the bedcovers with the most terrifying monster. Only it's not bedcovers, but my skin. A fear like living in a ramshackle hut when there's a storm coming. Except the storm doesn't come, it's just there: always, everywhere, inescapable. Sometimes, the feeling that it's okay to live in this hut. And sometimes, in phases, the feeling of being wrong—the unfathomably deep, all-corroding horror of being wrong in myself down to the very last fiber. The urge to pluck out each of my cells with fine tweezers, one by one, and dissolve them in acid.

I wanted to tell you about my shock when I hear Meer. How much her voice resembles yours. Even though she wanted to become the complete opposite of you, in every way. Sometimes, when I'm talking to my friends, I secretly record my voice. My slight fear before I listen to the recording. My intense satisfaction with the words that sound completely different than they do in your or Meer's voice. My bitter revulsion at words that sound like yours or Meer's. Proof that I'm not my own.

For so long now, I've been wanting to tell you that four years ago—that time when I didn't visit you for six months—I was in a clinic because I'd stopped eating. I think, maybe, yes, I wanted to disappear. Not consciously, it wasn't a decision, it just happened. I didn't want to die; I just wanted this body to stop. Sometimes I woke at night with the eggy, sweet taste of French toast in my mouth. It tasted like sadness, like something that had been lost forever, and it tasted like a home.

3

The three of us are sitting in the cafeteria, you, Meer, and I. You're showing us photos of your room on your phone, the room we've just left. I look into your face. You're missing. I look past your face into the reflection in the window; my body sits there, half-transparent. My body looks like me. It doesn't often do that.

Meer asks me, quietly, while you're there next to us and talking about the view and how it changes every day: "Can you write up Grossmeer's life story for the funeral?"

Like always, she races around the bends without slowing down, then has to slam on the brakes and accelerate again like a snail, in too high a gear, and she repeats her question: "Can you write her life story? I can't do it," and I say, "Why don't you brake before the bend, like a person with eyes?" And then we fall silent until we're at her place. I curse myself that I couldn't just tell her I wasn't in the mood for "a quick cup of tea." Once we're parked at her place, sitting there stock-still, staring at the wall in front of us, I say, "You really are the most awful daughter imaginable, Grossmeer may be . . . in a home, but she can still . . ."

Meer gives me a tired look. She rubs her hand over her face. "I have to say goodbye to her," she says. "While she's still partly there. While there's still something to say goodbye to. It can happen really quickly. And do you realize how much work it is? When she dies, we'll have so much shit to take care of. It's just a matter of time. I've started writing it. But I just can't."

The light is dim inside her apartment. We sit down at the table, which is covered with files, receipts, and notes. She hands me a piece of paper:

Rosmarie Häfeli, née Sägesser, 1935-?
Rosmarie Häfeli—maiden name Sägesser—came into the world on November 14, 1935, in Ostermundigen near Bern.

I laugh. "That's all you've got?"

Her mouth tightens.

"Yes, that's it. Like I said, what am I supposed to write? Something like: in spite of her many brothers, she helped out a lot in the garden. From an early age, she learned the hard way what it means to be a woman. From an early age, she was interested in the great wide world, but only made it as far as Bümpliz? Or: She met her husband at the onion market. But alas, he died young? After his death Rosmarie traveled the globe, saw Niagara Falls, Victoria Falls, the Silk Road, Machu Picchu, and the Great Wall of China? Or how about: After her illness—whenever that may be—she was finally able to go to the happy hunting grounds? But unfortunately she could no longer remember her life. Because while her grandchild was fucking the nursing staff, Rosmarie was disintegrating? Is that what I'm supposed to write?"

I stare out of the window. "You've forgotten . . . you've forgotten the first Rosmarie." We fall silent. I need to do something with my hands, so I demonstratively unpack the pink pullover, it's almost ready, I begin to sew on the sleeves, Meer says in irritation, "Put those damn needles away, it makes me nervous." Then she goes into the kitchen.

She comes back with a different face and a pot of black tea. She sits down and is silent. Leans across the table, takes my hand. Her hand is cold, and I flinch. "Please," she says. I fight the impulse to pull away.

"You're so cold," I say quietly.

Meer pulls her hand back. "I'm always cold. If it's not summer, I'm always cold. It's like I've got a coldness in my bones, like ice, that I can't get rid of. Alex always says—well, it doesn't matter. I'm cold a lot."

"Did you already have it when I was a child, this coldness?"

"I've always had it." She pulls up a chair, swings her legs onto it, draws one knee in. She stares into her emptiness. "There was this time we went for a winter walk along the Aare. It was beautiful, the weather, I mean, crazy beautiful. The sky blue and everything else white. The banks of the Aare had frozen over. I was playing tag with Nico. Just a little, on the riverbank. Straying a little onto the ice. Meer—Grossmeer—said, 'If you two fall in, I'm not coming to get you, I'll tell you that right now.' Peer didn't say a word. And of course, the ice cracked under me. It wasn't deep, so it wasn't too bad. I just went into the water up to my knees. But it was damn cold. I tell you that, it was ice-fucking-cold. And we had to finish the walk. Me with my shoes full of icy water. We didn't turn back. Meer said, 'What did I tell you. This is what happens.' And I was frozen, so frozen. Just shivering. Nico tried to warm my hands in his. But it didn't help. When we got home. I was trembling, my lips were blue. Meer ran a warm bath. When I was about to get in, she said, 'No, not you. Look at your socks.' And I looked at my socks. They were my Sunday outing socks. We always had these awful Sunday outing getups. I had to wear woolen underpants. A ribbon in my hair. That fucking ribbon. And the socks, in winter: white, good wool. The best we could afford. And from the ice, a sharp edge, I don't know. There was a loose thread in the Sunday outing socks. And Meer said, 'You can only have a bath once you've darned your socks.' I was . . . I was shivering so violently. I couldn't darn the socks. I couldn't thread the needle. Just couldn't. Nico had bathed already, he wanted to help me. But he'd never threaded a needle. So he couldn't help me either. And anyway. I know. If it'd happened to him. He wouldn't have had to darn the socks himself, because boys don't have to." She pulls her gaze out of the emptiness and turns it on me.

"You've never told me that," I say.

"But the coldness was in me even before that," says Meer.

I inhale deeply and agree to write Grossmeer's life story. But it needs to be long, I say.

"Why?" asks Meer.

"Well, Grossmeer would never keep things brief with that many people listening to her."

Meer sniggers. Then she asks whether I want to have dinner here. "You could look through the boxes with Grossmeer's photos and everything while I cook." I nod.

"Alex is coming today too, though," Meer adds. I nod.

"When did you last see Peer?"

"We spent the weekend together."

I nod contentedly.

I'm sitting in her chaos room, Meer's cooking, I'm small, sensing Meer through the walls. In a box marked "Rosmarie / Sägessers" the photos lay jumbled together. I start at the top. There you are, Grossmeer, as a brand-new Grossmeer with my still-tiny self. You as an Indigenous person of North America at a "Parade of Cultures" just after the war. You as an exhausted laugh with a still-tiny Nico. You as a young, lovestruck grin next to a bicycle on a moor somewhere.

There's Urgrossmeer as harvester in our garden, among the still-young raspberry bushes, with a bundle on her back and a wicker basket at her waist. Urgrossmeer as woman, in a white, white wedding dress. Urgrossmeer as joy in the newly built chicken coop. Urgrossmeer's gnarled hand as size comparison next to a long nail.

Urgrosspeer as pride next to a cutting that will probably become a tree. (Which? Perhaps the weeping beech?) Urgrosspeer as man next to the excavated foundations of our house.

Urgrossmeer as vegetable-prepper over a basket of potatoes. Urgrossmeer as a person in her Sunday best. Urgrossmeer's first-ever picture; she as hazy fog.

Behind the box of photos is a box marked "Witches etc. Photographic material." It contains drawings of prisons and stakes, copper engravings of torture instruments (poor-quality, yellow-tinged copies from the overpriced copy shop around the corner from Meer's). A young woman exposing her genitals to a faun. Obscene witches smearing themselves with balm, sitting around a fire, enveloped by night and animals. And again and again, women being burned at the stake, encircled by devils or clergymen. My favorite: the fresco of a tree, surrounded by women and ravens. In its branches, oversized erect penises. The lovely old fable of the witches who steal penises, hide them in tree nests, and feed them oats so they don't flee.

The memory of how, four years ago, I gave Meer the definitive text on witch-hunting—*Caliban and the Witch*—mingles with another memory: I must be about nineteen, and I'm sitting on the beach with Meer. We're on holiday, I've just finished my school-leaving exams, and we've just argued. After a long silence, Meer says, "You know, the way you talk to me often makes me feel stupid, uneducated." My answer: "Well, you are. Uneducated." This comes to my mind together with the guilt, the knowledge that she would have liked to study and hasn't to this day, that she enabled my studies with her poorly paid work and that this is one of the reasons why we now inhabit two different worlds. I only realized years later that a strange rivalry exists between me and her. That I didn't study *for* her, but rather *in place of her.* I knew it had been a very difficult decision. Me, I mean; *I* was a difficult decision for her. I was an accident. She knew that if she had me, she couldn't finish the diploma she had begun studying for at night school.

Perhaps that's why it always annoyed me so much when she said things without thinking. Because beneath it lurked my immense guilt; *she's uneducated because I exist.* Later on, she wanted to become a midwife. She always talked about doing it, but never did. For a long time, I believed she could have educated herself if she'd really wanted to. But back when I believed that, I knew even less than I do now about what it means to have children.

I sit down at Meer's cluttered desk. She was a witch fanatic even when I was a child, but the fact she's collected all these witch pictures is news to me. My gaze falls on a gray folder on the bookcase: "Family Tree." Strange, I think, that's not one of the family trees Grossmeer showed me. A few moments after opening the folder, I hear the front door, and Alex comes to greet me. I tell

Meer I'll need to look through the files another time, that my eyes are tired from work. "Sure," she says, "you've got my key." In response to Alex's gaze, Meer says, "Kim's writing up the life story." Alex smiles. "That's sweet of you."

It's still strange, seeing them kiss. Meer misunderstands me. She thinks I don't like Alex. But that's not true. Anyone with hair that red, who can so calmly stand up to Meer—she is, after all, significantly older than Alex—and who's been working in an admin role since school without losing their sense of humor, deserves my respect. I'm mostly annoyed at myself, at my bourgeois wish that Meer only had Peer. We drink one and a half bottles of red wine. When Alex is there, they both vie for my affections. They suggest we all go to Pride together sometime. I say I'm not going to that commercial circus. A brief silence. Meer fetches dessert. Migros budget brownies. She doesn't apologize for them.

I get thrown out at nine; Meer has to work again tomorrow, she says. "Hair never stops growing, you know, it's not like books, waiting for you to open them."

4

Dear Grossmeer. Wow. If you knew the lengths Meer has gone to *not* to write your life story. Instead, she's written a family tree, over two hundred pages long. An excavation of your possible roots. Today, Saturday, I went to Meer's apartment. I knew she was visiting you at the home. Next to the box "Witches etc.

Photographic material" I found another folder marked "Women in Switzerland / text material." I grabbed it and the gray "Family Tree" file and copied both in the copy shop around the corner. While I was copying, I took a quick peek and began to get a sense of what Meer had been writing.

It's your family tree, Grossmeer, but on your meer's side. Quite a patchwork, written on the typewriter initially, then mostly by hand, with corrections, comments on Post-its, and crossed-out sections. Some of the handwritten biographies are clean, composed in a steady script, which leads me to presume they're at least the second draft. In others, the writing is less careful; it changes, becomes swifter, broader, the sentences are rarely complete, and there are more corrections. In the earlier biographies in particular there are drafts in Swiss German—presumably she started in that. But the clean, typewritten versions are all in a Swiss version of Standard German, which Meer writes in when she's making an effort to use written language. On the way home, I tried to get a better overview of all the material.

I became increasingly amazed. I can't believe that Meer, my meer, your daughter, has written this. The family tree begins in the fourteenth century, like the Sägessers' family tree, our male line. Meer begins with the plague, the "Black Death." I googled the dates of the historic pandemic—they're correct: mid-fourteenth century. She has written up all the biographies from 1334 until you, tracing the line of our women, the ones who are missing in the male family tree. The places these foremothers wander like ghosts stretch from the heart of Switzerland via Germany to Florence and Cuba. There are words I've never heard Meer say: *unpretentious, elysian, Utopia*. She describes—for almost ten pages—an abortion performed with historical instruments and tinctures; and later on the stillbirth of a calf, during which the mother almost dies; countless variations of recipes for plaited loaves; an almost unreadable rape; a hallucinogenic drug scene in which an old woman flies through times and dimensions; and here and there, she includes illustrations from Silvia Federici's *Caliban and the Witch*: a soldier's whore, a herb witch, a prostitute who was forced into an "ordeal by water," a body that is half tree/half human, an enslaved Black female who gets branded, and so on.

Four years ago, I had thought Meer wouldn't understand *Caliban and the Witch*. It's a very academic text, but a feminist-Marxist classic about the history of the female body during the rise of industrial capitalism, and I knew how much this topic interested Meer. Partly, I also wanted to include her in the university education I was benefiting from. I never asked afterward whether she had read it, not wanting to put her in the shameful position of having to say she hadn't understood it, that it was something for "educated folk." Meer used to read witch books even during my childhood. But they were poorly researched historical novels or differential feminist pamphlets, which propagandized women as being superior to men, which understood femininity as something purely biological, existential, as the exact opposite of masculinity. Back when I was beginning my studies and feeling the need to distance myself from Meer, that was how I thought she understood femininity. My postjuvenile arrogance. The woman who spent years researching, poring over history books, and combing through internet forums in order to secretly compose a family tree, that's not the Meer who raised me, not the woman I thought I'd emerged from. But see for yourself, Grossmeer.

5

The first four biographies are typewritten, correction-free, clean, presumably drafted multiple times.

Barbara Zürcher, née Staub, 1334-1380

Born in Brettigen. Barbara was nicknamed the splodge by her eight brothers on account of the huge, ugly birthmark what was on her cheek. Plants were her best friends. When she turned thirteen, the Black Death was hot-footing it across Europe. Because beautiful girls attracted the plague, Barbara's sister Margreth was beaten to death. But it didn't help: all the villagers briskly died of the plague. Barbara only survived because, through shame, she always slept curled up behind the cows. She then had to marry a distant "uncle," a man named Hans, so the village and land would stay in the family.

Meer goes into some detail describing the aftermath of the plague, and Barbara's life, when she seems to be constantly pregnant.

Hans Zürcher was furious with Barbara, because only their daughters lived to adulthood. Of eighteen pregnan-

cies, three boys died before birth, four during birth,
two in childhood and one in adulthood. After a few damp
summers, Barbara was beset with visions. The <u>rye mother,
death and fire</u> were everywhere. Her anxiety attacks grew
worse and worse. Eventually, Barbara locked herself in
with a sack of ergot fungi from the cornfields. When she
came out, she was transformed. She told Ottilia, her
favorite daughter, that beings from a faraway planet had
come and shown her how to free the good spirit from the
ergot. Ottilia soon noticed her mother now only talked
to plants and the grain fungus.

Jakobine Elsener, née Zürcher, 1374-1394

A kind of Ronja the Robber's Daughter, with a down-to-
earth manner. Jakobine her life was brief and self-
determined. As she watched her father, Hans, snarling
at her mother, Barbara, and her sniping back at him,
she swore she would never marry. Jakobine was a coarse
woman and liked getting her hands dirty. She didn't give
a tinker's cuss about her family's growing wealth, from
their large quantity of land. She taught herself how to
set traps, predominantly to catch birds: bow and glue
traps. She spent hours on end fiddling with mistletoe
berries and resin to make the best glue.

But Hans Elsener his eyes. She hadn't factored these
into her little milk book. Hans Elsener's eyes were an
elysian thing. So green and lovely, like when you dive
deep into Lake Aegeri and gaze up from below the water's
surface into fingers of sunshine. Nine months later,

Jakobine was dead. Father Hans and Husband Hans were
devastated.

Magdalena Ledergerber, née Elsener, 1394–1469
Grandfather Hans and Father Hans loathed Magdalena like
the plague, because her mother had died having her. Magdalena was strict, God-fearing, purposeful. Even though
she was illiterate, she became the village bookkeeper.
She single-handedly created a system for the organization and recordkeeping of cattle, expenditure and rev-
enue, harvests. With this, Magdalena made quite a bit of
money for the family.

Meer describes Magdalena's "milk book," her meticulous
documentation and organization, reminding me a little of Urgrosspeer's crop rotation plans. After Magdalena, there's another
Barbara, whose biography appears in multiple different versions,
which leads me to suspect that she occupied Meer's attention for
quite a while. Here's the beginning of a version written in dialect
about the second Barbara's life:

Barbara Züllig, née Ledergerber, 1432–unklar
Fohlks awlways sine Barbara Züllig as the wysust wum'n
fro her kin. Klohsr to her grate-ahnt Ottilia Zürcher
tha her ohn muther, Magdalena, thats bileev en godd wer
mor tha a bohdee culd suhfur. Awlredy yuhng, Barbara
tuuk intrehst in her grate-grate-grandmeers erb garden. Ohld Ottilia tawt the bryte gurl awl her wysdum.

```
Wun day, Ottilia brawt yuhng Barbara, 16 yeres ohld, to
tha garden haus. "Arr you redi vore yore legassy?" she
ahskd, all sollum. Barbara noddid her hed. An so Ottilia
tohld the yuhng gurl abohwt her vizhuns, that an ayngul
had kame and shohde her the erbs seekrit spirrits. The
ayngul tawt her hou to rilees the guhd spirrits vrom
the ergot kore. Leev the ergot in haut wawtur, an ohnly
the guhd spirrits kame owt. The eveel spirrits stade
in, afrayd ov wawtur. An Ottilia mayde a salve, tha she
smeerd a Barbara, her armes an beneev her nohs.
```

Meer has always struggled with writing, and spelling never was her strong point. Some words are crossed out and rewritten up to four times, in different ink. Many are dialect words, which presumably she looked up in Duden or the Swiss German dictionary and replaced with the "proper / Standard German" words. For example, *Schoos* with *Schürze* (not *Schoss*) or *Scheichen* with *Bein*. Like many Swiss people, Meer sees Standard German as refined, elevated, educated, a school language, not a foreign language, but an alien one. At school she was one of those who got left behind, and at just sixteen years of age, she had to do an apprenticeship to become a hairdresser.

Back when I was about twelve years old, I came home with an essay for which I'd received a very good grade. I showed it to Meer; she was even prouder than I was and stroked my head lovingly. I'd been told by the teacher to correct the few mistakes I had made. On one, he had written: "This is dialect. Replace it with

the correct Standard German word." I had written that someone's bad knee *bravte*. I asked Meer, "What's Standard German
for *braven*? Apparently it's not good German."

She stood up, suddenly furious, grabbed the Duden dictionary you gave her when she got married (it wasn't new, but from
a used bookstore), and threw it at me. "Look it up yourself,
lazybones!"

I couldn't find the word in Duden. There was *brav* as an ad-
jective, but no verb. *Braven*, I was able to translate for myself
only later, is the Bern German verb for "to get better, recover,
heal."

Here's the cleanest (and I therefore presume: final) version of
Barbara Züllig's life story:

Barbara Züllig, née Ledergerber, 1432-unclear
Barbara Züllig was always regarded as the wisest woman
in her clan. She felt closer to her great-aunt Ottilia
Zürcher than her own mother, Magdalena, whose unending
benedictions got on her tits. Even before Barbara had
outgrown her kiddie clogs, she took a keen interest in
her great-grandmother Barbara Zürcher's herb garden.
Old Ottilia taught the eloquent child everything what
she knew.

One day, Ottilia led sixteen-year-old Barbara into
the garden shed. "Alrighty, are you ready to take on your
legacy?" she asked solemnly. Barbara nodded. Ottilia
told the young woman that an angel had appeared to Barbara Senior and shown her the secret spirits of herbs.

```
Above all, the angel had shown her how to release the
good spirits from an ergot kernel. If you leave the er-
got to steep in hot water, only the good spirits come
out. The bad ones stay in the fungus, they're afraid of
water. Ottilia then made a poultice, what she applied to
Barbara's inner arms and beneath her nose. Barbara soon
came over all funny and had to lie down for a bit beneath
the cherry tree. For a while she was out of sorts, but
then she saw the light in the leaves rain down on her
like liquid rock crystal, and her feet flowed out of
her faded stockings, and her hair braided itself into
the roots of the cherry tree. And as she flowed out of
herself, the tree charmingly absorbed her.
```

This trippy experience is followed by two pages describing Barbara's marriage to her odious husband. I picture Meer hammering these pages into her typewriter, occasionally looking up words or synonyms in her well-thumbed Duden. From time to time, she has Barbara say Standard-Germanized French words, like she picked up the "paraplui" (umbrella) or Barbara was "eschoffiert" (incensed). I'm moved by this. It seems Meer placed a more sophisticated language in Barbara's mouth than she was actually able to speak. At the same time, there are glimmers that Meer, as the writer, wanted to show she could master the language of the "have-it-alls" (Swiss German for "blue bloods"). Except that this wasn't the language of the German aristocracy; but that of the Bernese patricians. I don't know whether Meer knows this. The thought makes me sad. And the fact that I'm reading this with the conviction that I know better and am feeling sad for her—this makes me ashamed. I know she would have liked to know more, about all of this, about everything.

After one year of marriage, Barbara has had enough. She runs off and joins a professional army, becoming a sex worker.

Barbara wasn't the prettiest, but nor was she the ug-
liest, and she had all kinds of noblesse. And she was
quite intelligent, which she valued over looks. So she
wasn't one of the prostitutes with the highest number
of tricks. The lower-ranking soldiers were generally
paired with the lower-ranking prostitutes, and after a
while, Barbara found a firm footing.
     The highest-ranking whores were so haughty and proud
that they turned their noses up so high the rain practically fell into their nostrils. These girls, the most
beautiful and biggest-breasted, were claimed by the
loudest and most masculine soldiers. Thank God Barbara
wasn't one of them. Because the soldiers of the first
rank usually felt the need to legitimize their masculinity even in bed, and were boorish as hell. Nothing
scared them more shitless than making fools of themselves in front of a whore. Erection problems? Put it
in the vault. If the prostitutes didn't keep schtum,
they were swiftly reminded who was boss. Barbara's most
beautiful colleagues frequently complained about how
violent their soldiers were, and how they constantly
had to rhapsodize about certain body parts. No, Barbara
was happy not to be one of the top prostitutes. But she

wasn't one of the lowest-ranking whores either, that were given the stupidest and weakest soldiers. She was glad of this too, because the lowest-ranking soldiers also felt the need to overcompensate. Barbara was a contented midfielder.

After some years had passed, Barbara knew most of the herb wives between the Baltic Sea and the Alps. Combined with what she had learned from Ottilia, this made her into a library of knowledge. She helped the soldiers with wounds and erection problems; and supported herself and the other prostitutes with contraception and abortion. Barbara had just one little one, from the early days. Clemens. He was a fine fellow.

There are a few crossed-out pages here about how Barbara leaves the army, follows her calling, and goes to live with an old herb witch in the Black Forest. There she learns to read and write, and acquires even more knowledge about the female body. After the old woman dies, Barbara goes to Frankfurt, a city that, in the mid-fifteenth century, invested in the development of health care. Or so Meer wrote. I google it. She's right.

With the money inherited from the old witch, Barbara bought a little garden on the outskirts of Frankfurt and began to sell medicinal herbs and offer healing. With her herbal knowledge, she swiftly made a name for herself as a "sage femme." If ever there was somebody she couldn't help physically, she gave them some ergot spirit, Barbara Zürcher's ointment, and accompanied the

patient on an inward journey. Before long she was able
to afford a practice in the city center, and a maid to
tend the herb garden in her stead.

By the age of thirty-two, Barbara had run three gardens and supported the city's doctors and midwives as a
"sage femme." She also specialized in difficult births
and wound healing. The city authorities valued and supported her work. After helping the daughter of the
wealthy Klaus Humbracht survive a five-day breech birth,
she was rewarded with a house in the vieille ville.

As Barbara grew older, she dedicated herself more and
more to gathering her knowledge (she wrote a medicine
book) and to educating young women. She trained midwives in her house on the outskirts of the city, while
her house in the center became an unofficial refuge for
unmarried women in "unfortunate circumstances." The
patrician families she was connected with (Humbracht et
al.) protected her from the church. She was a thorn in
the clergy's eye, and her house was demonized as a place
of fornication. But she could live with that. To put it
plainly: she couldn't give a flying fuck.

In her forties, she was called out of bed one night
by the Humbracht family. An acquaintance of theirs, a
prince's son, had been gored by a boar, which must have
hurt like the blazes. His entire left side was one big
split. Barbara bathed and cleaned him and prayed over
the evil wound, stitched what she could stitch, and
repeatedly rubbed in her healing ointment, which was
swiftly devoured by the red wound-mouth. She knew that

her powers wouldn't be enough to heal the nobleman. Suddenly he awoke, delirious with fever. Barbara pressed him back down onto the bed and commanded: "Don't move, you need to rest. You're safe now." The nobleman obeyed, relaxed, and looked into Barbara's eyes, the blue-yellow eyes she had inherited from Hans Elsener, and it was as though they recognized each other. She stayed three days and three nights by the nobleman's side—his name was Alexander—toiling away. Once the prince's son was finally through the worst, she went outside and ran into the forest. There she screamed, screamed at the world:

"All these years I've abandoned myself. I've sacrificed myself, as we're expected to. I'm a healing hand without a body of my own. I agreed to care for your wounds, you pig-filthy world, to coddle and cosset you, and now I finally see: you're one great incurable wound! Fiddlesticks! I gave my d'accord to love you, you bad-tempered potato of a planet. But do you know how tiring that is? I'm no longer the soldiers' bicycle, and I'll save these rich ball sacks no longer. These lips have no more demonic smiles à la reserve. It's enough to drive a person to despair, trying to like you and the brainless creatures you bear. Enough is enough! Tell me, you pigsty of a planet, why aren't I allowed just one crumb of happiness? You torment us poor dregs whenever you can, so wouldn't it be fairer if I had never met Alex, this prince who's so far above me? This snowdrop, twenty years younger, who'll have his head lopped off at war or be poisoned on home soil?"

Barbara fell silent and stood there. It was as dark as

inside a cow's rectum. The only answer was the rustling
of the forest.

She went to see the prince a few more times, and his
wound slowly healed. But she didn't want to cure him too
quickly. After his long convalescence, the two met in
the forest another five times. Then he was sent by his
father to the English court. On the journey over, he got
a dirty splinter from the ship's railing that caused a
blood poisoning from which he died. Barbara never found
out. It took a very long time for his features to fade
from her memory. Barbara kept three images of him with
her until the day she died beneath a hawthorn tree. The
white, downy skin of his bottom beneath her rough hand.
The way he turned around on his gray horse after each
of their rendezvous; his anxious gaze and then the re-
alization: SHE'S STILL THERE! And finally, the feeling
she had when they embraced: all of my love, Alex, all
of me, forever. I build my dreams around you and paint
them scarlet-red.

In her old age, Barbara asked two of her grandchil-
dren, Maximillian and Ottilia, to come with her on a
final journey south. She wanted to see the mountains
one last time. They set off in a carriage from the
Humbrachts. After hours of silence, they reached the
middle of a beech forest. Barbara took her grandchil-
dren's hands and said, "My darlings, I'm sorry. You're
my descendants. Carry my legacy, carry it as far as you
can. I'm sure there will soon come a time when everything
is different, when what we've built will fade away. My

darling children, I'm so sorry. Always remember: that
our paths crossed, that we were in the same place at the
same time, and if you add up all the possible places
and all the possible times and all the possible bodies, that's magical. Maximilian, don't be too hard on
yourself, you'll bite into enough hard bread as it is.
And you, Ottilia, grab people, beat them with the chamber pot if necessary, the abyss won't come, we are the
abyss. The light doesn't only appear in the afterlife,
we are the light. The Lord hasn't left us, he's left us
the choice."

Barbara then signaled to the coach driver, who stopped
in the middle of the forest, and just like that she ran
into the trees. Maximilian and Ottilia were gobsmacked.
Then they ran after her. But Barbara had already been
swallowed by the forest.

Dear Grossmeer. Your daughter wrote all of this. Aren't you a
little bit proud? It's past two in the morning now, my eyes are
sore, I look over the pages again, read a few handwritten notes:
"Add stuff about midwives, Frankfurt," or, "Ask Alex if makes
sense." I picture Meer trying to write your life story, brushing
her hair back, tying it up again and again like she always does
when she's exasperated with a task. And I think I know what
she's told herself: that she's finally going to chronicle her meers'
family tree. The material she began to collect in my childhood.
She'll trace the line of her female ancestors—all the lives that
aren't recorded in the usual family trees; that simply appear out
of nowhere—and when she reaches her Meer, you, she'll finally

be able to write up your life. And I'm almost 100 percent sure that when Meer reached Barbara Züllig, she was gripped by a writing frenzy. I know a writing frenzy when I see one: the incalculable, blazingly bright bang of a world suddenly opening up before you, from one moment to the next, at your desk, between sitting there and sitting there. And as for Meer's language, I'm convinced that this Helvetic German is a conscious one-finger salute to Standard German. I'm very tired, but I feel connected to Meer in a way I never have before. I'd like to read one more biography.

It's about Barbara Züllig's only son, Clemens Züllig. He helps her with her work and becomes her right-hand man, managing the apothecary and the administrative side of the midwifery training that Barbara offers. When he's around thirty, he falls in love with an unmarried patient, Johanna, who comes to the Züllig house to give birth. After several years of happiness with her, one evening he goes to his meer (who is illustrating her medicine books and sticking in dried herbs) and shares his suspicion that he's infertile. Barbara laughs. Is that all that's bothering him, she asks. Clemens says yes. Barbara replies that she had already suspected as much. This is her advice:

"As you know, you're a soldier's brat. I had you when I was seventeen. During those first months with the army, I didn't yet know how the female body works. We were based near Strasbourg, where I met an herb wife, a backstreet abortionist. I lay down beneath a chestnut tree, the old woman busied herself with her cauldron, and I began to plead for your forgiveness. I said: I'm sorry I can't have you, but I live in a world where I can't offer you a decent life. All I can offer is war and poverty. I readied myself. But then I sensed you could feel it. And I couldn't do it. I went back to the military camp and made my decision: I'll have you, but you'll be my first and last goof. And I'll devote myself to gathering knowledge about our bodies, so in future I can determine what happens inside me."

Clemens looked at her for a long while. "As always, Ma, you're talking in riddles." Barbara grabbed her son's chin and said, "Aren't there enough fatherless children already? I believe your seed is less valuable than your fathering." And so Clemens became a loving father. His and Johanna's family grew as more and more women came to the Züllig house in "unfortunate circumstances." The children whose bonus-parents they became: Adelheid, Maximilian, Hans, Maria Catharina, Verena Maria, Elisabeth, Carl, Kaspar Josef, Ottilia, Ida Agatha, Johann Peter, Johann Jordan, Clemens Adelrich, Johanna Elisa, Georg Carl, Agatha Maria, Clemens Anton, Arnulf, Balthasar, Marie, Arbogast, Adalbert, Magdalena, Kaspar Oswald, Chlodewech, Huldrich Sebastian, Elfrun, Ida Maria, Johanna Christina, Siegfried Kaspar, and Barbara.

6

A week later, Meer brings you a cake. Just like that, without a birthday. The cake is decorated with marzipan tennis balls.

You're a little girl, completely still with joy. "How did you know I always wanted to play tennis as a child?" Not even Meer can find a good lie to answer this question. She leaves the photo she brought you in her bag. Meer took it two years ago; you at seniors' tennis, looking happy, proud, sweaty.

I speak with the nurse who is Nico, my dead uncle. I say, "Why doors that are painted like walls? And doors disguised as bookshelves?" First Nico says, "Flight impulses," then sentences that start with "we," and then, "People with dementia don't have a problem with the dementia, just their surroundings." I say, "So why the flight impulses?" Others say, "Confusion, not discontent." I say, "Trapped." Others say: Technical terms. I say: Feelings.

I do what I always do when I can't bear something: I have sex with the first available person. Here, that's Nico. The calm with which he leads me to the visitors' toilet on the fourth floor and tells me it's not the first time. I come, his cock so deep inside me that I know he can feel the heartbeat at the end of my rectum, that he must be able to feel it, my little heart that I can't feel, that I feel only through his flesh, that I feel only briefly, right now, because it's impaled, throbbing and racing, on his urethra.

We smoke out of the window. He's so hairy the smoke gets caught in his chest hair. I say that no one has a personality in this place, that even the nurses never say "I," but only ever "we," that it's infantilizing and it irritates me. He says I must love my grossmeer very much, given how often I'm here. I say nothing.

"What's it like?" he asks. "What?" I ask. "To be like you," he says. "What's it like," I ask, "to be like *you*?" He shrugs: "Completely normal. I just am." "Well so am I," I reply. "I just am. For me it's nothing. It's only something to others."

I watch him walk off to the nurses' station, adjusting his white work trousers, and I see the masculinity. I see the pure, entire masculinity of this world, which always acts as though it were just one body, as though it were only forming the reality of this one body and not all realities constantly, including those of the hairless, the pawed, scaled, slimy, single-celled.

I pay for you to visit the hairdresser. You specify, down to a hair, what kind of cut you'd like. I see myself in the mirror behind you. I think about how, in this system, I'm still most likely to be seen as gay. And because there's this illness that spreads rampantly among my people, or rather, because there's the narrative that it spreads predominantly among our bodies, but I want unprotected sex, because otherwise I can't feel myself, I shell out nine hundred francs a month for PrEP (pre-exposure prophylaxis). And because I'm not a boy inside, my body costs me another three hundred francs a month for shaving, creams, makeup, and another eighty still for other pharma. I see how happy you are with your short hair, and I think about how much cheaper a gender-fluid body is than a dementia-ridden body, and that we're both regarded as sick by this system, yet neither of us are accepted by the health insurance plans.

I take you on a walk away from the home. We come across a meer with two children, and we come across a front garden with Meertrübeli.

"Meertrübeli," I say.

"Yes, you can't miss them."

"Do you remember the story about the Meertrübeli bread you didn't eat because you were so angry?"

You look at me, astonished. "But that was my meer, with the Meertrübeli bread, that's not my story."

I'm sitting on the train from Bern to Zürich, reading about Barbara Züllig's granddaughter Ottilia Züllig, who was politically active and loved her adopted brother; who because of the rise in misogyny had to close the Züllig house; who joined a protest march with the female silk workers and was never seen again. Who, at night, when she couldn't sleep, sang the song "Even in heaven, that land of no sinners, we were just poor silk spinners."

I read about Ottilia Züllig's daughter, Maria Euphemia, the last midwife in the family, who suffered under the political changes. She was ordered by the city—in other words, the men, who were now hijacking medical knowledge—to draw up a list of pregnant women, to name suspects when a child was abandoned, and to keep a network of secret informants in her lodgings in order to control the women. Maria Euphemia had work clothing specially tailored, with trousers and pockets, because this was far more practical. Bonnets hindered her too, she said; they were essentially blinders. She eventually wore these clothes all the time, and was soon nicknamed "the ladess." I read about the terrible gang rape that Maria endured. Or rather, I read parts of it. It seems like Meer was determined to place all the patriarchal contempt for the female body in these pages. There are twelve men, and Meer takes a whole page for each of them. There are painstaking descriptions of how Maria was held down, the sounds made by each man, the stench of his penis. It's written from Maria Euphemia's perspective, including the thoughts with which she stopped herself from falling into despair. She fixes her gaze on a lilac bush. I want to skip over the last few men, but then I force myself to read after all: This violence is part of Meer's project. Because Maria Euphemia falls pregnant out of wedlock, she's accused of sleeping with the devil, and so she flees Frankfurt, which for many centuries had been a pocket of liberalism, and goes to Florence. She takes with her only the medicine book of her urgrossmeer Barbara, and her child, Catharina. In Florence, she passes herself off as a widow.

I read about Catharina, who grew up in Florence, birthed eighteen children, became devoutly Catholic, and hated her meer, Maria, for her witchcraft (abortions).

I read about Catharina's daughter Raphaela, who suffered from anxiety; who was persecuted by a twelve-headed monster.

I read about Raphaela's daughter Lucia, who had panic attacks in which she was plagued by horrific birds that looked like human beings; they were blind but saw everything.

I read about Lucia's daughter Lila, who was devoutly religious, who spied on her young neighbor through a hole in the wall and masturbated, then took this to confession in the hope Jesus Christ would appear to her, and if not Jesus Christ then at least Paul the Apostle or another saint, so she wouldn't look so bad compared to her friend Marcella, to whom saints were constantly appearing.

And I read about Lila's daughter Claudia Bianchi and her friend Ira. I'm fascinated by Claudia, who in contrast to her meer, grossmeer, and urgrossmeer, had a very unusual life. She fled Florence and traveled across Europe amid the turmoil of the Thirty Years' War.

Claudia Bianchi, 1596–1650

Claudia spent almost every day with Ira Marinero. They frequently stayed with Ira's grandparents, who lived in San Donato in Collina, a little village in the mountains around Florence. Their mothers both had an especially clear line to God. These visits to the grandparents were intended to protect Ira and Claudia from fornication. After all, fornication is always so much more common in the city. The two girls liked being in the countryside, where they could escape their mothers' stern gazes. They ran through the chestnut forests and told each other numerous variations of the same story. This is how it went:

The narrator (alternately Claudia or Ira) is in San Donato. It's early in the morning, and everyone is still fast asleep, so the narrator goes out to walk alone.

She makes her way through the forest and comes across
an unfamiliar stream. Following it uphill, she reaches
a waterfall cascading into a pond. A sturdy warhorse
is stood next to the pond. The narrator stays behind a
bush. And what she sees takes her breath away. There
in the pond, beneath the waterfall, is an honest-to-
goodness knight, bathing. The finest figure of a man
you can imagine. A long blond mane and a broad back, so
broad you could breakfast off it. His spine is lined
by two mountain-mighty chains of muscle, and the cool
water runs eagerly down this rolling landscape. Then he
turns around. He's as beautiful as all the antique stat-
ues in the world combined. Each time one of the girls
tells the story, it gets a little longer. In one, the
knight plunges beneath the water. On the next telling, he swiftly emerges, whips back his golden hair,
and the droplets of water moisten the narrator in her
hiding place. The next time, he spots the narrator and
gives her a stern look. He approaches her. Then the water comes to just below his navel. Then to the edge of
his pubic bone. The water glistens iridescently on his
astral body. Then the line of his groin appears above
the surface of the water. Then the knight says: "Well,
aren't you a little rascal, hiding behind a bush like
that and spying on me. Just you wait . . ." Then curly,
wiry hair emerges from the wet, until . . .

The following sentences are crossed out so vigorously that the paper is perforated in places. I'm only able to decipher the final sen-

tence: "... Then they go at it hog wild." I laugh joyfully, imagining
Meer feeling like a "rascal" as she wrote this passage, I imagine
her spurring herself on, feeling your gaze, Grossmeer, and writing against it. I remember her once telling me about the "female
gaze," how proud she was to know this feminist, film-theory concept (and I of course was equally proud). Around a year ago, we
had a conversation about her youth. She said she grew up believing that women didn't have sexual needs. That for a long time
she thought she was sick for "lusting after" men or women at the
open-air swimming pool. It wasn't until her early twenties, when
she was living with a friend and walked in on her masturbating,
that she talked about her sexuality for the first time. "You don't
know how happy I was to see Fränzi like that, with one hand between her legs, the other in her mouth." Had she herself never
masturbated before that? I asked. "I had," she said, "but still. You
used to hear these awful things. They said if you touched yourself, you'd get pimples, or consumption, that you'd dry out, that
it's a sickness, contagious, and that if you did it regularly, you'd
die." She never masturbated at home, she told me. She always
felt like Grossmeer could see. She only masturbated in the toilet
at the swimming pool.

When Claudia and Ira weren't telling each other stories
like these, they played hide-and-seek or fooled about.
Once, in the city apartment, Claudia found a big old
book while she was hiding. It was at the back of a wardrobe, covered in a thick layer of dust.
    The first part was an herbarium: on one side, the
pages held pressed, medicinal plants, now crumbling,

and on the opposite side, text in a language the girls didn't understand (they could read, but only the biblical Latin that Claudia's devoutly religious mother, Lila, had taught them).

The second part contained gruesome drawings. Gaping wounds, open fractures, bandaging instructions, and lots of lists. The lists—as the girls discovered through comparison—were different combinations of the plants from the first section.

The third and final part was the one the girls looked at most. There were drawings of naked women, of children in the womb, of splayed legs, of vulvas, of scissors that cut between the vulva and bottom, and many more unheard-of things. One weekend where they were going to stay with Ira's grandparents, Claudia secretly packed the book. The two friends would go as far as they could into the chestnut forest, to the mountain stream, and read the mysterious book. They hid it in a disused chapel in the forest.

One hot summer's day, they were at the river again, their noses in the book. It was proper sweat-inducing weather. They looked at the drawing of a child that lay transverse in the womb. They were sixteen. Suddenly, Ira banged the book shut, stripped down to her bare skin, and jumped into the stream. "Come on, you little chickenshit!" Ira called, but Claudia just sat there impassively. They didn't talk any more that day. In the evening, at the grandparents' house, Claudia broke down, and she wept through three whole days and screamed in one long fit of rage. She tore out all of her hair and acted like an ill-bred wench. When her mother, Lila, came by with a priest in tow, the man of God swiftly grasped what was wrong: the young, beautiful girl had been possessed by the devil himself. But the exorcisms he performed were all in vain. When Claudia was put into a carriage, her last word before turning silent was: "Order!"

Claudia ended up in a variety of institutions, all of them religious, of course. After six years she escaped and made her way northward, through the chaos of the Thirty Years' War. Eventually she ended up in a poorhouse in Bavaria, where she lived for a long time with beggars, prostitutes, sodomites, murderers, and deserters. She remained mute.

On a warm April evening in 1646, one of the clerical attendants tells her about the landscapes he encounters in his dreams. He tells Claudia a great deal, because she's such a good listener. The most beautiful landscape he has ever seen, he says, was a lake in the Black Forest. What was the most beautiful landscape she's ever seen? Claudia stood up and told the man that the most beautiful landscape she'd ever seen was Ira Marinero's skin, Ira's sixteen-year-old thighs stood in the mountain stream, Ira's breasts in the sweat of that August day. This was the most beautiful and terrible thing she'd ever seen, because it was so close and yet so unreachable. The holy man stared at her. Her voice, because of her thirty-four years of silence, was more a squeak. He hurried out of the wing of the building, leaving the door open, ran to the disciplinarian in his living quarters by the poorhouse, and cried: "She speaks! The mute speaks!" By the time they returned, the mute was already long gone.

7

—Hello?

—It's me.

—Oh. You. I'm really stressed right now, I had to take on two shifts today because Jacqueline had a "migraine" again, then my favorite clippers broke, and then I paid the invoices for Grossmeer. It's so expensive. The depressing thing is, even when I work more I still don't earn enough for all Grossmeer's shit, and there's so little rent coming from the house, it doesn't even cover the maintenance.

—I don't think I'm coming to see Grossmeer this Saturday. I need a weekend to rest.

—Okay. Sure, I get it, it's a long way from Zürich to Ostermundigen . . .

—I've been coming every weekend.

— . . . even though your grossmeer is on her deathbed . . . Is this because you don't want to see the nurse?

—What nurse?

—Are you in love with him or something? . . . Why are you always so sensitive?

—We just have sex. But you know that already. Drop it.

—He asked after you yesterday. And last week too.

—What did he ask?

—I see how you two look at each other. It's the only time I see you like that.

—It's called sexual attraction, Meer, so I very much hope you don't. Besides, he's from a Kurdish background, and a nurse, so it wouldn't work between us anyway.

—What's that supposed to mean? That's racist and . . . what-chamacallit . . . that thing you said to me last Easter . . .

—Classist?

—Exactly, classist. Why can't you be with a Kurdish nurse?

—I didn't mean because he's Kurdish . . . Yes, you're right. That was fucking racist, sorry. The whole thing just reminds me of Fabrizio. I can't hold another grown man's hand while he comes out to his macho, conservative-scum family, and when it's someone "like me" there with him, the shit really hits the fan. I wish I didn't have to pay any attention to nationality, but I need someone who's familiar with these issues, who . . . I have to protect myself a little. I'm just—"special."

—How do you know his family's macho?

—I . . . Well, I don't, I guess. I'm sorry.

—Is that why you broke up with Fabrizio?

—He broke up with me.

—That's not what he told me.

—Oh. So the two of you still meet for coffee, or what?

—No, we ran into each other at the station. I just said I thought it was a shame he broke up with you, that I still liked him, that I wasn't like Peer. And then he said—it was clearly emotional for him—he said it was you.

—That it was me . . . Ma, listen. When I was in your office for Grossmeer's obituary, I found the family tree.

—Yes.

—Not the Sägesser family tree. Your family tree, the one you . . . wrote, in the gray folder . . . I read it, I mean, I'm reading it.

—Look, I'm so tired and I have to open up the salon tomorrow morning. We can talk on Saturday.

—Ma, I . . .

—Listen, I still need to dye my hair today, it just won't do, you know, a hairdresser with dark roots showing, I can't just go to work looking however I like.

—Sure, I know. Hair doesn't wait. Good night.

8

I stand by the open window. The beech tree rustles. A soft metallic rustling, like thousands of tiny aluminum foil leaves. When I close my eyes, it sounds like I'm standing at a riverbank, as though I'm standing far away from here. Before me lies the life of Ira Marinero. The first part is written neatly by hand, probably a redraft. The second is full of corrections, even more so than Claudia Bianchi's life.

Ira Marinero, 1596-unclear

When Ira's mother, Marcella Marinero, catches her packing her things a few weeks after Claudia Bianchi's breakdown, and asks where she's going, Ira says she

plans to free Claudia from Mariazell, the convent for
madwomen. And that she also happens to be deeply in love
with Claudia. After that, her mother set the city's
morality police on her, so Ira had to lay low with a
school friend. You're afraid of scandal, thought Ira,
and scandal you shall have, Mother. This is how it came
about that Ira applied for a prostitution license at the
Office of Decency.

The Office of Decency—l'Ufficio dell'Onestà—was
founded in Florence in 1403. Like everywhere in Europe,
the population numbers collapsed after the Black Death
and stayed rock-bottom. In addition, furthermore, homosexuality was spreading like a second plague. The Office
of Decency was a surveillance and enforcement commis-
sion that set itself the aim of increasing the population, and, in the process, bringing homosexuality to an
end. They organized information events, where presenta-
tions were given on how to be a good man or a beautiful
woman. (This is all true, by the way!) As a woman, you
couldn't laugh too loud or walk with too broad a gait
or look directly into a man's eyes, and as a man, you
couldn't cry in public, and essentially you just had to
father as many children as possible.

Meer, Meer, I think, laughing into my room, you've become a
proper research fiend. I skim over several pages about how unmarried men over thirty were taxed at higher rates, due to the
Onestà, and how women who bore numerous children received

gifts, like a salami or half a pig (depending on how numerous the children were).

The Office of Decency also increasingly took over the support and control of public whorehouses. The thinking behind this was: Young men wouldn't take one another as lovers if they had easier access to women. So the brothels became important institutions in the promotion of social order, or rather, of compulsory heterosexuality. It went so far that the Onestà even gifted boys a free visit to the brothel on their sixteenth birthday.

Back to Ira. She had no intention of working as a prostitute. Because she could read, write, and do arithmetic (her mother had taught her something, at least) she swiftly found work as a bookkeeper in a brothel. She proudly wore the yellow armband that marked her out as a prostitute. And she made sure to be seen with the band of whores by a friend of her mother's. Revenge really is sweet.

The work was utterly delectable. Ira's youngest sister had secretly brought her the forbidden book from the chapel in the mountains, and with this mysterious, foreign book, Ira was able to help the prostitutes with their numerous health problems. She had grown especially fond of Elvira, a young girl from North Africa. Ira had saved all her money, but it still took three years before she could afford the journey to Mariazell. When she finally arrived there and asked for Claudia, she dis-

covered that Claudia had fled a few months before. Ira
was so angry she bit out a tooth. She went back to the
horse and carriage in a daze, and returned to Florence.

On the journey home, Ira began to write poems in which
she asked the universe where Claudia was, which fox had
last seen her or which moss was growing over her legs.
Time passed. One day, while Ira was tending to a bad head
wound that Elvira had sustained while turning tricks,
the girl asked whether it was true that Ira could write.
Ira said yes. Elvira fell into a reverent silence, then,
once Ira was done tending her wound, said, "If I could
write, I'd write up my life story." Ira didn't respond,
but thought: I can write, but I don't have a life I'd
want to write up. Washing contraceptive sponges and a
foolish vengeance, that's my life. Writing is wasted
on me!

Once, in 1630, while the plague was still rife, Ira
saw her mother at the edge of the streets the prostitutes were permitted to walk; old Marcella Marinero,
with a plague boil in her hand. The little old mother
straightened her arthritic back and called from the
other side of the road: "My child, I'd like to embrace
you, but I'm sick. I'm sorry. Won't you take off that
ghastly armband and come home, to your proper life?"
Ira turned around and went back to the brothel with her
women. For the first time ever, she felt like she belonged. Later, when she was supposed to abort a child
for Elvira, the young woman asked whether there wasn't

perhaps a different tool than forceps. Because it always
hurt so goddamn much. Ira had already found a decoction
in her forbidden book that she hadn't yet dared try,
because she didn't know two of the herbs. She had been
able to identify all the other plants from the pictures.

Meer describes how the decoction killed Elvira's baby, but didn't
get it out of her body. There's a ten-page description of how Ira
had to scrape it out with the forceps after all. I start to feel sick.
Elvira only just survives this unbelievable agony, and is severely
weakened. The next time she gets pregnant, she doesn't want to
get rid of the child. Elvira dies during the birth, and the child
survives. Ira cries for three whole days. She takes on the care of
Elvira's child.

After her friend's death, Ira resolved to write up Elvira's life. But when she sat down, she realized she
knew almost nothing about her, even though she'd been
the person closest to her. Elvira had barely told her
anything, and Ira had almost never asked. They had simply battled through life side by side. What kind of life
have I led? thought Ira. I've turned myself into stone.
All she remembered were Elvira's jokes. Elvira always
told the shallowest jokes, which Ira found simple as
hell, perverse, crude, though no cruder than the other
prostitute jokes that *did* often make her laugh. She
wrote down Elvira's jokes. And because she couldn't
remember Elvira's life, she began to write down the

other prostitutes' life stories. For seven whole years,
she documented everything, asked the women about their
lives before prostitution, their dreams. Late one evening, when she went into the kitchen with the intention
of getting herself a hunk of bread—she was carrying her
whore biographies and planned to work on them at the
bench by the stove—a young newcomer asked what she was
holding. Ira answered: <u>The Collected Disappearance of
Florentine Lilies</u>. After significant pleading from the
prostitute, Ira opened her book. She read out only her
favorite jokes; the others depressed her too much. More
and more of the whores gathered around, until eventually almost the entire crew was sitting in the kitchen.

"Cupida Assatanato's favorite joke: What does the
leper say to the whore? Leave it in, I'll be back
tomorrow."

"Stella Regina's favorite joke: A terrone comes into
the cathouse and says: I ain't got two scudos to rub
together. The whoremonger says: In that case, you can
rub your own."

"Gloria Golosa's favorite joke: A college man bought
himself a new pair of trousers, but they were too tight.
So he shaved his legs."

"Maria Rossi's favorite joke: Two popes run into each
other on the street."

"Fica Fichissima's favorite jokes:

"Tried to open a brothel for soldiers with no legs, but the motto SPRITZ AS YOU SITZ didn't go down well.

"Tried to open a circus next to the brothel, but the motto CUNNING STUNTS NOT STUNNING CUNTS didn't go down well.

"Tried to open a brothel next to a chicken coop, but the motto FUCKS NOT CLUCKS didn't go down well.

"Tried to open a brothel for lepers, but the motto USE IT OR LOSE IT didn't go down well.

"Tried to open a whorehouse next to a leper house, but the motto SCREW, DON'T MILDEW didn't go down well."

Fica Fichissima was the name Elvira had given herself for her clients. The whores were still slapping their thighs and roaring with laughter as Ira stepped out onto the street. She hadn't laughed at all. Ira stood there indecisively, clasping the lives of her favorite sluts to her chest, her forty-eight-year-old chest. The year was 1644 and it was cold, and she stared up at the sky, and felt the kind of immense sadness for which there just wasn't space on Earth. She was young again, standing in the ice-cold mountain stream and seeing Claudia sitting there motionless on the riverbank, unreachable.

Ira went to her room, where Elvira's child was waiting
for her. Ira had named the child Elvira. Then she packed
up her belongings, laid aside the yellow armband, took
little Elvira by the hand, and left Florence.

I catch my breath. I read about how Ira travels on foot to San Donato in Collina, to the empty house belonging to her late grandparents, and how she makes a home there. She raises the child
alone, earning a living as a healer with the knowledge from the
forbidden book. One day, a ghost appears in her garden, tooth-
less, hairless, wearing only a tattered vest. The ghost embraces
Ira and says:

"Ira, it's me, Claudia, I've been searching for you,
Ira, I wanted to see you, and so I set off, but a war
raged around me. I roamed only at night, to be invisible,
so I wouldn't end up back in the poorhouse. I talked to
the moon, told it everything I knew about myself and
the world, made my way through swamps, ate cattail and
sleeping fish, and only seldom went through the vil-
lages. I pinched clothes from washing lines and plucked
turnips from gardens, I walked through the fields of
Europe, where I ate daisies and dandelions and sorrel,
I went into the woods, which became my bedrooms, and ate
berries and roots. And everywhere, war. I went north,
west, south, east, and this war was everywhere. I saw
mountains, Ira, mountains of corpses. I heard screaming, a howling and wailing, and I can still hear it
now. I saw people steal clothes off the dying, not even

waiting until they were dead, pulling rings off fingers before rigor mortis set in. And I did the same. I've seen the face of our Earth—and it's grotesque. I've seen war slash open the Earth's skin, I've seen the Earth's entrails. We're living on a grave, and the fruit we eat grows from our dead. Here, Ira, this swallow brooch is for you. A Bohemian gave it to me as he lay dying when I crossed the battlefield. I was supposed to take it to his son, but he didn't live long enough to tell me his name. As the moon is bound to the earth, and humankind to the body, so am I, Claudia, bound to you, Ira Marinero."

9

Dear Grossmeer. I'm sitting next to you as I write this. Half an hour ago, I finally gave you the pink pullover. You told me you were always forced to wear pink as a little girl. But that you're not a little girl anymore. You laid it carefully but firmly on the windowsill. Then you got into bed and demonstratively fell asleep. I couldn't help but smile. It's Saturday again, and it's beautiful. Outside, I mean. I'm sitting in the armchair next to the window, you're lying in the bed and snoring. It occurs to me that I could actually tell you this stuff. That there's the possibility, now, to speak. I could tell you I miss you more than I know you. I could tell you the list of things that will remain of you. I wrote it last week. But it's far too long. I could tell you a selection of the words you'll leave behind.

Kömerle for "shopping"

Küechli for "rascal" ("You're such a Küechli!")

Gsunntiget for "getting gussied up, wearing one's Sunday
    best"
Abläschälä for "to wheedle an object out of someone by
    talking in a charming way" ("Oh, that's lovely, where did
    you get that? Oh, what a shame it's not on sale anymore.
    Do you use it often?")
Meertrübeli

These words have always been there. Attendants, witnesses to
my existence, hidden treasures in an otherwise transparent body.
On, in, and around me. Back when I was a foreign body among
all you unforeign, native bodies; back when I was a plant, these
words were already old; they were here a long time before you.
But now they've begun to disappear. Nobody says *kömerle* or
abläschälä anymore. Though Meer still says *abläschälä* sometimes, in a feigned, theatrical way, like someone turning a sweet
over and over in their mouth. I think she says it because it's connected to the few lovely memories of you, because you once
abläschälä'd a packet of biscuits off the neighbor, who was better
off, and you were lovingly caressing Meer as you spoke.

I'm no linguistic purist, so this isn't me wailing about the
disintegration of language. I just want to preserve these words
because they come from you, because they came out of you, crept
out of your mouth on scuttling little spider's legs, and crawled
into me. It feels as though the words saw me, my distant lands,
as though they traversed the zones I can't express, the ones I
still conceal from you and Meer, through fear your gazes would
tear them to shreds. But because they've seen me, these words,
I know they've also seen you, and Meer too. They were in you,

and with them you were able to say, understand, describe something of your own. And it's the same for Meer and me; that's why we still use these words. And even though the words come from an "inside" and go into an "outside," they don't drag into the open what they've described, these invisible regions of ours. They keep their own secret regions protected for each of us. And I don't know why, but I find that so comforting and so beautiful and so sad that I can't help but cry, here, now, next to you. I'm never closer to you than in these words.

I could tell you that half an hour ago I asked Nico what his name is. He was playing with the tiny white lake of sperm in my belly button. I was half lying, half sitting, on the changing table in the bathroom, and Nico said: "Ardan." And he asked what my name was, and I told him. I could try to tell you how I said "Ardan" and how Ardan smiled. That I said, "Look, Ardan, look," just to say his name, and pointed at the sperm slowly trickling across my stomach, and how Ardan collected my droplets on his hand. I could tell you that we looked at each other while he was still inside me, while he slowly turned soft, that his penis felt as though it were transforming, melting from a wooden hardness into honey, that Ardan dripped onto my hip bones and then—so unhurried, like a fleck of sunlight tiptoeing across a packed cellar—onto my thigh. I could tell you I asked about his coming out, whether it had been difficult, and that he answered (without commenting that this was a fucking weird question to ask in that moment, which it really was), that his coming out hadn't been difficult at all, that his father "wasn't normal" either, that this was one of the reasons why they had come here, and then I could tell you that he asked me whether we could go get dinner sometime, and immediately added: "Nothing fancy, we could just get a takeaway, the good Thai place by the station, it's nicely decorated, with real orchids, not expensive." I said no, and he didn't ask why it was a no, and I didn't say that I'm full of entrances, that like the residential home I have a thousand entrance doors but not one single exit, that I'm crammed full, that my body is still not completely my own and that there's no space left in me for him.

No matter how hard I try, I couldn't tell you how furiously Nico pulled out of me, how I dried up my sperm lake with toilet paper, how Nico pulled up his trousers, how he put on a different body language and a different face and passed me my underpants, which lay on the floor. How this gesture, the underpants-passing, had felt more degrading in its tenderness than all the times on sex-dates when, against my will, I had been hit, choked, jizz-faced, spat on, and verbally abused.

But no, Grossmeer, these things can't be said, not in the spoken language, not in the Meer language. I've never learned it, the telling, I've only learned the listening, the watching, and the talking that evades the things that really matter.

10

Dear Grossmeer. Even though you woke up after I didn't tell you all of this, I'd like to write this moment to you again, because you'll forget it anyway.

While I was writing about Ardan, you snored more and more loudly until eventually you were awoken by your own snoring. You looked around a little accusingly. When you saw me, you said, "Kim, love, where am I?" I knew immediately that this was a lucid moment, that you were with yourself, and how rare that is, so I laid my notebook aside and said, "In the home, Grossmeer," and you pulled yourself upright, tucking a second pillow behind your back. "Oh yes. Have you been here long? You won't believe the dream I had, I was lying here in bed and my meer was standing in front of me, gigantic, and she was asking: Where did you hide my kirsch? I know it was you, so tell me or I'll beat it out of you." I said, "Oh no, a nightmare." And you said, "No, it was nice to see my meer. And you, how long have you been here? Hasn't your hair grown long. Is it dyed? We always used to dye ours." I take out my hair band and my hair falls down over my shoulders. "No, it's not dyed. But look, I'm starting to lose some of it." You look at me in surprise. "Really? You must've inherited that from your grosspeer. He was bald by the time he hit thirty, these things always skip a generation, you know."

I sit down next to you on the bed, consistently amazed by how soft it is. You can really sink into it. My weight makes you shoot upward slightly and involuntarily slip toward me. "Grossmeer," I ask, "why do you think you were born on the same day as the first Rosmarie?" You laugh. "Little one. You and your questions." You stroke my hair. As carefully as you can, like I'm a kitten. You seem content. Your skin remembers your constant manual labor, never stops protecting itself, turning itself into calluses. A strand of my hair gets caught in a skin crease. You notice it too late, move your hand away and tug my hair. "Oh, sorry. These paws of mine. Oh, girl's hair." I sigh. "I know, Grossmeer. You always wanted two sons." You give me a stern look. "It was a different time, you know. A girl was expensive. The dowry. Girls couldn't work." I shake my head. "But that wasn't the case anymore when Meer was young. She wanted to work, and she was able to till I came along." You laugh, a little disparagingly. "Sure, as a hairdresser. Now, Nico, he really made something of himself. At the bank, Nico—" I interrupt you: "Nico drank himself to death"— "Nico really did well for himself at the bank."

I lie down next to you on the bed, make myself as narrow and long as possible, put my arm around you. You hold my arm, your thumb twitches nervously over it like it twitched over my legs when I sat on your lap as a child. "Grossmeer, I remember so little of my childhood. I did some research, and apparently when something bad happens, the brain can refuse to remember anything from that period. I'm wondering whether something bad happened in my childhood. You know, I have these recurring dreams about the chicken hutch. I'm too small to . . . the doorknob." You laugh, disbelieving, almost sympathetic. "Little one. You had the most sheltered upbringing imaginable." You talk about the geraniums. I try to think about nothing. I picture a completely empty lake. Swimming. Drifting. Drinking. Meer's earring that cast waves of all the colors in existence against the wall. Bloodbeech. My toes in the earth of the garden. My skin is sand, sand that's being carried away. Suddenly you, my hair in your hand: "That's nice, like that." I straighten up, look at you, you look at me, you smile.

11

—Hi.

—Oh, hi, it's you, I'm so tired, Jacqueline had an attack of arthritis and within an hour she couldn't even lift the scissors, so I had to do two persons' work, her daughter came in the afternoon, you remember her, she did her training in Germany, well, in any case we still haven't done the tax declaration either, you know how I love doing that, it's not my responsibility, but always ends up falling to me, doesn't it, and you?

—I'm okay. Ma, I wanted to ask you about the family tree.

—Oh, we already talked about that two weeks ago.

—No, Ma, we *didn't* talk about it two weeks ago . . . Is this even about Grossmeer's life story? Or was that just a ruse to get me to read the family tree?

—What is this, an interrogation? Hello, is that the cops listening in?

—Meer. You wanted me to read this family tree. Didn't you?

—Perhaps I wanted . . . Look, I've been working since I was sixteen years old. When I was an au pair in Fribourg, at seventeen, I used to have one day off a month, and once I went to Villarvolard, and that's when I first read about Catherine Repond. After that, I began to research witches. There's been a war against us for centuries. Thank you for *Caliban*, by the way, it helped me a lot! And you know, I really value your opinion. You've become a real man of learning. A . . .

person of learning. Sorry. Hey, another thing. The nurse was really abrupt with us this week, not like before, he's usually so chatty . . . I know it's none of my business! It's just, I was thinking about it and I'm worried about you. Since . . . Fabrizio, it seems you've really isolated yourself. You used to do so much. Go to concerts and readings and so on. You used to talk about your friends, Dina, Mo, what are they up to nowadays?

—It's just that I'm working now and I go to see my grossmeer every Saturday.

—So what's getting you down? . . . Fabrizio would have . . . wanted you . . .

—Look, Meer, I'll tell you what happened with Fabrizio, and then the subject's closed once and for all, okay? I broke up with Fabrizio because I wanted an open relationship, because I wanted to fuck around, because I . . . My body needs that, okay? And Fabrizio wanted a bourgeois relationship, with two identical nightstands in a newly built apartment, and a Labrador, and he talked in "we" sentences, okay? And yes, he wanted to be with me, but he also wanted to be with his family, and his peer and I—we couldn't be in one room. He wouldn't even look me in the eye. Is there anything else?

—No.

—Good. You said you were tired. Your bed's calling.

12

Sofia Ferrari, 1666–unclear

"I am Sofia Ferrari, my mother was Elvira, and my grandmothers were: Elvira Innominata, Ira Marinero, and
Claudia Bianchi. My grandfather was the city of Florence. My mother was named Elvira for one of her mothers,
and she was so poor she couldn't even afford a last name.
Her first mother, Elvira Innominata, died of my mother's
big head. Elvira's second mother, Claudia Bianchi, died
in 1650; after she and Ira had lived together for four
years. Ira and Claudia and Elvira had a "game," as they
called it. It was a kind of rehearsal. It was fun, sometimes. It could occur during a completely everyday moment; during a boring dinner, or working in the garden,
or even when they were asleep. The key phrase was 'If
they come.' When one of the three women said that, the
others had to immediately stop what they were doing and
rehearse what they would do if they came. You know, just
in case they came. So, if they came, Claudia, being ill,
would confess—only *if* they came—to having bewitched
Ira—when they came—and feign a devilish fit—once they
came—and Ira would—once they had come and overcome
Claudia—take Elvira and flee.

"And so, after you came, Ira fled to the <u>Pauperes
Lombardis</u>, a group of Waldensians—Protestant crack-
pots who lived in Piedmont. She had to leave behind
everything she loved: Claudia, the mysterious book of

witches' wisdom, and <u>The Collected Disappearance of</u>
<u>Florentine Lilies</u>. All she could take with her was her
daughter Elvira and the brooch that the dying Bohemian
had given to Claudia. Ira and Elvira lived in communes,
where people shared all their worldly possessions. In
1655, when my mother, Elvira, was eighteen, the majority of Waldensians in Piedmont were slaughtered; the
survivors fled to Val Chisone, but were driven out from
there too, by King Louis XIV. In 1660, Elvira married
my father, Luigi Ferrari, and, having had enough of the
starry-eyed idealists' strict way of life, they left
the Waldensians and settled in Lausanne. And that's how
I came to be.

"I won't lay my life bare to your intrusive ways, I
belong only to myself, to myself and Elsbeth. I'll keep
myself to myself, because you too have come, my lords,
you have stripped me bare and shaved my entire body,
believing that the devil resides in the hair, because you
wrenched out my toenails and fingernails, because
you didn't let me sleep for days on end, because you cut
off my 'devil's organ,' because you strung me up with
ever-heavier weights on my feet, dislocating my shoulders to force a confession out of me. But I'm not your
witch. I can't influence the weather or conjure plagues
of mice, sour your milk or make your cheese crawl with
maggots. My monthly bleed was never poisonous.

"You accuse me of so much, and I'm guilty of none of
it. No mare or demon has ever taken possession of my

body. What you call a 'witch's ointment' or 'flying ointment' isn't sorcery. It's a simple decoction made from
the ergot fungus. My mother's recipe. You can't fly to
the Blocksberg with it, but you fly spiritually. I gave
this substance to those who came to me for help: I didn't
put a spell on them. And the blood beech I'm hanging from
now is simply one of nature's whims. I have never mur-
dered children beneath her boughs; I simply surrendered
myself to her. Why? Because trees are better listeners.

"I won't spend any longer than necessary defending
myself, because I already know my words will have no effect on you, you fool-born swines. My stake is already
ablaze. I know my defense is futile. But it won't have
been entirely in vain. What is said cannot be unsaid.
Sound waves travel on through the universe for eternity.
Here your flames lick my feet, here I the witch, Sofia
Ferrari of Lausanne, come to an end. Yes, I tried to make
magic: I tried to change your violent world. So burn
me. My efforts will ignite somewhere else. I have no
children, but my dog will carry my line forward. She's
a bastard, a shaggy-haired mongrel, her blood a mix of
street mutts, wolves, and other tramps. She holds my
story; she has licked me awake her whole life long, the
life inside each of us has ignited the other, and at this
very moment she is carrying my legacy over the hills,
eastward, away from this hate-filled place."

13

When I get home from work that evening, I'm filled with anticipa-
tion. I sit down immediately on the bed, and continue reading the
family tree. For the first time, I'm disappointed. Meer continues
with Selma Schwarz, in the Zürich area around the year 1720, who
has a club foot and whose only talent is baking. The sole ray of
hope in her life is the stray dog that brings the swallow brooch.
The next lives depicted by Meer are uneventful; farmers' wives in
Zürich's Affoltern district. Only one life stands out: Emma Zurbuchen, who, at the age of sixteen, grows a beard. Otherwise, it's
just descriptions of everyday life as a farmer's wife: cleaning, cooking, washing, planting, harvesting, bearing children, and carrying
children to the grave. And each winter, the fear of starving and
freezing. I tell myself that these accounts matter too. And yet I notice how much I long for something extraordinary, how swiftly the
ordinary lives bore me. I think Meer wanted it to be boring because
she herself finds it boring. And yet she wanted to write it down regardless. The plaited loaf recipes are passed down from mother to
daughter, with minimal changes, and they ultimately save the family from starvation: a country aristocrat gets a taste for the bread
and buys it regularly. And the brooch Claudia Bianchi took from a
Bohemian private is a constant presence, passed down from mother
to daughter.

The first life in which Meer once again permits some extraor-
dinariness is that of Johanna Zurbuchen.

Johanna Zurbuchen, 1774–1851

When Johanna is three months old, her mother drops her
into a vat of boiling milk. She is rescued by one of her
brothers. "Would've been one mouth less," grumbles their
mother. Johanna survives, but her entire body is scarred.
With fourteen winters, she leaves the farm and travels
by foot to Zürich. She takes a fresh blouse, her bonnet,
and her grandmother's swallow brooch. As she searches
for work, it proves advantageous that Hans Kaspar Escher-
Keller has just gone bankrupt, dragging almost all of
Zürich down with him. The Eschers—one of the city's
most influential families—will employ any worker that's
an outsider and unaware of the citywide hatred of the
family. Johanna knows her way around a kitchen, especially where baking is concerned. The Eschers love her
plaited loaves, and before long she has a secure role as
a baker.

Heinrich Escher is determined to improve his family's
reputation. (His grandfather got a maid with child and
ran off with her, and his father has been involved in
all kinds of financial corruption.) Heinrich speculates
on land and, in 1803, buys the Buen Retiro plantation in
Cuba and sends his brothers Ferdinand and Friedrich out
to manage it. The personnel expands, and soon there are
eighty field slaves and five house slaves. As with all
good, earthy Swiss people, though, it's not long before
the two Eschers are struck by homesickness. And so boss
brother Heinrich, the sly old fox, sends Johanna down to

cook traditional dishes: Rösti with fried eggs; blood
sausage with roasted potatoes; veal in creamy mushroom
sauce; and, of course, plaited loaves.

The first time Johanna sets eyes on Michel-André, she
thinks he's her own reflection. Michel-André is tall,
with dark skin, and he's one big scar. Not from milk,
like her, but the whip. They spend the most wonderful
year of their lives together. Short nights, long, far-
too-long days with stiff, bad backs, clandestine rendezvous beneath palm trees, promises in a language all
of their own, a blend of colonial French and Swiss German. And then Johanna—forty-three by this point—gets
pregnant. And Michel-André is bitten by a snake. He dies
on the spot. Ferdinand Escher (who knew about all of
this, of course, but didn't want to send the braided-
loaf master home) heavyheartedly lets Johanna return to
Switzerland. Together with the other slaves, she buries Michel-André, and places the swallow brooch in his
grave. On the journey home, she stands at the railing,
cries, and all of her hair falls out into the sea.

Back in Switzerland, she brings a girl into the world:
Michelle, a small, anxious creature with alert eyes and
excessive hair growth, like her grossmeer Emma. Johanna
continues to work with the Eschers until her death, and
they protect her from the accusations of having borne a
child of the devil.

Among the sheets of paper, I find a document with "MyHer-
itageDNA" written on it in large, bold lettering. The words

"Mesoamerican," "West African," and "Italian" stand out. I immediately lay it aside.

Michelle Gfeller, née Zurbuchen, 1818–1841

Unwilling to be constantly branded a "monster" by the kitchen staff, Michelle ventures out into the world at an early age. She makes ends meet by selling the hair of her preserved beard to men who don't have enough beard hair or head hair of their own. She becomes the main attraction in an early freak show, has a brief marriage with a completely hairless man, and bears two children that she takes to her mother, Johanna, in Zürich. She sets off to Berlin to become an actress, but never arrives.

14

I leave the care home, fleeing you and Meer and your arguments, walk around aimlessly, give myself a hit of Ostermundigen, and suddenly my old detour gets hold of me, the route home from kindergarten that I tied into ever-bigger loops in order to avoid coming home at all. I didn't remember it, but my legs know: the wave's coming up now, and that rough spot, and where I always went to the right, beneath the fence. I stand in front of our old house. I haven't been here in almost twenty years. The old cliché: the house is always much smaller than we remember. I picture my urgrosspeer building the house, digging out the cellar, spending months on end drawing up plans, sawing the planks of wood, sweating through his shirt and pants every single day; his only shirt and his only pants. Actually, though, I can't picture it.

The current tenants have let the garden grow rampant; it froths over the fence. And there's the blood beech, big and dark. Without realizing it, I'd been afraid of this moment. I often pictured myself going back: to the place where it started, where I started. I had envisaged a dramatic scene. The homecoming. How the house would open itself up, the garden quivering, the blood beech unfurling, embracing me. The place revealing to me the things I can't remember. Now I'm standing here, and there's a house, there's the garden around it, and in the garden there's the blood beech. That's it. The things are silent. I turn around.

When I get back, you're still arguing, you and Meer. Meer's face is blotchy, she's accusing you of not having mended her teddy bear, her favorite teddy, saying you laughed at her when she cried over his head falling off; you say the teddy was completely past it, unmendable, more tatters than teddy. I turn on my heel again, go to the bus stop, the proper one, and continue reading.

15

Ida and Dorothea Gfeller, 1841-unclear/unknown
The twins grow up in the Escher household in Belvoir, Zürich-Enge, and look like two peas in a pod, but are as different as one cowhide from another. Alfred Escher (old Heinrich's little lad) becomes one of the most important men in Switzerland, and his household expands

too. The two girls grow up working around the house.
Pragmatic Ida toils in the kitchen with her grandmother
Johanna. Empathetic Dorothea is initially a chamber-
maid, then from 1858 on looks after Alfred Escher's newborn daughter, Lydia Escher. When Lydia loses her mother
at the age of six, Dorothea becomes a second mother (if
she wasn't already) to the future millionaire heiress.
Ida marries a shoemaker from Bern, moves there, and is
kept busy giving birth and doing household chores that
she finds really tiresome.

Dorothea stays by Lydia's side night and day, even
though the young aristochild has many other governesses
that teach her aristocratic things. But Dorothea combs
Lydia's hair, laces her corset, and dries her tears.
Lydia, sweet-hearted little Lydiäli, grows into an intelligent, outspoken young lady who can move sans dif-
ficulté in upper-class circles.

By 1883, though, there's been enough freethinking.
Lydia is forced to marry Friedrich Welti, the lad of powerful Bundesrat Emil Welti. Following his marriage into
the rich Escher family, Friedrich's career gets vaulted
to success; he becomes a manager, gets into the insurance industry in a big way, and becomes a patron of the
arts. He shares his interest in the arts with Lydia. But
she is languishing away at home. She wants to talk about
art, politics, and society, and she wants to change the
country. Instead, she's stuck deciding what color the
geraniums will be and what fish will be served that evening. Her husband's impotence puts a strain on her too,

not because she particularly wants to have sex with him, but because Friedrich blames her for it. Lydia whispers that secret only into Dorothea's ears. Nobody else knows. At a soirée held at their house, Lydia meets one of Friedrich's former classmates, Karl Stauffer-Bern. He's charming and funny, he paints, sculpts, and writes poetry, and he's the first man to take Lydia seriously.

In 1889, when Friedrich can no longer handle the pressure of siring a son and heir, the couple move to Florence. Dorothea goes with them, of course. Taunted by his own body, Friedrich invites Karl so that he at least has a drinking partner. He goes on frequent business trips, leaving his wife in Karl's care. The servants—Dorothea in particular—watch Lydia and Karl's affair with clasped hands, bowed heads, and contented smiles. No one says a word. No one apart from an overambitious stable boy, a total nincompoop that writes to Herr Friedrich. He returns immediately, but the lovers have already departed for Rome. Upper-class circles across Central Europe are outraged.

It isn't long before the long hand of Father Bundesrat Emil Welti wrenches the two lovebirds apart on a piazza in the heart of Rome. Karl is sent to prison; Lydia to the insane asylum. Dorothea is wracked with worry. Lydia's diagnosis is: "systematic insanity." Karl is arrested under the allegation of "raping an insane person."

Both are brought back to Switzerland by their families. Frederick agrees to divorce Lydia on the condi-

tion he pocket 1.2 million francs from her inheritance
(the equivalent of a state treasury at the time). But
Lydia only discovers after signing the agreement that
she'll never again be allowed to see Karl, her soulmate.
The scandal would apparently be too much for Friedrich.
Karl commits suicide in Florence with the soporific
chloral hydrate. He is thirty-three. In December, Dorothea finds Lydia on the kitchen floor alongside an open
gas tap. Before taking her own life, she founded the
Gottfried Keller Foundation to promote the arts and the
"autonomy of the female sex."

    In 1892, Dorothea goes to Bern to see Ida, her twin
sister, that's widowed and lives outside the city in a
tiny apartment with seven of her twelve children. On the
evening Dorothea arrives, the two sisters are sitting in
the shabby kitchen. Their backs are crooked, like bean
plants no one has thought to tie up. They are silent until Ida gives her sister a word to the wise: "We toiled
away while you were preening your princess's hair in the
palace. Don't think you'll be resting on your laurels
here. You'll have to work to eat."

Meer's family tree has finally arrived in Bern. The way it orbits
around and repeats itself and still hasn't arrived at the wound reminds me of the infinite loop of your sentence: "The first Rosmarie was so beautiful, everyone loved her." The way you return so
often to your sentence reminds me of a shamanist concept: that
in a traumatic moment, a part of the soul splits off. And yet the

mind returns repeatedly to the trauma—as though there were a splinter it needs to reintegrate. This also corresponds with observations in modern psychology. If a trauma gets triggered—in other words, if the person in question is reminded of the situation (even by really small things like scents, colors, words)—their body numbs itself. They can no longer feel their arms or legs, and report "falling out of their body," fainting—anything to avoid reliving the same pain. The situation that can never be fully told, that refuses to be woven into our own life narrative, it's simultaneously everywhere and nowhere, always intruding but never available, filling everything up and yet always empty.

What I'm trying to say, Grossmeer, is that there's an emptiness, and I don't know whether it's mine. Perhaps this emptiness is inherited, perhaps it's a blank space that gets passed on, into which each person in turn loses their own. A void where every generation weaves their own threads into the emptiness. I don't mean that in an ethereal-psychological way, but very concretely. I too only exist because the first Rosmarie died. And there's so much absence from even before that. And perhaps this entire text, this entire writing urge is a placeholder, the creation of a place where this emptiness can finally be held. Not a text, but a place to write: "Here is something that can't be said." Which isn't the same as remaining silent. We need sentences in order to be able *not to speak* about our trauma. I've spent my whole life believing I have to fill up our emptinesses, carry them, endure them, pass them on. I believed it was the task of my family, of our entire culture; that it *is* our entire culture. I thought I was a surrogate body, enabling those who are absent, those who died too soon, to live out their sacrificed lives. It was always a betrayal to think of giving up this task. Everything was always a betrayal, a betrayal of you, of all my meers, of our existence. Even saying "Johannisbeere" instead of "Meertrübeli" is a betrayal. Writing is a betrayal; writing about the two of you, a double betrayal; writing in Standard German, an immeasurable betrayal.

Derrida says that language functions through absence. The word *beech* only means "beech" because other meanings are absent; because it doesn't mean "birch," or "book," or "belly," or "blood"; because it doesn't mean nothing and it doesn't mean everything. To write, therefore, is to rearrange the absence in a new way. And writing in itself always means the physical absence of the person writing. If I were really there, if I could be with you, then I wouldn't need to write you a letter. But even this Derridean certainty dissolves in the raging of the language ocean, in the thunderstorm of tongues, because the Swiss German word *Buch* means "belly," but also "beech," as in the "beech at Irchel." In the belly of language, everything is digested, and if a person wants to take paths that are on this earth but not of this world, they have to eat their voice—a swallowed voice can call all the swallows from their winter, can sing all the swallowed tongues into existence.

I began writing this, Grossmeer, with the intent of casting a healing spell, of conjuring a little magic; of giving the woundless pain a wound; of giving a mouth to that which has disappeared, passed, but not gone; an "and," an "It was like that *and* I live on," "Irma disappeared *and* she is here now." I began these texts with the intention of building a witches' cauldron containing all kinds of caring magic. I wanted to heal without striving to "cure," without searching for a pristine wholeness, a purity. Perhaps *healing* is the wrong word, perhaps it's actually about scarring; the tissue forming its own, new, visible seams. Because I don't want the tissue to grow back without a trace. For that which is absent to disappear without a mark of its absence. I'm not striving for a full stop that concludes a sentence, but rather a semicolon that says, "Here is a border, but also a continuation," one that lets the sentence flow on and yet leaves an empty space between its two punctuation marks; I would like to take this narrow spiral, where I'm circling around the void in the center, and carry it onward.

To Derrida, writing is *pharmakeia*, pharmacy: the administration of a *pharmakon*, a substance that can be both poison, a drug, malicious, and also a remedy, a medicine, healing. But *pharmakeia* is also—as I recently discovered—an old word for "witchcraft," for practicing with substances that can both create and heal wounds. Everything is connected, Grossmeer, inextricably linked, and yet the witches' thread has been cut, so we have to pick it up again and learn from the dead; listen, conjure, write, dance around the tree of stolen penises, fabulate, weave. We have to create networks that keep us in the world: in this world, in yours, and in all the worlds that may still be possible.

16

Meer called on Thursday and said you were getting worse. So I'm visiting you again today, Saturday. Meer isn't coming until later. I step into your room, you're reading or at least pretending to, you look at me and say, "Good morning." You don't recognize me. I sit down beside you, give you the bar of chocolate I brought, introduce myself: "I'm your grandchild"; I introduce myself multiple times, and you ask me, more and more insistently, to leave your room, and say you don't accept presents from strangers. When you still don't recognize me after five minutes and I don't move, you get angry, you curse me. I put the chocolate down on your table and leave the room. I go to the nurse's station, ask for Ardan, he says he's busy, I grab him between the legs and say I want to blow him, he says he's not a plaything. Plaything, plaything. You gave me groceries made of plastic in miniature form and played "shopkeeper" with me. Once, when I was at your apartment, I played at cooking. In the middle of the game, something broke. I held the plastic food and cried: "But none of these are real things! They're all fake." Plaything. I can still remember the feeling, as though I'd awoken from being under a spell. I knew I'd been pretending to myself. I sat on your lap, you comforted me. Your coarse hands on my cheeks; they glistened with my tears and snot. You didn't clean them until I stopped crying. Only the chestnuts still functioned as magic playthings, they could become anything.

Sometime later, the chestnuts lost their enchantment too. I've now finally remembered how it happened: I had taken the chestnuts home with me, despite not having any toy pots, but Meer let me use her pans. And there—in the grown-up pans? Under Meer's gaze?—just like with the Migros toys, all the life suddenly vanished from the chestnuts, and I realized they were just boring chestnuts. That's when I knew how people grow up. I cried and went to Meer. She gave me a tissue and said she was busy, that she needed to do laundry. When I didn't stop, she snapped at me: "Pull yourself together, you were screaming all night too, I'm tired." That's when I stopped crying and began my hatred of Meer—a silent, tiny, concealed hatred I kept tucked deep inside me; a fragment of ice beneath a trapdoor. I would take it out secretly, in the chicken coop, in the blood beech tree, whenever I was angry with her, and turn the ice over and over in my hands, it was beautiful as a jewel, and brutal, like a handful of winter's night. This was my secret; that I didn't give my whole being to you and Meer, but held something back that belonged only to me, that was only me. When I sensed that you or Meer were in a bad mood, when I opened and abandoned my body to be with either of you, because you needed someone who was there solely for you, I did it in the knowledge I had this fragment of ice beneath the trapdoor. I spent my entire childhood hiding this from Meer, giving her the love you never gave her, and I knew I couldn't let her see my hatred, or she would die. She made me so there would be someone to love her unconditionally. And if she dies, I die too. I had to keep Meer alive with my tiny life.

Now I'm sitting alone in the home's butcher shop, where all of you, or "we," play "housewife" and "shopping." The plastic meat glistens at me. A piece of outsourced body-memory. I wonder where in my body the Migros-product-memories and the chestnut-memories were archived, because they've always been there; I just didn't have access to them. I wonder where in your body your memories are. Where I am in your body. I was afraid of this moment, Grossmeer, the moment when you no longer recognize me. I've been preparing myself for it, this whole time I've been writing to this You, so that part of you will stay with me.

Meer texts that she's in the home, and where am I? We meet, I tell her you didn't recognize me. Meer asks a nurse to accompany us. The nurse says, "This is your daughter, Frau Häfeli, she was here yesterday too." And Meer says, "I'm your daughter, Ma, I was here yesterday too. It's me." You get anxious, and protest that your daughter's dead, that you only have a son. Meer says, "No, your son's been dead for two years, I'm your only living child, it's me." You start to breathe heavily, and fall silent, the nurse grabs Meer by the wrist and says, "No, Frau Häfeli, you're right, of course, we were wrong." Meer's eyes flash. "Yes, that's true, I'm sorry, you just have a son, it doesn't matter." Your eyes widen: "So where is he?" Then Ardan comes in, carrying a tray full of medication, "Nico," you say, spreading out your arms, "my son." Your hands are damp with Meer's tears, I hold Meer's hands, my hands are empty.

17

I stand in the bathroom, look in the mirror, take off my makeup. I look at the cotton pads, at the small, dark clouds made from the black that was just on my lashes, making them beautiful. I look into my face, my bare face, I see your nose, I see Meer's eyes, I see Peer's chin. Someone once told me, before shooting his load onto my face, that I could actually be a handsome man. He meant

it as a genuine compliment. After he had come and gone, I stood
before the bathroom mirror then too, to wash off the sperm that
clung in small clumps to my eyebrows. I told my mirror image
that beauty isn't gendered; that a beauty exists beyond masculinity and femininity. I said it many times over, and for a long time.
I see the photo of you, pregnant, with a five-o'clock shadow. I
see you in the wedding dress. I see you in the wedding dress in a
river, dead, floating away. I see you surrounded by orchids, I see
Meer in knight's armor going up a mountain, I see myself standing in the night. I go to my bedroom, straighten the pillow, and
read the final biographies.

In these biographies, I think I can feel Meer already thinking
about you. Or maybe she's too close to the women, and has even
seen photos of them. She makes another massive detour, one last
effort, it seems, not to arrive at you. For my ururugrossmeer,
Johanna Schmied, 1868–1915, there's a date of birth, marriage,
death. Then page after page describing the work in the silk spinning mill, meticulously researched processes. What Johanna ate
(predominantly potatoes, stinging nettles, beans, cabbage), what
she never ate (an orange, sirloin steak, and chocolate, even though
one of her daughters worked in the chocolate factory). The life
of her twelve children, of whom four died before reaching adulthood. How Johanna was very interested in insects, particularly the
mud-dauber wasps in her courtyard, more so than in her children.

It's similar with Rosmarie Aeschi, 1884–1944, my ururgrossmeer.
Here, Meer researched the work in the chocolate factory in Bern's
Matte district, and calculated how many calories Rosmarie burned

going home for lunch (a bowl of soup), all the way from the factory in Länggasse. She wrote how it wasn't worth it calorie-wise, obviously, because Rosmarie burned more on the walk than she got from the soup. Meer describes the alcoholism of the man from whom Rosmarie fled into religion. She is the first in her family to eat an orange, during the Christmas of 1922. Rosmarie Aeschi's ladybeard.

My urgrossmeer's life story is composed by hand, but only in list form.

Ida Sägesser, née Aeschi, 1900–1989

—Earliest childhood memory: the smell of freshly peeled potatoes (earthy, juicy, tangy) and an image: the long, pale ribbons of potato peel that dangle down from her mother's grubby hands into a bowl, to be used later (waste nothing!).

—The last little joy: a nip of kirsch liqueur. But she frequently forgets whether she's already had a glass, and is often sozzled by the time her daughter Rosmarie peeks in on her and confiscates the kirsch. Irma, her grandchild, always lets her have the liqueur.

—The final triumph: that she notices when Rosmarie dilutes her kirsch. That she, Ida, tucks a new supply of kirsch into the toilet cistern, where Rosmarie will never find it.

—Her greatest shame: that her last and most beautiful child, Irma, falls pregnant out of wedlock at the age of sixteen and is sent to Hindelbank women's prison.

—Her greatest fear: that her children aren't religious enough to get to heaven.

—Her biggest secret (which everyone knows anyway):
that sometimes, when her husband is out, she dresses in
his clothes, looks at herself in the mirror, and feels
so beautiful she could die.

—The thing she finds hardest: that at the age of nine,
her first daughter, Rosmarie . . .

—Her greatest joy: that her second daughter, the
second Rosmarie, was born on exactly the same day as the
first Rosmarie: on November 14, sixteen years later.

Rosmarie Sägesser, 1919–1928 (the first Rosmarie)
Rosmarie is earthily beautiful with an earthily beautiful smile, and adored by everyone. She has unbelievably
blond hair, like a cornfield just before the harvest, and
alabaster skin. She comes into the world on November 14,
1919. But at the age of nine, Rosmarie falls ill. They
can't afford a doctor. The neighbor, who has a doctor
for a brother and therefore understands a little about
medicine, says it's nothing serious, just a really awful bout of the flu. But it gets worse and worse, and
before long Rosmarie is coughing so much she can barely
breathe. Ida pawns her wedding ring and sends for a doctor that gives her some medicine. Ida sits at Rosmarie's
bedside, gives her the medicine, and says, "Everything
will be okay now." Then she goes to the kitchen to make
chicken soup. By the time Ida returns, Rosmarie has
choked to death.

Ten months later, in 1929, Ida has a baby; unfortunately not a daughter, but a son, that she baptizes Robert. The following year, in 1930, Ida has another baby; unfortunately not a daughter, but a son, that she baptizes Phillip. The following year, in 1931, Ida has another baby, unfortunately not a daughter, but a son, that she baptizes Benoit. The following year, in 1932, Ida has another baby, unfortunately not a daughter, but a son, that she baptizes Moritz. The following year, in 1933, Ida has another baby, unfortunately not a daughter, but dead. The following year, in 1934, Ida has another baby, unfortunately not a daughter, but a son, that she baptizes Hans-Peter.

The following year, in 1935, Ida finally has the girl she longed for. The girl's name is Rosmarie. She was supposed to come into the world in late December, but is born on November 14. Three years later, Ida has another girl, and her name is Irma.

Rosmarie Häfeli, née Sägesser, 1935– (the second Rosmarie)

—Born: November 14, 1935

—Trains as a nurse

—Meets her husband at the onion market

—Has two children, Irma and then Nicolas, who she always preferred

—Likes traveling

—From 1975 onward, sings in a women's choir

—Goes back to work in 1980, which is unusual

—Loses her husband and mother in the same year, both
unexpectedly

—Starts to work more and treats herself to an increasing number of trips to exotic lands

—Dotes on her grandchild, Kim, who she often looks
after

—After her retirement, she finally fulfils her childhood wish and plays tennis three times a week for as long
as her health allows

—Suffers from severe dementia, like her mother, Ida

—The first thing she forgets in dementia is her
faith. Probably because she finally has an excuse to
turn her back on the religion forced on her by her
mother

I hold the final piece of paper in my hand, with your life, Grossmeer. It's written on a typewriter, and the edges are tattered. I
imagine Meer inserted it into the typewriter and pulled it out
again multiple times. So that's where you come to an end, I think,
after the tennis. And then comes Meer and then me, and in me
the line comes to an end. I think back to Clemens Züllig, Barbara
Züllig's son, who was unable to have children. But I'm not like
him. I don't care for the people who need me. I only visited you
once you had already started to disappear.

18

—Alex Garibaldi speaking?

—Er, oh, hi, Alex, you're at Irma's?

—Hey, Kim—Irma's in the shower right now, she should be out soon . . . How are you?

—Well. Pfff. I guess Meer told you?

—Yes, I'm really sorry. That was a really difficult situation last Saturday. But I get the feeling Irma is also relieved, in a way, that Rosmarie's now—that the final turn has finally happened.

—Mm-hm.

—You don't feel the same? . . . Oh, here's Irma. Sweetheart, Kim's on the phone. Bye, Kim.

—Hello, Kim?

—Hi, Ma. Listen, I'm pretty tired, it was really tough going in the archive today, the climate control wasn't working in one of the rooms, and a few hundred files started to go moldy, they're all ruined. I finally reached Grossmeer's life story and I'd like to know about Irma, your aunt. Did you ever do any research on her?

—No, I can't tell you any more than I already have.

—But you—

—Kim, you've already asked me, and I told you everything I know.

—Okay, okay, there's no need to raise your voice.

—I'm not raising my voice, I'm just defending myself.

—Well, why do you have to defend yourself so aggressively?

—Kim, have you finished the family tree?

—I'll ask you again: Was the thing with Grossmeer's life story just a ruse? You didn't even want me to write it, did you? You just sent me into your chaos room so I'd find the family tree?

—No, I really can't write it. And if you go poking around in other people's rooms, you should be a bit more careful. The file was put in the wrong place. But seeing as you've already read it, you might as well tell me what you think.

—Well, it's . . . I'm impressed. It's crazy. It's great. You did all of it?

—Thank you. Yes, of course.

—But . . . the thing with the DNA really annoyed me.

—But that's not made up!

—Precisely. The very fact you did a DNA test.

—Well, I just wanted to find out. To know where we come from.

—And do you? Know where we come from?

—Yes, we have a lot of Italian in us, a bit of African—

—That doesn't mean anything!

—Why are you getting so sensitive?

—What kind of people use blood or relational logic to structure an argument? It's fascist, Meer, this fascination with your own blood and family tree, saying it defines you is pure fascistic ideology.

—But it doesn't define the women in my text, that they have African blood. It's simply the case that they do. And us, that we have it. It's your blood too, remember.

—Yes, I'm not debating that. Just this pseudo-intellectual substantiation—your text doesn't need it.

—It's simply too hard for you, monsieur, to imagine you can't so easily—wait a moment. What is it, Alex, I'm . . . Yes, start. The orecchiette. No, use the zucchini, otherwise they'll spoil. Listen, Kim: I'm not an academic, remember? Sometimes what you say goes over my head.

—Hey, is Alex living with you now?

—How do you mean?

—She's always at your place.

—Yes. She's here. I mean yes, she lives here.

—Okay. Thanks for telling me.

—Why should I tell you?

—Why wouldn't you tell me?

—You don't tell *me* everything.

—You know who I'm *not* having sex with right now and why I broke up with Fabrizio. It doesn't feel like I'm hiding much. Why did she move in with you? She only moved six months ago.

—Kim, sweetheart. The thing is, I didn't want to tell you on the phone . . . Alex is pregnant.

—What?! Why?

—What do you mean "why"? There's no "why," she just is. She's younger, and the baby's doing well.

—Whose is it?

—Well, not mine, obviously.

—So why doesn't she move in with the baby's father?

—There is no father. We want to have the baby together. Yes. We want a child together.

—At your age?

—Listen. I'm fifty-four. Men do it all the time, and no one says a damn thing. I was really young when I had you.

—I thought you didn't like children.

—Who says that?

—Grossmeer. And Peer.

— . . .

—The fact you would want a second family . . .

—Kim, sweetheart, it's silly talking about this on the phone. But listen to me—

—No. We should talk another time.

—Kim, it's completely different from you and Peer.

—We should both calm down and talk another time.

—I am calm. I could talk about it now, I watched the video you sent me, I would only speak in I-sentences—

—Okay, so *I* can't talk about it right now.

—Okay . . . And about the life story, do you think you could finish it by—

19

Dear Grossmeer. We're sitting at the fake bus stop, next to Herr Füglister, and Ardan has just gone inside the residential building. He and I brought you out here, we sat down next to Herr Füglister, and it was a bit cramped, but I'm quite slim. To you, Ardan was Nico again, and I wanted to take advantage of that.

After you spent several minutes telling us about your geraniums, I gave Ardan a nod. He took your hand and asked: "I have a question that's important to me. Can you tell me what happened back then with Irma and her baby?" You looked across at the linden tree, a little confused, your lips moved silently, and only in that moment did I realize the question I'd given Ardan was unclear. Irma could be your sister or Meer, your daughter. Both Irmas, and with both there was a difficult issue regarding children.

"Nico," you said, "that's all so long ago, you know how long ago that is . . . I told Irma: Don't get rid of it. She was weak, Nico, you know. She might not have looked it, but she was a delicate little flower, actually, inside. I knew if she got rid of it, or tried to, it would haunt her for the rest of her life. Even for me, back when I . . . It was completely . . . That's why I said: Don't do it. I knew she wouldn't be able to cope with it like I had." Ardan looked at me questioningly, and I nodded. He said he was going to fetch some tea. You didn't want him to go, so I said, "Tell me about your geraniums, you have geraniums on your balcony, don't you." You let go of Ardan and talked about your geraniums, how you water them when you go traveling, and how you travel a lot, that last year you were on the old Silk Road, and how you want to go to Iran next, that geraniums are heavy feeders, they're always hungry, and the best fertilizer balls are the ones from Gesal, they last six months.

Now we are sitting here, me, you, Herr Füglister. Herr Füglister talks about his wife, she must be waiting for him, he says, you talk more about your geraniums. I sit next to the two of you and type this into my smartphone. I can't bring myself to talk with you both, I can only bear to sit here this close to you because I'm writing. Darkness slowly falls, and somebody will probably come to take you both inside soon, presumably Ardan. My thigh touches your thigh, warming me. I'll sit here and write to you for as long as I can, I'll sit until I'm sitting in the dark.

I also wanted to tell you that I once came to Bern alone, to do "research" for my book. I visited places that are still present inside me. I visited Dählhölzli Zoo: the wolves, tomato frogs, and polar foxes. I went to Ostermundigen train station. I went to the Matte district, to the old chocolate factory where Rosmarie Aeschi worked. I didn't tell you I was in Bern.

I also wanted to tell you that Meer asked me to write up your life story, and I wanted to tell you that I'm not going to do it. It's her responsibility, and I can't take it on. But I wanted to tell you about Meer's family tree, where she tries to gather you and herself into an ancient line of women, meers, heroines. I saw how Meer evaded you, for centuries on end, how she followed up every lead in order not to reach you for a little longer. How Meer's text moved me even though I wanted to think it was bad, and how I only noticed, through Meer as a mirror, how I've evaded you in my writing too, and now I think evasion is perhaps the only way a person can get close to you.

I wanted to tell you how much you mean to me, how often I think of you, I wanted to tell you that for me you represent an evolutionary border, Grossmeer, like the polar foxes' fur, which they've developed over hundreds of generations, for winters as cold as minus fifty degrees, which makes them out of place in our era—our era, which some people call the "Anthropocene," others the "Capitalocene," and others still the "Chthulucene." The body knowledge that was important for many generations, the long, shaky line, comes to an end in you. The knowledge carried in bodies of how to do laundry in winter without freezing off your fingers; how to clean windows with newspaper; how to mend things that have been broken, darned, battered, and torn countless times; how to sleep even though it's so cold that the piss freezes instantly in the bedpan; how to slaughter a chicken that's your favorite chicken; how to make use of its entire slaughtered body, innards, bones, feathers, brain; how to sing even when you're hungry; how to give birth without an epidural; how to carry your children to the grave; how to avoid crying, always, because otherwise the water in the body will overpower and overwhelm you, how to avoid crying when things are at their worst; how to find an apology-grief, about the death of a favorite chicken, for example; how to have faith in something outside of yourself; how to carry on, not for yourself or in order to achieve something, but, yes, perhaps for your family.

Some time ago I was wandering aimlessly through Bern on the hunt for memories, "prowling around," as you'd say in the Meer language. And then I saw you. You were standing on the other side of Länggasse. I stopped, froze, broke out in a sweat. What could I say? I have no excuse. I knew you would be furious. I knew I was guilty, guilty of your unhappiness, your loneliness, guilt guilt guilt. "Why haven't you come to visit me, if you're in

Bern?" I knew I had failed; that I haven't fulfilled the purpose for my existence. Your white hair, fine like white mold. Your rough, paw-like hands clutching the shopping bags. Your stern gaze. You didn't recognize me. I watched you walk away, this ordinary old woman on her way to do her shopping, her kömmerle, with a slightly cumbersome gait, her right shoulder slumping a little lower on every second step.

5

Coming Full Spiral

Water, water, take me where I cannot walk me.

———

If it's possible to say that in the queer and trans culture we fuck better and more, this is, on the one hand, because we have removed sexuality from the domain of reproduction, and above all because we have freed ourselves from gender domination. I'm not saying that the queer and trans-feminist culture avoids all forms of violence. There is no sexuality without a shadowy side. But the shadowy side (inequality and violence) does not have to predominate and predetermine all sexuality.

Representatives, women and men, of the old sexual regime, come to grips with your shadowy side and have fun with it, and let us bury our dead. Enjoy your aesthetics of domination, but don't try to turn your style into a law. And let us fuck with our own politics of desire, without men and without women, without penises and without vaginas, without hatchets, and without guns.

———PAUL B. PRECIADO

Everywhere we turn for comfort or for healing, we are met by the approved guardians of a knowledge that alienates us from our bodies and our souls. The smoke of the burned Witches still hangs in our nostrils; most of all, it reminds us to see ourselves as separated, isolated units in competition with each other, alienated, powerless, and alone.

———STARHAWK

Love hurts.

———NAZARETH

Dear Grandma,

we came from the north. We came yesterday, by bike, crossing the pass of the Lucomagno. Dina had gone ahead by car. I didn't think I would make it all the way up, but I did. When we reached the highest point it started raining, like, a lot. The water was so dense we had to go superslow. The rain fell in threads. I laughed loud, Mo laughed louder. After some time we stopped and decided to call Dina to come and get us by car. The rain slowed us down too much, we wouldn't make it before sundown otherwise. She picked us up saying she had had two beers already and had only been waiting for our call and was glad we called before her third beer.

After showering and drying and apéro-ing, Mo insisted on putting on nail polish, as a ritual of beginning our time here in Ticino, instead of a ritual of blood siblinghood. It was shimmery and turquoise and amazing, it was called *metallic mermaid*. I refused. Mo kept pushing me, begging cutely, then annoyingly. I don't put on nail polish anymore. Not because I wouldn't want it. I would want to. After pushing me too far, I told Mo hysterically: "I don't put on nail polish, because heterosexual men like you— who fancy themselves to be feminist and left and 'on the right side'—have started putting it on, in order to show your alliance. But by doing this you have claimed nail polish for yourself, in the same naive and arrogant way you claim everything, all the time, always, with the best intentions." Obviously the party was over after that. We ate pasta in silence and went to our rooms.

At two in the morning I still couldn't sleep. I heard someone go-ing to the toilet. I went to the door and opened it, in this very moment Dina also opened her door across the hallway and Mo was walking up from the toilet downstairs. We had a martini on the roof and I made a big apologetic speech. "I'm just jealous. You know, when I was younger I wished so much to put on nail polish but I never dared to, and even now—as I've been in my . . . emm . . . process for three years—I am still afraid, every single day. Not when I get dressed or put on makeup, not as long as I am in my apartment, but as soon as I open my door and enter 'the world.' I am sorry, Mo. I am jealous of the heterosexual men who wear nail polish simply as a political sign but who are not afraid of getting beaten and insulted and spit upon, those guys like you who are not afraid because you haven't experienced a life of daily, ongoing violence, of micro- and macroaggressions. And you know what gets me the most? It's that I have to be scared to wear nail polish, and you not. Because you can just take it off and be safe. But me, us, we cannot take 'these things' off. Because it isn't about what we wear, but about who we are. At least that's what this world teaches us." Mo listened quietly. After I ran out of words he said: "What made you think that I am not scared?"

I am always scared. I am still scared of you, Grandma, scared of what you will do when you read all of this. Which is why I am writing these letters in English, the language I taught myself by reading *Harry Potter* and watching *Lord of the Rings* as a teen-ager, the language of my sex-dates, the language that has other eyes than my mother tongue, the language in which I did not in-herit your eyes and your mother's and your mother's mother's eyes, the language in which I don't feel watched, the language that feels like a space of my own, no matter how incorrect, the language that you don't really understand.

Dear Grandma,

I'm writing these letters in the valley of Blenio, in the north of Ticino, in an old chocolate factory that doesn't run anymore, in the highest room, a room of my own. I share it with spiders, though, and the wind that carries the river in, a pigeon and some moldy fungi that thrive in the cracks of the wall. I guess I should say: It is a room of our own, but none of us owns it. I took some time off work to write these letters to you and to finally finish this project. I'm here with my two writer friends, Dina and Mo. Dina writes about her mother, her dying grandfather, and about her body, not bearing children. Mo writes about his father and how to not become his father, how by all means not to become his father. He, however, will soon be a father himself. I feel like the three of us are working on the same text. Just with different bodies. We talk about everything but the content of our texts. In the morning I walk through the forest, to the river close by, coming directly from the glacier. It's icy cold. The first time we went to the river, Mo just undressed and jumped into the river. I never would have thought that it's something one can actually do, to swim in a river that cold. But now I go every morning before I start writing, it is so vivifying, Mo sometimes joins, we scream-giggle from the cold and after bathing we stand naked in the riverbed, red-skinned from the cold, and he explains the ecosystem growing here (as in

an earlier life he was a natural-scientist-something): the lilacs that
are always the first to grow after an avalanche, the algae on the
stones, and other stuff I forgot. Dina sleeps late, reads gender
theory or Bourdieu in bed, smokes out of the window, waves
when we get back, smiling about us two "crazy" ones. I really
love the three of us. Sometimes we meet for a coffee or cook together, but mostly we are in our rooms or roam the forests on our
own. At least once a day I take my mountain bike and rush down
the valley and I try not to think about you. It only works when I
go superfast, so fast that my eyes cry.

Yesterday I talked to Dina about bodies and body-memory and
she reminded me of Annie Ernaux's late work *Mémoire de fille*.
We then talked about Ernaux's work as a body of shame, and
that shame is the most accurate force of memory. Shameful experiences are tattooed in our minds, they outlive in unequaled
precision all other memories. The memory of the "fille," which
Ernaux writes down over sixty years later, is the memory of
shame.

I realize that I too am a body of shame, a whole archive of it. But
that is not the text I am writing here. I shall have to write my
book of shame some other time. This text is my book of fear.
Fear stores situations equally "intensely" in our minds, I believe,
but with a different quality. Whereas shame is a high-definition-
hyperrealistic archivist, there is no clarity or precision to my
memories of fear. On the contrary, fear records blurry moods
rather than precise images. I feel like fear works with my whole
body, not with one single sense. I remember with some sort of

blind exactness the feeling of fear, all throughout my childhood, like some deep water I regularly woke up in, but I hardly remember exactly what I saw, heard, smelt, felt, or tasted.

While writing this text, Grandma, I realize that fear deletes what it records. It's like when you look into the sun, and then you can't see precisely what you just saw. Actually your notseeing, your blindness takes exactly the shape of what you just saw. It's a negation: on this spot would be what was too bright for you to see, your eyes say.

I was so afraid of throwing down one of these holy boxes of yours, the truckli. I was afraid of being alone with you. I was afraid of the first Rosmarie, I felt her in your apartment. My fear was an element, it was omnipresent. I was so afraid that I followed Farid's advice. I invented part 4 of this text. I wrote you into the home for demented people, although you still live at home, although you still know who I am. But you are at the beginning of dementia, like your mom. Maybe *inventing* is not the right word. Because I did not invent what you are to me, I didn't add anything to the relationship between you and Mom, I did not invent Alex, I did not invent the baby. I did not invent Ardan, he was a nurse in the clinic that I was in. So actually, I did not invent part 4. I just shifted things that happened or will happen into the presence of this text. Maybe this is what autofiction means: to drive through the realm of reality with one's own tempo, focus, and mode. Me, I just went faster: I shifted you into the home for the demented, where you will most probably have to go. I did this to be able to write. I needed a space—not even a fictional one, the home exists—where I could talk directly to you, a "you" that isn't really here. Maybe this is what is inherently queer about autofiction: to start writing from a reality that repeats the fiction that we don't exist. To start writing from a reality that isn't real to us, that puts us in the realm of fiction. To produce ourselves through writing, to invent literary spaces that are other, hyperreal, utterly needed realities. Maybe this is why so many of us write "autofiction," because we are still stories, because we aren't real bodies yet. And that's why still, after four parts of this text, it wasn't enough for me. There were still things I could not say in German.

Dear Grandma,

when I can't write, I do the same here in Ticino as I do at home: I go on Grindr. There are surprisingly many guys in this valley on Grindr. I have to think of Max Frisch's *Der Mensch erscheint im Holozän*. He writes about a remote valley in Ticino. I remember only one passage from this book, where he describes the young men of the valley. The narrator says that since the youngsters have motorbikes, they can get out of the valley after working in the forests and therefore Sodomy among them decreased dramatically. I love the image of old Max, making sociological studies about anal sex in the rural south.

The first evening Mo gave me two theoretical texts that he had been pressing me to read for a long time. He says he knows that I will "love" them. One of them is from Ursula K. Le Guin, this famous science-fiction writer that I should have read, for obvious reasons, and I always manage to pretend to have read, because

I read the Wikipedia article of the postgender novel *The Left Hand of Darkness* ten times. However: science fiction. Hmm. So, I did some Grindr instead. Apparently, fresh meat is rare here. Tourists just pass through, I suspect. Most of the guys texted me some creative lines like: "Sei turista? Posso mostrarti l'ospitalità della nostra valle?" There was a guy a bit farther up in the valley, around forty, who texted me a very cheesy text, about the moon, the earth, and my body. I snuck away, we met late at night, "up by the big chestnut tree where the two rivers meet," as he had texted me. It was not a joke, the chestnut tree was huge and very old. The guy did me very tenderly. His name is Cesare. His arms are full of tribal tattoos and he wears loads of trashy eso-rings with stones in all shades of red. After we did it, he took me to his place on his Vespa (blue), he even had a second helmet (with peace signs). He has pigs and hens, he grows organic tea (of course organic), and he's a shaman. We talked for a bit and he asked me to stay, but I didn't want Mo and Dina to know I was gone. However, the next evening we met again under the chestnut tree. This time I penetrated him. We went to his place, again on his motorbike, and then I stayed the night.

In the morning he had been up already, had looked after his animals and watered his plants. We had breakfast together. I never sleep well at someone else's place after fucking. He told me that he saw that my body was unusually heavy with others, that I was carrying. I said yes, someone that is dear to me will soon fall into dementia, is basically slowly dying. He shook his head. He said the person I was carrying had been dead for quite some time. I was irritated. He asked me how I stood on the earth (I suspect he translated something word by word from the Italian). I said quite okay. He just listened, without judging, which irritated me, I then said, that I was of course still waiting to really arrive, here, that I still don't know what I am here for, but then, who does in my age, or at least my generation? He smiled at me with the most tender, toxic-positivity-annoying smile and said that at thirty, or whatever my age was, it was okay to slowly arrive on this planet. I broke into tears, ridiculously loud and uncontrolled and I told him about you. He then repeated, that he didn't think it was about someone who is still alive. "Who then?" I asked aggressively. He shrugged. He could do a ritual to try and see whom I was carrying, if I wanted to. Only if I wanted to. I said maybe.

When I got back, it was midmorning. Dina and Mo weren't there. Mo had left some printout on my doorstep. First I was annoyed, I thought it was the theoretical texts again that he had already given to me. But then I saw that it was a part of his manuscript. I went to bed, started reading. It was super atmospheric, the late '90s and early 2000s oozed out of it, after the first page I put on some Backstreet Boys and Britney (only ironically, of course!), and from there YouTube and Mo's text took me down into the rabbit hole. I read the loneliness and desperation of a childhood in the suburbs of a provincial town in the nineties. Of endless Sunday afternoons in the emptiness of the Swiss middle class.

Dina knocks. "Are you back?" she asks. "Are you back, baby?" I ask. "We went out of the valley to buy wine and more nail polish," Dina explains, "and I wonder where you might have been, oh most elusive bird of the night?" "Does Mo know I didn't sleep here?" "I didn't tell him." "Thanks."

Dear Grandma,

today it's been five days since I fucked Cesare. I was so agitated I couldn't write, although I jerked off in the shower in the morning, and at some point I just shut my laptop, threw the notebook on the bed, and started masturbating at the table. Of course, this was the moment Dina entered my room without knocking, wanting to complain about a journalistic text she has to write.

Ten minutes later I made two coffees and found her in the garden behind the factory. Weird silence, loud laughter. "Sorry, I wasn't able to write and had to let out some tension." Mo came into the garden, approaching us like a beaten puppy. "Can't write today. Mää."—"Neither can we," Dina said, and: "I caught Kim jerking off."—"What? Kim! Atrocious!" I stammered, "Do you peeps never jerk off when you can't write?" Mo said, "No. Never. I'm dead afterward. All energy gone. I don't even have sex in the evening, if I want to have a good writing flow the next day." Dina laughed pityingly and added: "As you know, my boy never wants as much sex as me, so I always jerk off, to calm down, to activate, to get inspired." We talked a bit about the link between orgasm and energy curves, the difference between male and female orgasms and if there is a nonbinary orgasm, linked to different hormone levels, and if this discussion was reducing sexuality solely to hormones.

As we were sitting in the garden, the cicadas going wild, the two of them talking, I realized that I perceive them as rivals. Part of me hopes that they continue writing, because I like their work, and I do think it's good. And exactly because of these reasons, another part of me hopes they will fail. So we won't have to apply for the same grants, the same prizes, the same funding. There is this sneaky, capitalist voice inside me that says that they won't try hard enough, because they have other things to be fulfilled with. Mo a kid and Dina her many friends, her journalism.

Some while ago I had dinner with Dina and her boyfriend. We had red wine and self-made tiramisu and weed on the balcony and talked about us, society, work. We talked about not having kids (Dina and her boy for freedom reasons, me for obvious other reasons). We had a lot of fun analyzing us and we even managed to push away the typical self-loathing of not doing something more meaningful with our privileges as thirtyish, well-educated, Central Europeans. We defined our generation as the apolitical self-fulfillers between the boomer generation and gen Z; we are the generation that hopes that they're not as content with patriarchal capitalism as their parents and not as discontent with it as the generation after them (watching the politicized climate youth with some jealousy, however). In the end my typical "I'll stay to clean the dishes," and their polite "No, of course not."

Shortly after this, Dina sent me a text, saying how nice it had been, without wanting to be too bourgeoisly polite. Then she sent me a quote from the documentarian novel *Het Bureau* by J. J. Voskuil about the career of a folklorist in the Netherlands of the fifties and sixties. The partner of the main character asks him, "Who would identify with their work? If you do something like that, you have to be sick." Dina added: "The proof that work once was not our soul's destiny!"

We were raised at the end of the twentieth century, in the short period of the "end of history," with the belief (and expectation) that we could become everything. But the end of history has ended, war and violence never really left, only left the self-image of "the West." But still, I grew up in an apolitical time of hyper-capitalist neoliberalism, and our goal was trying to make "it" as individuals. And in that goal, I am purely a child of my generation. And this is the place that I am writing you from, Grandma. The place that we have in common: to be common.

When I think of your life, I think of hardship, I think of no bread, and then hard bread. I think of Sunday walks in white Sunday dresses. I think of the armies of housewives whose main activity was rearranging and fixing the blankets and covers and clothes. I think of the half of society who wasn't paid for their work. I think of your pride, when you tell me how—after the kids were grown—you insisted on going to work, how you found work as a secretary, how my grandfather said, "Fine, go to work, I don't care, but don't think I'll touch the broom. And food is on the table at twelve and six o'clock sharp." How you had to hurry from the office to cook, how you took this gladly on you. I think of the feelings of you housewives. Of the enormous identification you must have had with your household. Of feeling like your house is your body. An untidy corner, seen by a guest, must have been like a slap in the face; all the shame and fear of not being clean enough, perfect enough, white enough. I think of having to maintain an image of a "good family." A good family is an ordinary family. Ordinary meaning: belonging to an order. The order.

When I think of your life, I think of a life lived for others, for your husband, for "society," for the people visiting and saying, "You have a nice apartment, your kids are well educated, you are valuable members of this thing we got there, this so-called society."

When I think of your life, Grandma, I think of the burden to have to be a good girl. I see with Mom, how much her life is trying to not be a good girl anymore. How much it is trying to be free of what a girl should do and can't do. A girl doesn't have to study. A girl will marry and have kids. A girl is faithful. A girl doesn't want things. A girl has to be content with what she gets. A girl is not loud. A girl is a girl. A girl is—above all else—pretty.

I wanted to write about you, Grandma, because your life is inside of me. And it will die when I die. I am your end. But I won't let you die. 'Cause this is textile magic: weaving presence from absence. However, writing isn't just sparkly magic. In all the different cultures where forms of writing were invented independently of one another, the earliest forms of scripture were always records of debts. How much did you give me, how much did I promise in return? That's why I think that literature and guilt are indivisibly interconnected. But—I also believe the forms of writing that interest me have always been those that don't want to be what they have to be. Texts that undermine their primary intention, projects that want to get free of their debts, writing that searches exit doors out of writing.

And still—writing in High German, writing in English, means I am betraying Mom and you, means I change class, I refuse the language of my ancestors, the Bernese German, I refuse the farmer language that does not have fixed grammar rules, that exists only in spoken form.

I'm sorry for all the times I didn't visit you. I'm sorry that I can't stand you much longer than a few hours. When writing, Grandma, I am with you. I wanted to thank you for not giving a fuck about my gender. For cooking vegetarian for me ("But eating fondue every day can't be good, can it?"). For this one time I was playing with the chestnuts as a four-year-old and they lost their magic and you listened to me and tried consoling me, but you couldn't do anything and you just held me.

Dear Grandma,

I didn't tell you about the talk I had with Mom. *The* talk. We went for a walk and I asked her, I said, I needed to know, finally, that this time she must talk to me about "it." Her body was crouching, like a hedgehog before it rolls itself in. "You need to know, you need to understand me. It was such a different time. Like on a different planet. When the women were too old to carry children the doctors would take away their uterus. They said for preventative cancer care. They took it out also of Grandma. After the operation, I went to visit her. She was extremely vulnerable. She hugged me for a very long time. I sat by her bed and held her hand. She fell asleep soon, and I watched the other women in her room, I saw on the shield at the end of their bed, that they had had the same operation. Everyone was whispering. But it didn't feel like they whispered to not disturb the other patients, but because they didn't dare to use their voices. There was a feeling like the room was filled with something huge, pushing us all to the floor. I couldn't stand it, I left the room and walked the hallways, I walked for a long time, until I realized that this whole entire floor was filled with women who had their uteruses cut out. I looked into a few rooms, and they were all lying there, women "after their best age," and all of these barely moving bodies were like one big dying body. The men in white had taken out its center. And they had replaced the organ that produces bodies with an organ that produces sadness. When I went back to Grandma's room, I understood. The women were not relieved of their uterus to prevent cancer, but to make them understand that they were now officially useless. Making and taking care of children had been their sole purpose. Now that we, their children, were finishing our apprenticeships, we could take care of our own. And so the mothers were of no use anymore. Their bodies were scraped out like a confiture glass. And that's when I swore to myself, I would never, never, just become such a body. Shortly after that I enrolled for the Matur for grown-ups. My parents didn't pay one single cent, because a daughter didn't have to get education. I was financing myself fully, going to school part-time in the morning and working late shifts, six days a week. And then I got pregnant. And I had to decide." We stopped walking.

"Did you try?"

"No."

"Did you want to?"

"It was such a tough decision, darling, you cannot imagine how it is. Everything was going so well, and all of a sudden—"

"Did you want to?"

"There was a day. Yes. I had an appointment." Waves of trembling shook her.

"I know I wasn't perfect, but I did try my best," she said.

"I know."

"After all, you are the person I love the most in this world."

"I know, Ma."

Dear Mom,

we had this talk some time ago. We had it before I even started writing this book. I've been thinking about it all along while writing this. Am I allowed to write this? Isn't it your story? Or isn't the question "Whose story is this?" much more complicated? Aren't we all interlinked in our stories, aren't our stories a matryoshka, aren't you in my belly, Mom, and Grandma is in yours and so forth and so on? And then who gives birth to whom here?

I am writing this with a cheap roller-tip pen and every here and there, when I'm stuck in a sentence, I let it rest on the paper, and the paper is active, it sucks up the ink, it sucked up the ink on the word *belly*, and while I watched the ink spot grow, I said the words I have for you, I whispered "Meer" and "Grossmeer," "Meer" and "Grossmeer" and on and on, I carried on these words deep in my mouth, like I would carry a baby close to my skin, and I realized that these letters have a mouth with which they say their sound, like all letters do, but my letters have a secret, second mouth, with which they whisper: Despite the odds, I live. And while carrying these words I realized that maybe that's the closest I will ever get to giving birth, and maybe that is good, because I know that I could never do what you have done, Meer and Grossmeer, no, I could never raise a child, I would go mad in the first few sleepless nights. And here is what I do instead:

I break the circle of children who kill their parents in order to be free, to become themselves. I don't kill my parents. I am giving birth to my mothers.

Dear Grandma,

it is two in the morning and I wanted to write to you about today. Dina's boyfriend came to Ticino for one night, the two drama queens are spending their night in a hotel, probably fighting over their relationship model. He wants to have an open relationship and fuck boys, she is theoretically okay with it, but is hurt by the way he told her, obviously being insecure if this is the beginning of the ending, he says no way, he loves her but is suffocating in this hetero-monogamous-biscuit mold, etc.

Anyway, me and Mo had the evening to ourselves. We wrote, and when we couldn't write anymore, we ate tons of the porcini we found. It was a new moon and I said we should do a bathing ritual to welcome the new moon-circle (which would have been too esoteric for Dina). At last, we landed drunk on the couch, huddled together, still cold from the water, and Mo showed me the cooking show of Snoop Dogg and Martha Stewart, we watched them make green-coated brownies (because green is environmental), then we watched them mashing potatoes, talking about Snoop Dogg's own vocabulary that neither his kids nor he himself understand, then they talked about Snoop Dogg's new Christmas album. Then I'd laughed enough, closed the computer, and said, "I read your text." I cleared my throat. "You actually never told me how your dad died." Mo laughed weirdly, saying, "Really? I never told you? Okay. I'm gonna tell you right this second." He told me that his father, one Tuesday afternoon when Mo's brother Nik came home early (Mo and his mother weren't there), shot Nik and then himself. Mo's mother found them. "It was the early 2000s. I was nineteen. Neither me nor she got counseling afterward. They cleaned up our house, we had a funeral, and then we continued." I asked, if he had any idea, why his father killed Mo's brother. I didn't add ". . . and left you alive?" Mo said, "Oh, my brother was his favorite son. I guess Dad thought he was doing Nik a favor. To not leave him in this horrible place."

I never told you, Grandma, that Mom went to a shaman herself, because she needed to know, how she came into being. Because Mom had always been afraid as a kid that you wanted to kill her. The shaman told Mom after the ritual that you had not been married when you got pregnant with her. At the time unmarried pregnancies—especially for poor women—were still extremely shameful and could even lead to imprisonment, which wasn't usual anymore, but still done, if civilians reported the "criminals" to the police. You were a farmer girl and didn't know any doctors who would abort, and anyway could never have paid it. You tried to abort Mom with a knitting needle, you experienced immense pain, and when it didn't work, got married very quickly. At least, that is what Mom's shaman told her. Mom finished saying, "Now I finally know, why I've always been so afraid of needles."

I have been afraid to write about this also, because I was afraid that pro-life, conservative Christians could use this as an argument for their cause. They could say: See, unborn children can feel fear, can feel their mothers wish to kill them. But here is what I say to them: Yes, maybe a very sensitive fetus can feel something like that, not in a hocus-pocus kind of way, but simply because it shares the same blood and hormone circle with the parent body. But that is not an argument against abortion, but against unprofessional abortion. Because there will always be abortions.

Me, of course, I am glad that Mom didn't abort me. But she had the choice, she chose me, and I think the only reason, why I can deal with this sometimes insanely shitty life, is because in the end, Mom said *yes* to me, even though it was a difficult *yes*. And I am not saying that her thinking of aborting me scarred me for life. It did scar me, yes. But not for life. Because I have loads of life, I have streams of life around my here-ness that are unscarred, unscared, untamed, and hyperfabulous, I have gushes of life that fucking love it here, I love this stupid species, I love this weird planet, I love this absurd body, I love all of this crap with all of the wicked woods of all of my hearts.

Dear Grandma,

yesterday after lunch, we dug out a pool by the riverbank, with our bare hands. I write "with our bare hands" not without pride. It makes me feel like a real person. Like someone with hands. Or someone in hands. Now there is a round "cold pot," big enough for two of us to lie inside, although it's not like we can stay much longer than a minute in the icy water. When digging, the water completely numbed my fingers. I had small cuts from the sharp stones. It's a nice reminder of us, digging out a pool. With our bare hands. Afterward, Mo put nail polish on all of our hands, we giggled like schoolgirls. While comparing which nail has the most even polish, Mom called. I didn't pick up. I called her later, I asked how Alex was, she said good, then added: moody and hungry, baby's fine. She told me that you fell over a carpet in your apartment, it's nothing bad, your knee hurts, but you are quite confused. She talked about homes for elderly people that she was checking. "I don't want her to live in a crappy place." I didn't say anything, I was licking the small cuts on my finger. Then she thanked me for the pink sweater and said that she never liked pink, because she had to like it, but now she found a liking. "I love the mix of different threads you made."

A few months ago I won a small literary prize for a text. I had handed in the very beginning of this text, the prologue about bringing the box of Lindt & Sprüngli to you. I didn't tell you that I won something, but you knew. Mom must have told you. She had read it in the newspaper. "You won a prize, I hear," you told me on the phone. "You know I still haven't read any of your texts. I would really like to read something. Because I am proud of you, you know." I changed the subject.

What I could not write in German is that my interest in writing about you isn't purely artistic, isn't simply psychopoetic. I don't just write about you, because I can't help it; I write about you because I'm quite certain that it results in the best texts I can write at the moment. It's the most efficient way for me to climb up the ladder. Literature is—apart from being a bourgeois branch of art—one of the few capitalist games where my hypersensitivity and fear are useful. Whoever denies the socioeconomic aspects of writing (however precarious they may be), whoever says literature is purely about the aesthetic expression of unspeakable depths is a rich kid that I wanna punch. What I want to say: I use you in order to swim out of the muddy class where I was born into, to swim to the shore. A shore.

Am I horrible? I guess. Am I the only one who thinks like this? I don't think so. The only difference between you and me is education; it's simply that I was born in a time, where the educational system is flexible enough to let someone like me study. If I hadn't studied, I would not have been able to write this text. I couldn't have earned enough to take this time off unpaid.

If we have a generational task, I think it is this: to start looking under the obvious wounds at the hidden ones, inherited ones (as so many of my friends do). And to let the traumata of our families finally gush out, a mixed-up flood of puke and poo and jizz and blood and squirt and tears. To cut the bloodline and not pass this shit on any longer.

After writing this last paragraph, I felt very bad, and I felt relieved. I had wanted to tell you these things since I won the prize with the prologue. After writing this paragraph, I went to knock on Dina's door and on Mo's door, it was late afternoon, I asked them if they were up for a drink. We got wasted pretty early on white wine, Mo made a risotto with the porcini we had collected, Dina told us about the book she was reading by Sheila Heti, who writes about her decision not to have kids, we listened to Knöppel, a Swissgerman punk musician, and I was very touchy, I kept embracing Mo and Dina. When opening the third bottle of pinot grigio, Dina asked the question that I had wanted to ask us for a long time: "What are we to each other?" I laughed, then said, "I feel like in kindergarten, we play family." Mo, putting a big spoon of mascarpone and then a whole Gorgonzola in the risotto, asked, "And who plays the kid?" Me and Dina answered simultaneously: "Me!"

Dear Grandma,

this morning I came back from the shaman Cesare, after we did the ritual he had proposed. He played the drum and chanted.

I was lying on a mat between huge crystals. My whole body
started shaking and I sweat like a pig. To finish the ritual he put
a singing bowl on my chest and put a small labradorite stone in
my wet palm. He said he saw my ghosts, that I am carrying quite
a load of ancestors that want something from me. All of them
didn't get to live in some way, by death or trauma. When I was
born, they felt their chance to come into a new life through my
body, because I have been very open, very penetrable from the
start. And that I had let them, I absorbed them in my body. One
ghost was very dominant, he said, but there were others, much
older ones. It didn't surprise me at all what he said. It surprised
me, that it didn't surprise me. "The dominant one, she will take
control if you let her," Cesare said. I nodded, kissed him on the
cheek, and left. I walked home through the forest, and it felt very
alive, and we talked silently, the forest and me.

After moving out of my parents' place, I moved around a lot, six
times in three years. With every move I had more notebooks. I collected them. My goal was to write about "it all," about masculinity
and discipline and violence and competition-society, about what it
means to be alive at the brink of the third millennium in this body.
Only after the sixth moving I stopped buying more notebooks and
confessed to myself: I didn't write a single line about all of that. I
had the longing to write, but I didn't know how. I kept the notebooks empty, in the way you kept your boxes empty.

I walked around a big rock and saw the chocolate factory appear
in the already-warm morning light, under the heavy shadows of

the mountains. From afar I saw Mo and Dina having coffee on the doorstep, they looked like a painting, they waved and I didn't wave, I pressed the fingernails into my hand like one presses the shutter button of a camera.

Dina said that Mo had said that I still haven't read "The Carrier Bag Theory of Fiction" by Ursula K. Le Guin. And if this was true? And if yes, how could I walk so peacefully? I sighed loudly, then moaned: "If it's that amazing, then why don't you make a résumé for me?"

Dina cleared her throat, got up, and held an improv-lecture-performance that blew me away. Apparently, Le Guin proposes a different way of looking at early humans than the one of the big hunter-hero-meat-eater stories. Namely the carrier bag theory of evolution. Meat, she writes, was not the main dish of early humans. Nay, nay. Believe it or not, our ancestors mostly ate vegetables, roots, berries. Things one collects. And rather than weapons, phallic knives, the earliest objects probably were containers, carrier bags, nets: something where you could keep your food. Keep it from becoming wet or eaten by other animals. An object, with which you can carry your carefully collected veggie-snack back home and store it, also. So this is the collecting-veggies-and-storing-them-kind-of-narrative. A story told in this manner doesn't have a one-way direction, a clear goal, one central conflict, a hero. Rather, it holds things. Like berries in a bag. They don't have one clear order. This way of telling stories gives things a space to be, to be kept, to be sheltered, to be shared, to be passed down, to come to life. "A novel is a medicine bundle," Le Guin says, "holding things in a particular, powerful relation to one another and to us."

I went up into my room and read Le Guin's text right away and the other text that Mo had been urging me to read: "Hydrofeminism" by Astrida Neimanis. Neimanis writes that in order to survive on land, our ancestors had to bring H_2O with them, and so they actually incorporated the ocean. We became evolutionary carrier bags of water. And the carrier bag way of narrating, I would say, is to put static things into flowing relations, in no specific hierarchy.

Me, I have always felt this waterness of my existence. I am a fluidity, my body resonates, I am in constant, deep resonation with you, with the past, with the ghosts you didn't bury, with the feelings you didn't live. Neimanis calls life on land the *hypersea*, a name to connect us to our roots, a word to name the interconnected way of life that has carried the sea onto the earth, in truckli called bodies. The hypersea. I feel like it is just another word for "Grossmeer."

In most European languages one differentiates between a being and its body. One talks of having a beautiful, thin, small, fat, ugly body—not of being a body, the old Greek-Roman-Christian notion mens sana in corpore sano. For me this body-and-mind dualism has always been painfully true, although I never believed it: I never was my body. It was too this or that, but never "me."

Of course, the body isn't just a box we carry ourselves in. To be a body, to be here, is to be water, 75 percent, but also, it's a constant practice. Writing this I have come into resonation with my languages, our bodies, and all the ancestors that made both bodies and languages. And of course, I don't mean "ancestors" in a biological way. Virginia Woolf is as much my mother as you are, the hypersea.

I take one of the notebooks, I go out, back into the forest, I walk fast, the mountains eat the sun already, I hear Dina and Mo in the garden, I lie down under one of the old chestnut trees and I want to write down Cesare's ritual and what he said, psychologizing me: "You are a carrier. You know that, and not only you. But you alone cannot heal everybody, you need to decide what to carry and how. And you need to find better ways to get rid of the rest." He said much more, but enough of ghosts and past, I will not write about this here. I open the first page of the notebook and I write: "THE SEARCH FOR IRMA." And I realize, that I had already started looking for Irma some time ago. I had written my friend Leo, who is a historian, if she knows anything about the women's jail of Hindelbank and what became of former inmates, and she had said yes, she'd actually had a seminar about it, and sent me some documents. I crossed out what I had written on the first page and wrote: "FINDING IRMA." Then I went to my emails, opened the document Leo had sent me. The first page was this:

House Rules for the Women's Workhouse in Bern

1. At five o'clock in the morning in winter (from October 1 to May 1) and at four-thirty in the morning in summer (from May 1 to October 1), all inmates are to be woken by a bell.
2. Work begins after prayer, three-quarters of an hour after rising.
3. Breakfast at seven o'clock, then work until midday.
4. Lunch at midday, recommence work at twelve-thirty.
5. Walk, if weather agreeable, from two to two-thirty.
6. At four in the afternoon, a fifteen-minute break for a snack, then more work.
7. Evening meal at seven o'clock.
8. Prayers at eight o'clock, then inmates are to retire to the bedrooms.
9. On Sundays, the wake-up call is later, at six in the morning, and breakfast immediately follows morning prayer; the evening meal is at six-thirty, and bedtime at seven-thirty.
10. Washing-up of crockery takes place according to rank, and rotates every week.
11. Daily cleaning of the bedrooms also takes place according to rank and weekly rotation.
12. On weekdays, <u>reading aloud only</u> is permitted after the evening meal. On Sundays, each inmate may read <u>independently</u>, and reading aloud is prohibited that evening.
13. On Sundays, all inmates go to sermon; the Catholics at a quarter to eight in the morning and the Reformed at nine in the morning.
14. The rota for use of the privy takes place six times

daily, three times in the morning and three in the
afternoon.

15. Anyone who requires use of the privy in the in-
tervening hours must seek the permission of the
supervisor.

16. The supervisors are tasked with ensuring that the
above rules are strictly obeyed. The patrolman and
custodian, as well as the custodian's wife, will
also check that the above rules are carried out in a
timely fashion. Exceptions are only permitted in ex-
tenuating circumstances and only with the approval
of the custodian.

Bern, January 2, 1889

Checked and authorized
by the Chief of Police   The workhouse custodian
Sig. Stockmar   J. Blumenstein

Dear Grandma,

yesterday we sat in the garden. I had shown some parts of this
text to Dina and Mo. Dina asked me if I had thought about publishing it. I reacted very weirdly, even for my standards. I said
"Yes" and "No" a couple of times and then left the garden.

A bit later I was making bread for us, and a quote from Jean
Genet came into my mind, which Annie Ernaux uses in *La place*.
It goes something like: "Writing is the last way out when one has
betrayed." To me, this isn't true. To me, writing isn't a way out

of betrayal, but it is the betrayal. Because I write about the things that we mustn't say. The unwritten rule: to never talk about feelings. How one truly feels about the others.

You, Grandma, had to replace your sister. Then Mom had to replace you, you filled yourself into her, because you couldn't be you. Then Mom filled herself in me. I was the next in line. I don't think this started with you, it started way before your life; I think this is our whole culture, this is patriarchy, it is *Hamlet*: to carry the tasks of your parents. To be loyal to your blood, to your family, means to not lead your own life. To be loyal is to carry the truckli of the parents, to empty oneself and put oneself into one's child. And foremost, to be loyal means to be silent about all of this, this curse; to name it is to break it, and that is why I am betraying you. Because you endured your whole life to be a replacement, and you were silent about it. I was meant to be Rosmarie number four, or Johanna number twelve, or Barbara number thirty. But I cannot be the next one, I cannot continue the silence, because I will not have kids. There will be no one to live in my stead. My belly will not fill with life, it is only full of blood.

I was doing some research about Hindelbank, when Dina came knocking. She has boy troubles. I was glad. About the interruption, not her troubles. "Did you know," I asked Dina, "that only in 1978 there were a handful of cantons who fought their right to handle abortions against the restrictive Swiss national laws? And that the law we have now—to abort without punishment until the twelfth week—only exists since 2001?" Of course, Dina knew.

Me and Dina lay in bed, her head on my belly. "So, how is your
sex . . . emm . . . topic?" she asked.
"Which of my sex topics do you mean?" I asked. Dina was
super uncomfortable.
"Your sex addiction?"
"It's not an addiction, it's not pathological, I just have a high
libido," I said.
"Oh, I'm sorry, I thought, emm. And then yesterday, when
you came home . . ."
"How are your boyfriend troubles?" I interrupted. She
talked and I listened, stroking her hair, that is always shiny and
dense and beautiful, and I am always jealous of it. From time to
time I asked something. When I realized that I was stroking her
the way you were stroking me as a child, I stopped doing it. Dina
stopped talking, lifted her head, looking at me, and said: "Please
don't stop." I continued and then she continued.

After some time Mo came in, he was in a very different energy,
he had smoked some weed earlier, he wasn't stoned anymore,
but didn't see the point in feeling miserable. He jumped on the
bed and convinced us that the only right thing right now was to
go collect porcini on the mountain slopes. And he was right, of
course, as always. He lectured in his biology teacher tone on the
symbiotic relationship between porcini mushrooms and the fir
trees.

The trees get stuff, nitrogen or micro-something, and the mushrooms get photosynthesized sugar in return. Me and Dina listened, well-behaved children that we are, and at least I stopped

thinking about what I had been thinking about before. I'm not sure Dina did. We climbed the mountain silently.

We climbed higher and higher, it was very steep and we found tons of porcinis. At some point we were in a competition of who finds the best, freshest, I felt like a fox in a chicken den. Suddenly we came to the tree limit, we went a bit farther up, then I shrieked, I pointed down, there was the river, our river, a tiny, shiny, silvery snake, and I was very certain that I was able to see our pool, but Dina and Mo said no, they smiled condescendingly. "The pool is much too small for us to see from here." I said: "Okay, if you think so." But I know I was right, bitches. On the way down Dina found a thistle that she gave me because it was pretty and I like pretty things and I wondered why I don't see her and Mo more often in my everyday life.

I went back to reading about Hindelbank. I read how the imprisonment was about "educating" the women, and they were even more severely "educated" if they did small "things," "behaviors to be eradicated," such as:

Uncleanliness
Disorder
Changing location without permission
Gossiping
Taking and stealing objects
Dangerous liaisons
Disobedience
Griping
Cursing

Obscenities
Bantering
Childish pranks
Laziness
Damage to property
Escape attempts
Escape
Violence toward guards
Angry outbursts

The historian wrote that this list got longer and longer over the years. They were forbidden to talk and write, except for special talking and writing times.

Dear Grandma,

When I had Dina on my belly and stroked her hair, I remembered once again how much I hated being held by you. By your big, rough worker's hands. Your skin felt like it had been one single wound and there was this coarse crust all covering it up, never healing. Your hand was always somewhere on my body—my arm, my thigh, my belly—and it was moving. Always, nervously, stroking. Like a cat's tail.

I suddenly remembered that one time, around two years ago, when I asked you (once again) about the first Rosmarie, you repeated your loop, like always, but then you suddenly said: "I remember Mom at Christmases. She would talk of nothing else.

Always the first Rosmarie. The heaviness. Everything. It was as
if all the objects had doubled their weight. I wished that I could
empty all objects in our apartment, so that they weren't so heavy.
And I kind of owe her, the first Rosmarie, no? If she had lived, I
wouldn't be here, would I?" And your hands, when you told me
about these Christmases. You were holding your own hands, as
if you were cold. Restless, ceaseless, almost hysterically caressing. Only now while caressing Dina do I get what this is. You
have always been trying to console yourself, to warm yourself,
to desperately make things good. I am sorry, Grandma, I didn't
understand as a child. As I didn't feel a difference between your
body and mine, you didn't feel a difference between my body
and yours, and that's why you caressed me so much: you were
subconsciously trying to soothe yourself. How arrogant of me to
hate your caressing. It was not meant for me.

And then a flood, another memory: One time when I was at
yours, asking about the first Rosmarie, you suddenly said: "Did I
ever show her to you?" I looked at you puzzled. You led me into
your bedroom. You opened the cupboard where you held all these
clothes that I had worn playing our girl-game. I realized that these
are Rosmarie's clothes, all of them. Without a grain of dust, clean.
From behind some skirts you produced a large photograph of the
first Rosmarie in an oval frame. Black and white. A pale girl, maybe
six years old. A controlled gaze. She really looks like Mom, especially the eyes. I understood then and there, why you never liked
Mom, why you always preferred Nico, because she reminds you so
much of the first Rosmarie. I thought: Now your anger must come.
The eighty-year-old anger with this Überschwester supersister

goddess. I didn't really look at the picture, I looked at you, looking at the picture. You said, softly, tenderly even, more to the picture than to me: "Look how pretty she is. Isn't she the prettiest girl?"

I don't know why I remember these things now. It feels like your "Rosmarie loop" is so dominant, that it even deletes memories in me that differ from it. Which reminds me of Dad's story, the story of his best friends, and how important it is to change one's story, in order to own it. He changed it, dramatically, the last time he told. He started, like always, with his two best friends, Bruno and Hans, coming on the morning of the first of August to ask him, if he will join them. They would go on "their" route. Dad said he doesn't quite remember why he didn't go. In the evening, their parents knocked on the door. "They didn't come back. You have to go look for them." He said that when they got there, he already knew, because there were freshly fallen stones. Then they found Bruno. Bruno's body, only a few bloody rags left of it, and the shattered skull. Dad said, like always, that at first he thought: Ah, there are Bruno his clothes. Until he saw, that these were not only his clothes, but Bruno's remains. And then, farther above, there was Hans. He was buried till the hip. He was unconscious, but alive. They dug him out. One leg he had lost completely, but the heavy rocks had hindered too much loss of blood.

Dear Grandma,

this is the last letter I will write to you. I'm still in Ticino. This morning was the first time that Dina came swimming too.

Tomorrow we are going home. I have already begun to think
about how I'll remember these days in the future. The pool, the
cold, cold water, the shaman, Dina and Mo. You know I still don't
know, I cannot—just—live. I still talk to the flowers on the side
of my roads as if they knew better than me.

Today after lunch I went to the river on my own, I walked up the
riverbed, far up, I was prenostalgic, I wanted to go farther up to
get a new memory, not linked to Dina and Mo. A memory that
was just mine. I had to climb around two waterfalls. I was completely naked. I finally reached a big waterfall I could not climb,
so I stopped. I yelled. I couldn't hear myself, the waterfall was so
loud. But I felt it, my voice, roaring in my chest and it connected
with the water, falling, and I connected with my body, calling. I
walked down again. It felt good to be outside, to be this region
of skin, to feel my voice rather than to hear it, and then I saw a
few lichens on the stones under my feet, and I remembered what
Mo had said about lichens; namely that they consist of symbiotic
relationships between fungi and algae, that as lichens they can
do what neither fungi nor algae can do, and I thought that these
algae, like us, must have come from the sea, and now they live on
trees, in relationships with fungi, so tightly, that they have given
up being algae completely, that they are no longer themselves,
but something entirely new. I thought about how to say goodbye, how to stop being an old form and how to take on a new
way of being. In order to talk to you, I had to find a way to let
you disappear, first in the home for demented and then in a language that is not linked to you. I needed to do that, so I could

love you, because I love you, but I can only love you when I can
write about you, and I can only write about you when I am in a
body of my own. I can only love you from afar. I went under the
waterfall, dove under the water, it was all swirls and curls around
me, and the last phone call with Mom ran through my head, the
phone call where she finally said what I had suspected: that Irma
was probably impregnated by her own father, Urgrosspeer, that
Mom suspects the chicken hut, that she knows that your mother
had called the police, that Urgrossmeer gave her own daughter
to the women's prison Hindelbank, that Urgrossmeer had told
Mom, because Mom asked her straight up, because Mom had
felt it, and that Urgrossmeer told her to never tell anyone. And I
didn't wonder anymore why you had named Mom Irma, why you
had given your daughter (who looks like your dead older sister)
the name of your younger sister who disappeared. I got out of
the water and I thought of Irma and that she probably still lives.
I imagined her roaming this country. I imagined her hating her
own family, that she never wanted to get back in touch with you
again. I imagined she doesn't want to be found. Or at least—not
by you, who didn't do anything, who kept silent.

I wanted this to be an homage to you. Because to me you are not
the second Rosmarie, you are the Rosmarie that lived. I thought
again of Ulysses, who isn't able to return home, not really. To
me, the *Odyssey* was never the story of a hero, but the story of
someone who survived the war of men, the *Iliad*, but being so
traumatized, that the way home wasn't possible. He is someone
else, when he gets home, and his home has changed too. The

circle I wanted to draw is more of a spiral. The ending line misses the starting line.

I got back, through the riverbed, downstream. I produced the apple I had brought, sat down, washed it in the river and cut it with the pocketknife Dad had given me. It was sour. Then I went in "our" pool. There, naked, shivering in the water, I was a fish, I was an awareness, I lay on the round pebbles looking at the sky and I could feel the reflection of the sky on the surface and I am a fragment of the sky and I see nothing but the blueness of the universe that is only blue in our eyes—did you know that the eye consists of 99 percent water?—and I would do anything to get up and take the softness of the water with me, like a fabric, like a star-light bright fuckingly epoch-making awesome postgender illuminated flowing dress, and walk the world in this wafting, swaying skin of water and light and universe, and then I hear them, Dina and Mo, they jump through the forest, yelling, throwing stones, stomping on the ground and hitting their chest like crazy people, and they yell but the river is louder, so much louder, and then we are all children, even Mo, who is always more of a dad, not in an annoying way, but in a very grown-up kind of way, he is the reasonable one with the nature stuff, Dina is the funny one with the politics, and I am the melancholic one with the grandmother. But not now; now I am the wild one, now I throw water at them and Dina gets undressed and Mo doesn't even bother, he jumps into the pool fully dressed and I laugh really loudly, hysterically almost, just so I don't have to cry, because I miss us already, because I know that tomorrow we are going home and we will be the reasonable one again, and the funny one, and the melancholic one, and I will have many sex-dates and a lot of work and no one to get wasted with pinot grigio a bit too early in the evening, and no one to write to about what I cannot say.

My mother tongue is talking. My father tongue is silence. And my own tongue are tongues, and my tongues are dripping, dropping, blurring, streaming, rooting, flowing.

Sources

PART 1

"Catillon the witch." La Gruyère Tourisme, https://www.fribourgregion.ch/en/la-gruyere/tales-and-legends/catillon-the-witch. Utz Tremp, Kathrin. "Catillon, eine Freiburger Hexe (1663–1731)." Staatsarchiv des Kantons Freiburg, March 2009.

PART 3

Hase, Andreas. *Bäume. Tief verwurzelt.* Stuttgart, 2018.

Jäggi, Jakob. "Die Blutbuche zu Buch am Irchel." In Naturforschende Gesellschaft. *Neujahrsblatt.* Zürich, 1894.

Kellner, Ursula. "Landschaftsbilder. Einfluss auf die Gestaltungen von Landschaft bei Heinrich Friedrich Wiepking (1891–1973)." Hannover, 2016.

Lutze, Günther. "Zur Geschichte und Kultur der Blutbuchen." In *Mittheilungen des Thüringischen Botanischen Vereins* (1892), pp. 28–33.

Nagel, Hanna. "Zur Kultivierung und Verbreitung der Blutbuche aus dem Fürstentum Schwarzburg-Sondershausen." In *Sondershäuser Heimatecho* 29, no. 12 (2018), p. 25.

Urmi, E. "Aus dem Leben der Buche." In *Briefe aus dem Botanischen Garten Zürich* 23, no. 6 (1989).

"Waldwildnis Possen: Mutterblutbuche soll mehr in den Fokus gerückt warden." In *Kyffhäuser Nachrichten* (5.7.2017).

Wimmer, Clemens Alexander. "Geschichte der Blutbuche." In *Beiträge zur Gehölzkunde* 12 (1997), pp. 71–81.

Wiepking, Heinrich Friedrich. *Umgang mit Bäumen.* Basel, München, 1963.

PART 4

Derrida, Jacques. "Plato's Pharmacy." In *Dissemination.* Chicago, 1981, p. 67.

Fässler, Hans. "Die kubanische Plantage der Familie Escher." In *WOZ—die Wochenzeitung*, no. 28 (July 13, 2017).

Federici, Silvia. *Caliban und die Hexe. Frauen, der Körper und die ursprüngliche Akkumulation.* Vienna, 2017.

Wottreng, Willi. *Die Millionärin und der Maler. Die Tragödie Lydia Welti-Escher und Karl Stauffer-Bern.* Zürich, 2005.

PART 5

Ernaux, Annie. *Mémoire de fille.* Paris, 2016.

Ernaux, Annie. *La place.* Paris, 1983.

Le Guin, Ursula K. "The Carrier Bag Theory of Fiction." In *Dancing at the Edge of the World.* New York, 1989, p. 165.

Neimanis, Astrida. "Hydrofeminism: Or, on Becoming a Body of Water." In *Undutiful Daughters: New Directions in Feminist Thought and Practice.* Edited by Henriette Gunkel, Chrysanthi Nigianni, and Fanny Söderbäck. New York, 2012.

Voskuil, Johannes Jacobus. *Schmutzige Hände. Das Büro 2.* Berlin, 2014.

Eggen, Peter, Andrea Baechtold, Rolf Schöpflin, Hermann von Fischer, und Anstalten. *100 Jahre Anstalten in Hindelbank: Festschrift.* Hindelbank, 1996. https://swisscovery.slsp.ch/permalink/41SLSP_NETWORK/1ufb5t2/alma991062153799705501.

Acknowledgments

I would like to thank (in alphabetical order):

Alok Vaid-Menon for the lesson to never, never forget humor;
Andrea for the Spätzli maker;
Andrej for the oils and the place in your village;
Old Angela for defending the obituaries;
Anthea for the sofa sanctuary;
Birgit for deriding classic novels;
Caro for the knitting and all your colors;
Catherine for the constant expertise 24/7;
Cédric for the Speedminton and your unspeakably strong shoulders;
Daria for the Volvo (RIP) and the monk's beard;
Deleuze & Guattari pour devenir ma bande de loups;
Dilan for the moon rituals and all that glitter, baby;
Dominique for the encoded postcards and protective spells;
Donna Haraway for them fabulous fabulations;
Doris Stauffer for the Lebkuchen;
Fabian for the consulting subscription;
Friederike for Walser's wood precision;
Gerhard Dönig for all the copper beech knowledge;
Harry Styles for unpop-ing the labels;
Ines for the introductory courses "Witchcraft for the Anxious,"
　　Parts 1 & 2;
Jelena for the cheesiest of all cheeses;
Lena for your fire, 'cuz I see fi-iiii-re only with you-uuu;

Leonie for all the taxi rides, to my Kirchberg hell and Flumsi
heaven;

Lorenz for the stone(s) and skiing and every zigzag of my skates;

Manuel for the sweet grass;

Marlies for the lady's mantle and pine cones;

Meike for not bending things straight;

Michel Foucault pour ton fouet;

Michi for the parmigiana and puzzles;

Nicole for the strolls;

Paul B. Preciado por dejarme mamar tu pene sin falo;

Regina for the larkspur and evening primrose and every key of
my piano;

RuPaul for the shablam;

Ruth Schw. for the train beers;

Ruth Stad. for the passion for jewelry;

Salome for your Moscato, which is so sweet and tingles the tongue
like nothing else;

Salomé for the co-weaving, co-spinning, co-dancing;

Sam Smith for all those diamonds;

Sandro for the hours of rowing yet to come;

Sebastian for the makeup tutorials and for sticking with it;

Silvia Federici for the de-nurturing;

Starhawk for giving me ground to dream my darkest, my earth-
liest magic yet;

Virginia Woolf for helping me swim in the unswimmable, and to
root in midair;

Thekla for the délices and the caramel glacé;

And Théo for everything, almost always.

Translator's Note

In the autumn of 2023, its stubbornly warm days reminiscent of the summer-autumn in this book, I found myself in the mountains above Lake Geneva, at a place called Château de Lavigny. I had been invited there on a fellowship to work on my translation of Kim de l'Horizon's debut, *Blutbuch*, which in English has become *Sea, Mothers, Swallow, Tongues*. The blush-stoned château, the former home of the Ledig-Rowohlt publishing family, echoed with the whispers of the legendary authors who had stayed there over the last century. Early each morning I would tiptoe downstairs, cross the dew-coated grass, slip through the gate, and go for a run through the vineyards. I always scanned the horizon for Mont Blanc, which seemed a fluid rather than fixed landmark: sometimes visible and sometimes not, depending on the weather or time of day, or perhaps its own whims. I imagined it cheekily shifting position, evading my gaze. It reminded me of "I am rooted, but I flow"—the words of Virginia Woolf—one of the epigraphs to this novel, and a fitting mirror to its genre-defying style and the process of translating it.

For a translator, a book like this is a gift. Infinitely playful, it extends an invitation to luxuriate in language. It is genre-fluid, gender-fluid, and overflows with neologisms. De l'Horizon's writing shifts frequently between registers, blurring the borders of fiction, nonfiction, and poetry; of fabulation and realism; of past and present. And yet it is also—and I say this lovingly—a torture, because of its inconsistencies and ambiguities. There are countless metaphors used to describe the craft of translation, and one is of carrying something—meaning, in essence—from one place to another. I interpret this as striving to create an equivalent experience in the English-language reader, even if it doesn't always occur through the same means, or at the same moment, as in the original text. With *Blutbuch*, the metaphor of transporting from A to B didn't feel right because the fixed locales of A and B, of German and English, appeared more fluid and hazier the longer I looked at them, and the words I picked up to transport were slippery too. Their layers of meaning multiplied and slithered out of my grasp. And in a way, this made sense: in this narrative there is no resolution or destination; it is a spiral, an unending process of becoming. This translation demanded a new approach.

Fortunately, before I began my first draft, I was invited in spring 2023 to participate in a workshop at Translation House Looren in Switzerland. Funded by Pro Helvetia, it gathered eleven translators who had been commissioned to bring de l'Horizon's debut into their respective languages. Up in the mountains outside Zürich, we spent four intense days—joined, on two of those, by the author—workshopping the text and its linguistic challenges. We discussed the finer details, such as the dialect terms and their meaning, and the wider issues, like gender identity and transgenerational trauma. Those conversations with colleagues, whose native languages included Catalan, Croatian, Dutch, Italian, and more, were greatly enriching for the work ahead, and I have carried their voices with me.

Unsurprisingly, even the title presented a conundrum. *Blutbuch* is a compound noun of *Blut* (blood) and *Buch* (book). The "blood" element has associations with bloodlines and inheritance, and also with violence, as experienced through transphobia, homophobia, and the forcibly-imposed gender binary. For the German-language reader, further associations arise as they delve into the narrative: the title also refers to the *Blutbuche*, the copper (blood) beech in the narrator's childhood garden (with this family tree element being an additional nod to bloodlines). And in the Bernese German dialect, *dä Buch* means "the stomach"/"belly," subtly suggestive of other recurrent motifs: emptiness and fullness in the body, the digestion of ideas. After playing with many possibilities for the English title, the author, the book's editor, and I found resonance through the multiword, poetic title of *Sea, Mothers, Swallow, Tongues*. It gives space to the novel's themes while also mimicking its linguistic and interpretative play.

One of de l'Horizon's core motivations in writing this book was to find a form of genuine self-expression in a language that is rigidly gendered. In German, nouns are assigned one of three grammatical genders—male, female, or neuter—through their articles, *der*, *die*, or *das*. Professional roles are often appended with *-in* to denote the female form: *der Lehrer* (male teacher) becomes *die Lehrerin* (female teacher). References to groups of mixed gender have traditionally defaulted to the male form in the plural, *die Lehrer*, while the female plural is *die Lehrerinnen*. In recent years there have been efforts to make the language more inclusive—for example, by adding an asterisk to the plural (*Lehrer*innen*) to include males, females, and those who identify as nonbinary—but this has been opposed by traditionalists and far-right groups.

Suffice to say, German is a language that doesn't offer an easy home to nonbinary bodies and identities. In English, there is arguably more linguistic flexibility for gender-inclusive terms. *They* as a singular pronoun, in my mind and mouth, is a relatively smooth

option, and one with historical precedent. Its use emerged as early
as the fourteenth century, and survived criticism from stringent
mid-eighteenth-century grammarians to become more commonly
used in modern Standard English as a gender-fluid pronoun. For
this translation, therefore, I needed to find ways of creating an
inflexibility in English that would echo that of the German text.
I chose to do this by keeping the cultural context of the original
as present as possible—by retaining and contextualizing some of
its phrases—and also by seizing the linguistic gifts that presented
themselves. For example, in German the noun for *child* is neuter,
"das Kind," with *es* (it) as the pronoun. I have rendered the child
as *it* in the English too, knowing that this would read awkwardly,
where in the original it does not. I actively welcomed this deper-
sonalization in order to suggest the rigidity that exists elsewhere in
German's gendered nouns. Though attributing a consistent male
or female gender to the child in the translation would have made it
read more smoothly, I feel it would have been unfaithful to the intention of the original. My choice also emphasizes Swiss German's
objectification of children and women; in the dialect, many of the
nouns for adult women take the neuter article *das*: "I didn't want
to be an object; I wanted to be a person, and grown up, and being
grown up meant having a gender, a male one. As a woman, you
were at risk of remaining an object or becoming an ocean. I didn't
want either" (page 13). The German also carries a sense of negative space—the uncertainty of the child narrator feeling pushed to
choose a gender—that I didn't want to lose. That *child* is a neuter
noun in German almost suggests that there is a neutral period before they grow up and need to choose. In the original, within parts
2 and 3, the narrator is either *it* or *the child*, and at the very end of

part 2 is referred to as *he/the boy*. Because I see gender-neutral and gender-fluid language as different concepts—to me, the former suggests an absence of binaries, while the latter speaks to an expansion, an unending ebb and flow—I chose, with the author's blessing, to also briefly incorporate *she* (in "On Playing Dress-Up," page 36) and *they* as pronouns (in "FlowingTogether," page 112).

A significant challenge in this translation was always going to be the original text's use of the Swiss German dialect; more specifically, Bernese German, from the narrator's home canton of Bern. Switzerland counts four main spoken languages: German, French, Italian, and Romansh. In German-speaking cantons, Standard German is the official written language and is taught in schools, while the Swiss German dialect, with local variations, is the main mode of communication in day-to-day life. A person's ability to speak Standard German accent-free is seen as an indication of their educational status, and this imbues language with friction and class dynamics. In the original, the narrator interweaves the Standard German they learned in school with the Bernese German they spoke with their meers. I chose to retain some of these dialect words, such as *truckli* (trinket boxes) and *meertrübeli* (currants), contextualizing them in order to offer the reader an idea of the cultural setting. In part 4, the use of dialect intensifies: Meer composes her first drafts of the witches' and whores' biographies in Bernese German, striving to create something entirely her own; she redrafts some into Standard German, then ultimately takes a defiant, self-empowering approach by combining Standard German and dialect. To emulate this, I have threaded informal, playful, slanglike phrases through a more formal register in the English.

The biography extract beginning on page 196 is the only part of the original composed entirely in Bernese German. This is the section I deliberated over the longest. When tackling translation dilemmas, it's helpful to think about the impact of the original text on the source-language reader, and to try and re-create this impact on the target-language reader. In this case, a Bernese German reader would fully understand the original; a Swiss German reader from other cantons would mostly understand it; and a reader in Germany might be able to decipher some meaning when sounding it out, but would likely feel alienated when reading it on the page. (To the uninitiated, Swiss German vocabulary and cadence can seem almost impenetrable, so great are the differences. I vividly remember, on my first school exchange trip to Germany at the age of thirteen, landing at Basel's airport—which exits into France, Germany, and Switzerland—hearing Swiss German, and wondering what on earth I'd been learning for the previous two years.) For this extract, I cycled through various iterations and approaches. Re-creating it in an existing English-language dialect would have made it too location specific. Leaving it untranslated could have blended well with the retention of dialect words elsewhere in the text, but would have alienated the vast majority of readers. Ultimately, I decided to create a new phonetic dialect, or rather an English sociolect, that holds influences from various regions and hopefully has a slightly rural feel, an important element to de l'Horizon. My hope is that rather than skipping over it, the reader will slow down and sound out the words to derive their meaning.

The novel's frequent shifts in register and style reflect the narrator's attempt to try on different linguistic identities. They are seeking to find a language—or a blend—that feels authentic. Here, language is many things; sometimes it is oppression, shame, or armor (such as the child's self-imposed "spell" of speaking in short sentences); sometimes, it is exploration or empowerment (such as Meer's blend of dialect with Standard German). Part 3 includes a compelling contrast between a stream of consciousness style and a formal, academic register.

So far in this note I've emphasized the challenges of the translation process, but I also want to highlight the joy. For just as this book carries the weight of responsibility to sensitively convey generational trauma and the oppression of queer and nonbinary people, so too does it offer a lightness. In a letter to their translators, the author encouraged us to be wild, transgressive—and to have fun. I felt this most in part 3, where *écriture fluide*, the term used by the author at Looren to describe this flowing, gushing, and washing through the borders of language, comes to the fore. Sound and cadence were key, and, with de l'Horizon's permission, I chose poetry over literal meaning. I soaked myself in the texts that had inspired them—Annie Ernaux and Édouard Louis, among others—and allowed my own textual influences to enter the mix. I developed new pre-work rituals, like somatic dance, and used voice dictation to create space for the delicious wordplay and neologisms that can result from mis-hearings. The more I allowed myself to relax and be carried by the energy of the narrative, the more gifts presented themselves in English, with *pontifiqueering*, *smother tongues*, and *cunning stunts not stunning cunts* being my favorite inventions.

De l'Horizon's journey through language(s) continues with part 5. In the original, this section was composed entirely in

English, a language in which the narrator feels confident. But neither Meer nor Grossmeer speaks English, so it is also the language in which the narrator feels most free. It represents their incomplete attempt to reveal themself to Grossmeer, addressing her, but not in a way that will be truly heard. In our Looren workshop, de l'Horizon emphasized that this part should appear in a different language than the rest of the book. In the original, the English is followed by a German translation created by the author using DeepL. This allows non-English-speaking German readers to understand it, but also serves as an additional voice and energy—described by the author as an "agency." Naturally, being AI-translated from a non-native-English text, it also contains some turns of phrase that are just slightly odd to German ears. Most other translators at the workshop planned to include this English section and to use AI to produce a translation in their own languages. For me, this was tricky—how could I convey the feeling of difference or liberation that this final chapter represents when the preceding parts in my version are also in English? If I were to translate de l'Horizon's English into something—an invented idiolect?—would it come across as forced? I feared that leaving the occasional non-native grammatical errors untouched could risk confusion for readers about whether they came from intention or rushed work. Torn, I returned to the idea of equivalency: German-language readers encountering de l'Horizon's English would, depending on their own fluency in English or lack thereof, either notice or not notice errors, or skip straight to the AI-created German. If they did skip the English, they would notice awkwardness in the DeepL version too (due to the aforementioned effect of translating from non-native English, via AI, into German). Ultimately, I decided to leave de l'Horizon's English text so that the reader can experience, for a short while, the author's voice directly. The space between our Englishes offers the additional voice and agency the author was seeking. I decided to trust that the reader would perceive the difference and sense there was a reason for it.

Anyone who has also read the original may notice additional text in this version, for example in the opening pages (the Sidhe on pages 11 and 12). These were created by the author especially for the English version, inspired by its rebirth as *Sea, Mothers, Swallow, Tongues*. I was mindful of finding the echoes of these new elements throughout the text, making the odd tweak here and there to help them take root.

Between the summer when I first encountered *Blutbuch* and writing this note, two and a half years have passed. As time went on, it became ever clearer to me that I couldn't pin the book down. Like Mont Blanc on those morning runs, like Grossmeer's memory as she succumbs to dementia, the narrative's language(s) and meaning(s) are too elusive. Instead, I had to trust the process and let the novel's ambiguity carry me along. I had to root myself, but flow. Just as the book itself has changed, so have I. Translating it has made me more courageous in my work as a whole, and for this I will always be grateful. I hope I have found a fittingly effervescent and fierce voice in English for the author, while also, with their encouragement, allowing my own to join the chorus. More than anything, I hope it will give a voice to those who feel silenced, a home to those who haven't found a welcoming space within systems of stark binaries. *Sea, Mothers, Swallow, Tongues* overflows with humanity. As I write these words, in a world that seems painfully divided, I know it's time to hand it over to you, the reader. I hope you find as much joy and empowerment in it as I have.

Jamie Lee Searle
Winchester, March 2025